SNATCHED

THE UNFORGETTABLE CRUISE

MARTIN M. NUZA

First published in paperback by
Michael Terence Publishing in 2022
www.mtp.agency

Copyright © 2022 Martin M. Nuza

Martin M. Nuza has asserted the right to be identified as
the author of this work in accordance with the
Copyright, Designs and Patents Act 1988

ISBN 9781800944756

U.S. Copyright Office
101 Independence Ave. S.E.
Washington, D.C. 20559-6000
Copyright Registration No: TXu 2-333-987

No part of this publication may be reproduced, stored
in a retrieval system, or transmitted, in any form or
by any means, electronic, mechanical, photocopying,
recording or otherwise, without the prior
permission of the publisher

Cover images
Copyright © Grigory Bruev
www.123rf.com

Cover design
Copyright © 2022 Michael Terence Publishing

Michael Terence
Publishing

The following is a dramatization based on actual events of true crimes committed on cruise ships. Names, locations and certain crimes have been changed purely for dramatic purposes.

Contents

Prologue: Breaking Free 1
1: The Journey 5
2: The Adventure 17
3: The Monster Awakes 32
4: Ocho Rios 52
5: The Monster's Wrath 57
6: The Devil's Call 81
7: The Search 91
8: The Anguish 107
9: Fishing 131
10: Below Deck 144
11: Grave Error 151
12: Vigilante 163
13: The Trap 177
14: The Betrayal 185
15: The last night 207
16: A New Beginning 223
Epilogue 226

Statement from Jim Walker 227
Statement from Kendall Carver 231
Statement from Jamie Barnett 234
Statement for Dianne Brimble 237
Statement for Rebecca Coriam 239
Statement for John and Chantal Hopkins 243
Statement for Shari Cecil 246
Statement from a Grieving Mother 251
Tips for a Safer Cruise 258
Acknowledgments and Special Thank You 260

Prologue
Breaking Free

A gentle breeze blows through *"W Flagler Street"* in Miami, Florida, as a number of people walk down the *"Miami-Dade County Courthouse"* steps, quenching the intense heat from this extra warm Thursday afternoon. Amongst them is Chloe Moore, a young but vulnerable 24-year-old woman, dressed in an elegant black suit with high heels. Her beautiful long blonde hair sways as she makes her way towards the sidewalk feeling a sense of relief as a heavy weight has finally been lifted from her shoulders. She clutches a piece of paper tightly in her right hand, completely lost in thought.

Michael, Chloe's ex-husband, wearing a formal suit, close to his thirties, removes his tie in frustration and remains standing at the foot of the courthouse steps staring down at Chloe walking away, clearly enraged.

The Judge has finally approved their divorce and Chloe is now a free woman once again. She married Michael over two years ago but soon discovered he was an aggressive, highly manipulative and controlling husband, who violently abused her both physically and mentally on a daily basis. Michael's only true love was for alcohol and drugs. Over two years of Chloe's life wasted, which can never be recovered, plunged her into depression and living with a constant fear of where and when Michael would strike next.

The thoughts mingle continuously in her fragile mind as she walks further away from him, perceiving his cold dark eyes staring at her from behind, "Why did it come to this? Why didn't Michael love me? What did I do wrong?" over and over again. She loved him dearly but knew she could end up dead as the beatings were growing more intense with every passing day.

Michael refused counselling and rehabilitation, culminating in Chloe's father, Ethan, stepping in and finally convincing her to file for divorce.

Chloe suddenly stops in her tracks and inhales deeply to gather her courage. She then impulsively turns around only to find his menacing silhouette still staring from the courthouse steps in the distance. She sees his fists are clenched, perceiving his all too familiar rage. She raises her chin up high and braves a smile, just to prove she is no longer afraid of him and he can no longer control her. They both exchange a soulless and emotionless stare, until Chloe eventually turns back and continues walking down the street feeling a sudden gust of cool breeze smothering her sweaty face. It makes her stop and take in another deep breath, this time a breath of freedom, feeling how the breeze refreshers her vulnerable warm face from the intense heat wave the city is experiencing today.

She closes her eyes and sheds a tear, clutching the folded paper tighter in her hand, sensing the pain of humiliation, believing she failed in her marriage not wanting to accept she was in fact the victim.

"Chloe!" shouts Alexis Young, a 23-year-old bomb shell of a woman, an attractive red head wearing a nice designer outfit with matching purse. She runs towards Chloe from across the busy street. Alexis is Chloe's only true friend; they have been supporting each other since an early age and have grown up like sisters.

Chloe opens her eyes and smiles just as Alexis arrives and gives her a massive hug of support.

"I am so sorry I wasn't with you at the courthouse," says Alexis with a tighter cuddle, "I should have been there, if only that damn cab didn't get caught in the downtown traffic." She leans back and smiles seductively. "I offered him my body if he'd run the red lights and get me here on time but I think he was from the other side, if you know what I mean." Remarking with a passionate but joking wink that makes Chloe giggle and laugh at her friend's stupid jokes that always brighten her mood in difficult times.

"It's okay, really," replies Chloe with a bright smile on her face, feeling a sense of security from Alexis's hug, "you wouldn't have liked it anyway, it was all so boring."

Alexis gives Chloe a mischievous smile "Was the Judge hot?" She remarks jokingly to cheer her up. "Did you give him the wink?" She asks, watching how Chloe blushes and gives Alexis a friendly slap on the shoulder, as they hold on to each other's arms and walk slowly down the street.

"He was a nice man, I think in his sixties, but still nice," replies Chloe, innocently.

"Maybe he was looking for a sugar baby," adds Alexis jokingly, "damn, I missed my opportunity to meet him."

Both Chloe and Alexis giggle and Chloe gives her a gratifying nod. "Thank you for always finding a way to make me smile and laugh, Alexis."

"No need to thank me, Chloe, after all, that's what besties are for," she confirms, taking two tickets from her purse and waving them at Chloe in excitement.

"What are those?" asks Chloe with anticipation.

"These are my present to you for surviving that awful marriage. Your wish come true. You always wanted to go on a cruise," she says handing the tickets to Chloe who is now clearly overwhelmed. "Well, I booked us on a cruise for next week. Nothing but sun, mojitos, spas and lavishing hunks for one whole week to fulfil our every desire. We are going to the Caribbean!" she shouts at the top of her voice and they both scream in excitement.

Chloe hugs Alexis with joy. "You are the best friend ever, thank you."

"No thanks needed," replies Alexis but she cannot help noticing Michael staring at them from a distance. "Just be sure to smile from now on as you have your whole life ahead of you. That chapter of your life with Michael is over now."

Michael punches his fists in anger as he remains standing at the top of the courthouse steps watching the two women staring back at him. He knows he is losing his power over Chloe, but he controls his emotions as many people are walking in and out of the courthouse.

Chloe and Alexis hold hands as they give one last glance at Michael. "He won't harm you ever again," mutters Alexis softly at Chloe. "If he does, I promise you, I will kill him this time," she remarks and then smiles at Chloe. "Come on, I'll buy you lunch."

"You got these tickets, the least I can do is buy *you* lunch."

"Nonsense," replies Alexis, "today is *your* day. You can buy me lunch some other time. Let's go to Roberto's Italian just two blocks away. His lasagne is out of this world and God knows we both need a good Italian wine right about now," she says, grabbing Chloe's hand firmly and taking the lead as they walk at a faster pace down the street feeling energized and full of life.

1
The Journey

At the entrance of a lovely driveway in a picturesque suburb of Miami, in the city of Weston, a postman opens a letter box with the name "Moore" written on it and introduces a number of letters inside. A number of children ride their bicycles on this bright sunny morning and some of the neighbours go about their daily activities as the postman looks up at the *"Moore's"* semi-detached two storey home. He dreams of one day owning a property like this with its beautifully cut hedges and white picket fence.

Inside a large garage filled with all sorts of stowed away items in many shelves, a parked SUV and a gym built on a corner with a treadmill, weights and a punching bag, is Ethan Moore, Chloe's father. He's a Police Detective who is 45 years of age, wearing a sweatshirt, shorts and sneakers, relentlessly pounding the punching bag. Hanging proudly on a wall there are a number of old framed photographs: *Ethan Moore posing with his black belt in a Martial Arts competition. Ethan Moore standing proudly on a podium cheering as he holds a winning trophy in the air. Ethan Moore wearing a Miami Police Sergeant's uniform posing with his Police partner Hank Shaw in their black and white patrol car. Ethan Moore firing a hand gun in a police firing range. Ethan Moore with his late wife Amber and a young Chloe on a happy occasion.* On one of the shelves there is a gold Detective's shield and service handgun tucked away in a holster. Many medals and ribbons proudly decorate another wall, showing an achievement of Ethan's countless wins throughout the years for his Martial Arts and weapons firing, a true sportsman and top-class Police Detective who has partially converted the garage into his own man cave.

The connecting door to the house opens and Chloe walks inside carrying a tray holding a glass of beer and some snacks, wearing casual clothes. She clearly enjoys watching her father train and carefully sets the tray down by a counter. "I think I can hear the bag begging for help," she says loudly with a great big smile on her face.

Ethan stops and wipes sweat from his face, giving Chloe a loving smile. "I didn't hear you walk in," he says reaching for the beer.

"You never do when you are so concentrated on beating the shit out of that bag," she replies and takes a bite from one of the snacks.

Ethan stands tall with a brave smile, glancing over at the photograph of them on the wall. "Your mother always told me the same thing," he replies emotionally, smiling vehemently at his wife's smile in the photograph.

Chloe smiles proudly at the happy photograph. "I miss her, too."

"I know you do, pumpkin," he replies and then puts down the glass and erratically tackles Chloe, pinning her to the floor. But she quickly overpowers her father and manages to pin him to the floor instead.

"You are slipping old man," she remarks teasingly, trying to keep him pinned down.

"Who are you calling old?" he yells arduously, and then taps the floor to give up. She quickly releases him and they both give a proud look at each other and she helps him to stand. "You taught me to defend myself well, dad, but God, you stink. Better hit the shower before Alexis arrives for the barbeque, you have less than an hour to get ready."

Ethan kisses Chloe on the cheek. "Yes, mother," he says jokingly and walks into the house through the connecting door, leaving Chloe all alone to take a moment where she glances around the garage, remembering all those happy moments she once spent in here training with her father all those years ago. She looks at the treadmill where she once turned the speed so high it nearly caught fire. She glances over at the dumbbells and larger weights, where she played all sorts of pranks on her father while he used them. She then punches the bag in a highly professional manner and smiles, remembering how Ethan taught her the techniques of fist fighting while her mother used to watch and cheer her on, every afternoon.

"Come on, Chloe!" her mother used to shout at her. *"You can do it, that's my girl!"* Remembering, holding back her tears, she walks closer to the photograph of her family together and silently starts to cry, clearly missing her mother dearly. "I miss you, mom," she whispers and caresses her mother's smiling happy face in the photograph.

***

Lounging on deckchairs in the backyard garden beside the pool, Chloe and Alexis, both wearing colourful bikinis showing off their bronzed and toned bodies, enjoy homemade cocktails as they sit back and stare up at the beautiful blue sky. Ethan happily flips burgers on the grill, wearing an apron over a clean shirt and his blue bathing shorts.

"I hope you like these babies cooked to perfection, cos they are just oozing with love," he proudly shouts out as he places three buns on the grill. The constant sizzling of the meat being slowly cooked along with the beefy aroma and the smoke rising up from the grill is what Ethan loves the most about barbeque afternoons, a tradition they do every week during the summer. A time he can enjoy with both his daughter and Alexis, who's become part of the family.

"You cook'em Ethan, show them who's boss!" shouts Alexis teasingly.

"Remember not to overcook mine like last time, dad," reminds Chloe as she sips her cocktail.

"I know, pumpkin," replies Ethan as he tenderly prepares a juicy hamburger with green salad and mayonnaise and hands it to Chloe.

"My master chef," giggles Chloe as she takes a bite and savours the burger in her mouth. "I am in heaven right now."

Ethan prepares a second juicy burger and now hands it to Alexis who quickly takes a bite and is amazed by the richness of the flavours. "You have outdone yourself today, Ethan. It's one of the best burger's I have ever tasted."

"Thank you for your positive comments, ladies," replies Ethan as he now prepares his own burger and takes a great big bite, savouring the burger in his mouth. "I should have been a chef. These are really good," he remarks and sits down on his lounge chair beside the girls and takes a sip from an opened can of beer sitting beside his chair.

"I am happy the divorce finally came through and that bum is no longer a part of your life, honey." Ethan says and raises his beer to make a toast. "To having control over your own life again."

"To freedom," replies Chloe as she clinks her cocktail with the beer.

"To getting back two years of lost fun," remarks Alexis as she also clinks her cocktail with their drinks and they all take a sip of their drinks.

"Thank you for all your support, dad," Chloe shyly says to Ethan with a tender smile on her face. Then she turns to Alexis. "And thank you for sticking by me through those dark moments in my life and keeping me sane."

Alexis leans over and gives Chloe a loving hug, holding back her tears to remain strong. "No need to thank me. That is what friends are for," Alexis says as they keep hugging.

Ethan holds back his tears as he proudly watches with satisfaction, knowing his daughter will be well looked after by

Alexis. "Just promise me one thing, pumpkin."

"Anything, dad," replies Chloe who now leans back on her chair.

"Enjoy yourselves but for God's sake, don't fall for the next deadbeat you meet, especially on that boat!" he replies with a warm smile.

"Jesus, Ethan, she's not a baby and it's a ship we're going on!" replies Alexis giggling with Chloe to make her feel alive and happy.

"I stand corrected, a ship, not a boat!" he says and laughs giving Chloe a loving smile. "But you are still my little girl, always will be, and I will never stop worrying about you."

Chloe cannot hold back her emotions any longer and cries, leaping up from her chair she gives Ethan a great big hug, wrapping her arms tightly around his neck. "Thank you, dad. I love you."

"And I you, Chloe," replies Ethan proudly also shedding a tear.

Alexis cannot help it and also cries but remains watching in silence.

"I promise I will call every day to let you know I am fine." Whispers Chloe into Ethan's ear as they both cry together.

"I will make sure nothing happens to her, Ethan," says Alexis confidently.

"I know you will, Alexis," replies Ethan with a fatherly smile. "You are like Chloe's oldest sister and I know you will both be just fine on board with all that sun surf and open bars."

"I just can't believe we're sailing tomorrow. Jamaica, here we come!" shouts out Chloe with anticipation.

"I will definitely drink to that!" yells Alexis and downs her cocktail in one shot.

Chloe drinks her cocktail, too, and sits back on her chair.

There is something troubling Ethan in the pit of his stomach, but he just smiles at the girls with a sense of concern, not wanting to ruin the moment or their weeklong vacation.

***

Ethan drives his SUV along the heavy traffic down the Port of Miami Tunnel. Chloe and Alexis are sitting at the back, glancing through cruise brochures, completely energized, hyperactive with anticipation as their vacation is about to begin. Both are wearing casual sexy summer wear while Ethan has on shorts and a shirt.

"The beaches in Ocho Rios are so beautiful there's even horseback riding and snorkelling," explains Alexis with excitement staring at the stunning marketing pictures in the brochures. "We're gonna have so much fun, I just know it!" she adds and she and Chloe high five.

"I can't wait to visit Grand Cayman Island. I hear George Town is a hidden gem!" remarks Chloe and puts her brochure down. "I think this vacation will be good for me. Get my mind off to a new and much needed, fresh start."

"Just promise me you won't speak with strangers and you *will* call every night, so I know you're both okay," requests Ethan firmly keeping his eyes on the busy road ahead.

"We promise," replies Alexis mischievously, "besides, now that Chloe's single again maybe she'll meet her Mister Right. They do say cruises are best known for their romances."

"The whole idea of going on this vacation is to celebrate my divorce and being free again, not to get hooked with another man," confesses Chloe with a mischievous grin on her face.

"I know that look," giggles Alexis.

"What look?" asks Ethan expressing concern.

"The here comes trouble look!" Alexis says and they all laugh.

Ethan eventually drives into the impressive parking lot and carefully parks his SUV at the "Cruise Line Terminal Parking" where hundreds of vehicles are arriving and parking all around them. He turns off the engine and takes a deep breath as he observes how hundreds of people are making their way into the nearby massive terminal building carrying many pieces of luggage for their cruise.

"Well, here we are," he says and looks back at the girls. "You ready?"

"Oh yeah!" replies Alexis and together with Chloe they quickly exit the SUV, leaving Ethan now watching an empty back seat.

"Of course you are," he whispers with a sigh and promptly exits the SUV. His attention is drawn to the impressive luxury cruise ships berthed along the entire port, but to one in particular, *"The Poseidon of the Seas"* docked nearby which is the ship Chloe and Alexis will be boarding soon.

"She's a big sucker, isn't she, Ethan?" asks Alexis who is also admiring their cruise ship.

"I'm surprised the cruise is only five days," he replies, totally perplexed, "it would take anyone five days just to explore the whole ship."

Chloe opens the trunk and begins taking out four large suitcases from the back. "As long as we know where the pools and the bars are, we'll be fine," she says.

"And the buffet restaurants," adds Alexis as she helps Chloe with the luggage and soon the four suitcases and on the ground. Ethan snaps out of his trance, as there is something bothering him about that ship. He shuts the trunk and locks the SUV.

"You got everything?" he asks checking the four suitcases.

"Yes, two a piece," Chloe says happily as she examines their luggage and pats her purse to ensure she hasn't left anything inside the SUV. "Yes, that's everything."

Alexis takes her two suitcases and begins rolling them towards the busy terminal building, where hundreds of people are shuffling in all directions. Ethan takes the remaining two suitcases and begins to roll them also towards the terminal building while Chloe walks beside him with a great big smile on her face.

"I just don't understand why you need so much stuff," he says, pulling the suitcases. "I mean, you are only going for five days, yet you've packed for an entire month," he mutters as he struggles with the suitcases trying to keep up with an experienced Alexis who is ahead of him walking at a faster pace.

"This is nothing!" replies Alexis with a happy smile on her face. "Just wait till we return from the cruise next week!"

"We are going on a shopping spree and bringing back an extra two more cases each full of great stuff," adds Chloe super excited and the girls both yell with joy.

"God help me. I will need to build you a new wardrobe!" jokes Ethan making the girls laugh as they continue walking ahead.

***

Over twenty minutes have passed since they arrived and Ethan, Chloe and Alexis are patiently waiting at the front of a long line inside the massive Terminal Building. Over fifteen other lines hold hundreds upon hundreds of other passengers who are also patiently waiting for their turn to be attended by the small army of "*Check in*" friendly cruise attendants staff members at their counters. Each staff wearing their distinguishing cruise uniforms and showing their pearly whites with their welcoming smiles. Ethan looks behind him only to be amazed at the long line of passengers who continue to arrive and are patiently waiting. The couple that are being attended to in front of them leave, and it's now their turn.

"Good morning and welcome to the check-in desk of The Poseidon of the Seas," says a smiling attendant at Chloe, who is next in line. "My name is Clarisa. How may I help you today?"

Ethan, Chloe and Alexis approach the counter rolling their four suitcases along smiling at Clarisa.

"We have a reservation," replies Alexis, who hands Clarisa some printed documents and their tickets, "Alexis Young and Chloe Moore."

Clarisa checks the documents and types on her computer keyboard where on her monitor the names Alexis Young and Chloe Moore promptly appear.

"Yes, here you are," she says confirming their reservation. "You are in stateroom 6505, on deck seven," she adds and punches the *"print"* button on her keyboard where a printer is activated and, in a few seconds, two plastic bracelets labelled *"All inclusive"* are printed along with an official one page document. She collects them all and hands them over to Alexis. "Please be sure to have these bracelets on you at all times," she adds and waits as the girls securely fasten the bracelets on their wrists while Clarisa smiles at Ethan.

"I am just here to say farewell," says Ethan shyly to Clarisa.

"We will take good care of them for you, sir. There is nothing for you to worry about," says Clarisa professionally. She smiles back at the girls checking the bracelets are secured. "They are waterproof and soft to the skin so make sure you don't remove them as you have paid for the all-inclusive package which gives you full access to any of the bars on board where you can get as many drinks as you like."

Chloe and Alexis hug in excitement, "Yes!"

"I will now need both of you to look into this camera so we can take a picture of your faces," she says pointing to a small web camera mounted above the computer's monitor.

Alexis gets into position and smiles at the camera. Clarisa hits the *"Enter"* key on her keyboard and takes Alexis's picture. It is now Chloe's turn and she gets into position and smiles at the camera. Again, the attendant hits the *"Enter"* key on her keyboard and takes Chloe's picture. Soon two boarding cards are printed out, one with Chloe's picture and details and the other with Alexis's picture and details. Clarisa collects the cards and hands them over to the girls.

"These are your boarding passes, which you will need to have on you at all times when you disembark or board the ship during port calls. It will also open your stateroom door."

"How is security on board the ship?" asks a concerned Ethan.

"We have a highly experienced security team at hand, sir. Part of their duties are to cross check every passenger entering the ship in any of the ports by swiping the code on the cards and checking that the pictures match the passenger in front of them. So no one will be on board who is not supposed to be," she says, perceiving Ethan's concerns. "Would you mind putting the luggage on the counter please?"

Ethan promptly puts the four cases in a special slot on the counter. The attendant puts tags on each of the suitcases so they are delivered to stateroom 6505.

"When you are ready, please make your way to my colleague standing at gate 6 and he will direct you to the gangway," confirms Clarisa gesturing over to her colleague standing at "Gate 6" on the other end of the ample building. "Will there be anything else?"

"I think you've covered everything quite well," replies Chloe.

"If you need anything while aboard remember to go to the Guest Services desk where my colleagues there will provide any assistance you may require. Enjoy your cruise and thank you for choosing to sail with us today," replies Clarisa with a wide and bright smile.

Ethan, Chloe and Alexis walk away from the line and the next passengers now stand by the counter where Clarisa attends to them.

"Well, that was painless," remarks Ethan as they negotiate their way towards gate number 6 where a steward, wearing a smart white uniform, is directing checked-in passengers into the gangway leading up to the side of the impressive ship.

"It's supposed to be painless, Ethan, it's a cruise," replies Alexis.

"Are you sure you got everything?" Ethan asks as they reach a line by gate number six.

Chloe gives Ethan a great big hug. "Yes, dad. Relax," she replies. "It will be fine."

"I will be waiting for you right here when you return," he says, holding back his tears.

"My knight in shining armour." She kisses her father on the cheek. "I love you."

"I love you more," he says with a great big smile wiping a tear from her eyes. "What's this?"

At this moment a female ship's photographer is taking a picture of a couple near Alexis.

"Tears of joy," says Chloe shyly.

"I got an idea," says Alexis and quickly waves at the ship's photographer for her to come. "Excuse me, you mind taking a picture of us before we board?"

"Of course," says the ship's photographer who promptly arrives and smiles at Alexis. "Who will be in the picture?"

"Us three," Alexis says and quickly gathers Ethan and Chloe together and they happily put their arms around each other and smile at the camera.

"Hold that pose and," she says looking through her camera's viewfinder at the warm family pose and professionally takes two quick snaps, capturing the joyful moment, "got it!"

They thank the photographer.

"My pleasure, the pictures will be on the photo board on deck five later this evening," she replies and walks away to another passenger nearby who is waving at her to take their picture.

"Well, this is it," Ethan says to both Chloe and Alexis, and they all have one last big hug. "Better get going before you see me cry."

Chloe and Alexis both, simultaneously, kiss Ethan on the cheek.

"See you next week, dad," says Chloe and walks over to the steward at gate number six, giving Ethan one last wave.

"She will be a new woman when we return, Ethan," Alexis says with a positive tone.

"Thank you for this, Alexis. It's just what she needs."

Alexis winks at Ethan and smiles knowingly, she then turns and walks to gate number six where Chloe is waiting for her. They turn one last time back at Ethan and wave goodbye. Ethan waves, watching how the steward invites them both to go up the long gangway to board the ship. Chloe and Alexis hold hands and walk full of excitement up the gangway following other happy passengers boarding ahead of them.

Ethan's smile soon fades away, as that gut feeling he had, returns, making him feel uncomfortable, as if he knows that something terrible is going to happen but doesn't know what. He takes a last glimpse of Chloe and Alexis disappearing up the gangway, noticing that a team of the ship's security inspects the girls' boarding passes at a control desk, and soon allows them on board, where they eventually get lost in the busy crowds along the deck. "Five days," he mutters to himself and then walks away towards the building's exit, passing hundreds of arriving happy passengers shuffling in all directions to get in the check-in lines.

2
The Adventure

Hundreds of passengers and crew members shuffle about in this spectacular foyer, decorated elegantly to the last detail of perfection: A large fountain setting off controlled jets of water with a bronze statue of the God "Poseidon" holding his trident situated in the centre of the massive foyer. Four panoramic elevators that can travel all the way up to the 15th floor, each floor lit by thousands of tiny spot lights resembling stars in the night sky. A pianist, dressed in a black suit, elegantly playing classical music on a grand piano. An impressive busy cocktail bar serving drinks to passengers. A spiral grand staircase stretching up to the first floor. A broad selection of trees decorating the interior to give the setting a more peaceful and relaxing tone. Countless windows looking out to sea. Many comfortable couches and armchairs conveniently situated next to cosy tables strategically placed around the foyer, ensuring passengers can take everything in from the comfort of any seat. Lavish crystal chandeliers hang graciously from the enormous ceiling. Thick colourful carpets cushion the passengers' steps, giving them a sensation of floating in the air. Beautiful colourful lamps give an extra touch of colour to the already bright foyer.

Chloe and Alexis walk into this impressive foyer and are flabbergasted as they look around in excitement, watching the never ending ceiling.

"Oh my God!" remarks an excited Chloe.

"Welcome to The Poseidon of the Seas, ladies," says a waiter who stands beside them holding a tray filled with complementary glasses of champagne.

"Thank you," Chloe says watching the champagne with a smile.

"Like they say," remarks Alexis grabbing two glasses of champagne from the tray, "when in Rome!" She adds and hands one of the glasses over to Chloe as the waiter now walks to the next passengers.

"Do what the Romans do!" Alexis adds as they clink their glasses and sip the cold soothing champagne.

"I can't believe we are actually here," Chloe remarks, overwhelmed in exhilaration.

"Neither can I!" replies Alexis and they both look at each other and scream happily as they embrace and jump up and down expressing their joy while many passengers notice them and smile.

Watching the foyer from the second deck, the ship's doctor, Dr. Hugo Morales, a 35-year-old African-Dominican man, wearing his smart white doctor's uniform with a name tag that reads *"Dr. Morales"* notices Chloe and Alexis jumping with excitement in the centre of the foyer. He also notices the girls' attractive physiques, and leans over the railing to get a closer look at them.

His brown coloured eyes open wider as he clenches his hands tighter to the railings, like a wild animal locked up in a cage ready to escape.

His sight never leaves the girls as they continue to walk around the foyer, clearly capturing his undivided attention with their giggles. He touches a small scar on his right eyebrow with his right hand, as he thinks for a moment, never losing his focus from the girls for one second. He then snaps his fingers and raises his right hand in the air.

Viktor Pavlov, a good looking 40-year-old Russian steward, with stunning blue eyes, wearing a smart white uniform with a name tag *"Viktor Pavlov"* who has been patiently waiting nearby, immediately stands behind Morales with an emotionless stare on his cold face. Morales inconspicuously motions to Pavlov to observe the girls below. They both closely study Chloe and Alexis who are continuing to enjoy their champagne as they wander innocently through the grand bar, soon stopping to order some drinks, unaware they are now the centre of attention.

"Find out if they are alone." Orders Morales with a striking Spanish accent and a soft voice, so not to attract unnecessary attention from many of the passengers who are walking behind them.

Pavlov doesn't reply. He just nods his head and walks away leaving Morales passing his right index finger through his lips as he continues to study Chloe, not giving too much attention to Alexis.

Chloe and Alexis are being served Bloody Mary cocktails at the grand bar by a friendly waiter who quickly attends to other waiting passengers. "We better slow down, otherwise we are going to get plastered before the ship sails!" jokes Chloe.

"So what if we do?" asks Alexis who waves her plastic bracelet at Chloe. "Thanks to these beauties we can get plastered every single day while we're here!"

"And night!" replies Chloe and they both scream with excitement once again at each other and then down their cocktails in one shot, slamming their empty glasses onto the counter and break out in laughter. "I should have done this a long time ago," confesses Chloe, feeling sorry for herself and the hardship she had to endure at the hands of her now ex-husband Michael.

Alexis gives Chloe a supportive hug as she too understands her best friend's suffering.

"Welcome aboard The Poseidon of the Seas, ladies," says Pavlov with a striking Russian accent as he stands behind the girls with a seductive smile. "Named after the ancient Greek God Poseidon, God of the sea."

"Wasn't Poseidon the ancient God of earthquakes and horses also?" asks Chloe knowingly.

"You know your history well." Pavlov says, impressed.

"I majored in ancient Greek," she replies candidly.

"Then you will be happy to know that this ship is blessed to have the God's name to make our journey across the ocean, safer."

Both Chloe and Alexis are impressed with how professional and smart in appearance Pavlov looks in his stunning white uniform. They give each other an impish but secretive stare that only they know the meaning of; that this man is hot.

Alexis smiles, extends her right hand at Pavlov and takes a step forward. "I just love a man with an accent."

Pavlov takes Alexis's hand and seductively kisses it like a true gentleman. "My name is Viktor Pavlov and I will be one of your stewards during your stay with us."

"I am Alexis and this is Chloe," she replies with a blush.

"Is this your first time on our ship?"

Alexis gets closer to Pavlov and she can smell his striking aftershave, making her very interested in him. "There is always a first time for everything, Viktor," she whispers sensuously.

"It is a big ship," he replies knowing how easy this will be.

"The bigger the better, I say," replies Alexis with a wink.

Chloe kicks Alexis on the leg in order to make her snap out of her usual wild self, making Pavlov blush as he clears his throat.

"In that case, so you beautiful ladies, not get lost, please allow me to escort you to cabin, so you know where it is, and can freshen up. I be happy to answer any questions you may have about our beautiful vessel, yes?" he says in a seductive tone.

"Thank you, Viktor," replies Chloe.

"We are in stateroom 6505," says Alexis sensuously.

"Then we must go, deck seven, we will get elevator. Come."

Alexis smiles at Chloe and back at Pavlov.

"Lead the way, kind sir," instructs Alexis.

From the second deck, Morales observes how Pavlov escorts the girls towards one of the waiting elevators, noticing how Alexis is chatting up Pavlov while Chloe remains one step behind.

***

Pavlov escorts Chloe and Alexis along a labyrinth of narrow corridors passing many closed and open stateroom doors, also passing dozens of other excited passengers and a small army of crew members delivering suitcases to their corresponding staterooms.

Chloe observes the many interesting framed art paintings hanging along the corridors, together with a number of emergency fire axes inside glass cabinets in the event of any emergency. There are also detailed layout charts of the ship's decks hanging on the walls.

"How long have you been working on board this ship, Viktor?" asks Alexis.

"Just over three years now," he says.

"I bet it must get somewhat lonely at times."

"At times, yes," he replies honestly. "Tell me, you are alone?"

"Just the two of us," replies Alexis throwing her arm around Chloe's shoulders. "Me and my bestie for a whole week."

"That is nice. I am sure you will meet nice boys."

"Boys?" mutters Alexis in disgust. "Who needs boys when we can have *real* men who know how to treat a woman right?"

"You are absolutely correct, Alexis," he remarks as they finally arrive at the closed stateroom 6505 door. "And here we are."

"Would you like to come in and check if everything is where it's supposed to be, Viktor?" asks Alexis with an obvious flirt.

"I hope in some other time, as I must attend to other passengers now," he replies but takes her right hand and kisses it tenderly. "I will however say this, that we will meet again, maybe sooner than you expect. Until then, enjoy this ship," he adds and nods politely at the girls before walking away and leaving them alone.

Alexis leans backwards and lets out an emotional sigh. "I feel like Cinderella right about now."

Chloe takes out her boarding card and swipes it on the keypad to unlock the door. "Cinderella was a saint compared to you." She giggles as she swings open their stateroom door.

"I wasn't going to sleep with him," she replies seductively. "Well, at least not until he bought me a drink first," she adds with a giggle.

"Slut!" giggles Chloe as she walks into their room and Alexis quickly follows her inside.

"Will you look at this?" says Chloe in excitement exploring the stateroom that has two individual beds with beautiful animal decorations made out of folded towels resting at the foot of each bed. There is a porthole overlooking the blue skies outside. One couch. One connecting bathroom with a small shower. Two fitted small wardrobes and a mounted TV on the wall. A small desk with cruise letters and magazines. Their four pieces of luggage have been delivered and placed neatly beside the beds.

"Oh, I want to learn how to make this." Says Alexis picking up a towel folded to resemble a swan.

Chloe embraces Alexis and they both share a moment. "Thank you for always being there for me and for being here with me now," she says emotionally from the heart.

"Are you kidding? Who wouldn't want to be on a cruise and be pampered for a whole week?" she asks and they both laugh.

"Let's slip into our bikinis and tour this beast!"

***

Hundreds of passengers wave from many of her decks, as the ship slowly sets sail away from its berth, being carefully towed out to sea by two tug boats. Dozens of people watch proudly from the pier, waving back at the gradually sailing ship that is safely leaving the port. The ship's loud air-horn blasts repeatedly, as it says its farewell to Miami. Chloe and Alexis enjoy the moment as they are lost in the massive crowds, cheering and waving like crazy, wearing their sexy bikinis and sunglasses as they portray being the tourists they are. Amongst the dozens of people watching from the pier, Ethan waves farewell at the sailing ship, making sure the girls left safely. He smiles tenderly and looks up at the sky above.

"Watch over our Chloe," he whispers hoping his wife may somehow look after their daughter like a guardian angel.

***

Chloe and Alexis walk excitedly around the massive and luxuriously packed and ample promenade deck, where many named brands offer clothing, perfumes, gifts, children's items and food stores, conveniently located along the entire length of the ship, inviting the thousands of passengers to buy tax free products while enjoying appetising meals and snacks. The girls window browse and have the time of their lives, clowning around without a care of what anyone may think of them, as they behave like two teenage girls that have been set free, living the moment and making cherished memories as they fool around, giggle, laugh and enjoy life to the full. They even play tag and chase one another, nearly bumping into many passengers, laughing with joy until suddenly Chloe's attention is drawn to what she believes to be the most beautiful dress in the whole world, on display in one of the store windows. It's a pink cocktail dress with matching purse and high heeled shoes.

"Oh my God, I think I've died and gone to heaven," she remarks, touching the window admiring the pink dress with diamond accessories, and imagining she's wearing it.

"That sure is pretty," Alexis says as she grabs Chloe's hand and pulls her into the store. "Come on, let's try it on!" They giggle as they enter the store and one of the store attendants promptly greets them.

"We would like to try on that dress you have in the window please," says a serious Alexis trying to hold her posture.

"Right away," replies the friendly attendant. "Please, follow me." She escorts the girls to the fitting area located at the back.

Alexis and Chloe wander their eyes all around the beautiful store closely observing the many gorgeous clothes available. "I think I will be in here every day," she says totally ecstatic.

They soon arrive at the fitting area and the attendant gestures for the girls to sit on the comfortable chairs. "Please take a seat while I bring the dresses over," she says confidently and walks away.

"How does she know our sizes?" asks a curious Chloe.

"Are you kidding?" replies Alexis as they sit down. "They are trained to check us out even before we step foot into the store. Besides, with figures like ours, it's obvious what sizes we are."

The attendant soon returns with two matching pink dresses and hands them one each. "You may change in there," she says gesturing at a number of changing booths situated behind them. They immediately grab their dresses and walk into the same booth where they change together, something they have been doing since a younger age as they clearly hide no secrets from each other. Soon they walk out to a nearby mirror where they see how beautiful they look.

"You both look stunning," remarks the attendant.

"It's perfect," whispers Chloe feeling how it fits her body like a glove.

"We'll take them," says an enthusiastic Alexis to the attendant.

***

Sitting and enjoying an ice cream Sundae in one of the many snack stores, with their shopping bags resting next to their feet, Chloe and Alexis observe the never-ending stream of passengers shuffling about in the now busier promenade deck.

"These are amazing!" says Chloe savouring the creamy Sundae.

"The only problem is if we have too many we'll lose our figures and men may not look at us like they do now."

"Why must everything revolve around sex with you?"

"Maybe because I need it more than you do."

"Spoken like a true slut!" laughs Chloe, making Alexis laugh.

"Let's take another selfie, this time with the Sundaes," says Alexis taking out her cell phone and they make silly gestures with the Sundaes, capturing the happy occasion on camera.

"At this rate, you'll need to buy another memory card with all the selfies you're taking."

"I got that covered," replies Alexis taking a few more selfies of herself with pursed lips, "I brought three new cards. I figured, we're here only once so we might as well take hundreds of memories together."

***

At the impressive *"Windjammer"* buffet restaurant, an army of cooks serve rich cooked food ranging from: Chicken, Meats, Fish, Vegetables, Sushi, Indian, Chinese, East European and Soups to hundreds of passengers enjoying their meals while staring out to the open sea from their tables. The dessert station has an equally eye-watering selection of treats from all countries, ensuring every sweet tooth on board is indulged.

Chloe and Alexis continue to fill up their plates with a variety of salads and fish, unaware Morales is closely observing them from a distance. "Can you imagine how much preparation has gone into having so much food just laid out like this?" remarks Alexis amazed. "And the attention to detail is just unbelievable."

"Let's sit down over there," says Chloe. They soon reach an empty table overlooking the ocean, where they set their food trays down. Alexis takes out her cell phone and snaps a number of selfies with Chloe and the stunning ocean views in the background.

"I haven't had so much food since my mom passed away," recalls Chloe, taking a moment to recollect her thoughts.

"She was a great cook, Chloe."

"Yes, she was," she replies with a heavy heart as they sit down and get ready to have their lunch.

"And no matter where she may be right now, I am sure she must be watching over you and shouting, eat the whole plate," Alexis says jokingly, making Chloe laugh.

"One thing's for sure."

"What's that?"

"When we get back home, we're hitting the gym."

"That may be so but while we're here, let's indulge and worry about the extra pounds when the time comes."

They laugh and eat their food while staring out to sea.

Morales walks slowly, protected as he carefully blends in behind many passengers. Closely observing Chloe's firmed body he licks his lower lip with his tongue.

***

"I haven't felt this relaxed in a long time," confesses Chloe as she and Alexis stroll along the ample pool area in the top deck, feeling the cool ocean breeze against their bodies, feeling reborn.

"I am happy for you," Alexis says passionately.

Chloe holds Alexis's hand and squeezes tight, as a thank you gesture for her constant support, sharing this very important moment. "Two years in a shitty marriage can put an awful lot of strain on your health," she remarks knowingly.

"You suffered enough and now it's time to move on," replies Alexis with a comforting tone as they stare out to sea, observing how the calm waters reach out into the horizon wrapped by the never-ending blue skies above. "What do you say we check out that bar over there?" she hints seductively as she observes a sexy male bartender serving an enticing cocktail to a 21-year-old stud wearing nothing but blue bathing shorts and revealing an impressive six pack on his firmed, bronzed and toned hairless bare chest.

"Hell, yeah!" replies Chloe clearly checking out the stud from head to toe and they walk across the pool area, passing many passengers enjoying the large pool and Jacuzzi tubs situated in the centre of the deck, surrounded by hundreds of comfortable deck lounge beds where more passengers of all ages are resting, relaxing and enjoying the sun.

An army of waiters shuffle with trays, delivering drinks to many of the passengers while many young children are playing water activities in one part of the large pool, closely monitored by a number of the ship's entertainment crew who look after them.

Chloe and Alexis soon arrive at the bar and stand beside the stud.

"Can we get two mojitos, please?" asks Alexis at the bartender who nods his head at her and smiles, confirming the order.

"So, you like mojitos, huh?" asks the stud softly with a posh London accent, standing beside Alexis proudly showing off his firmed abs.

"Only when served right," replies Alexis seductively as she can't keep her eyes off his toned body.

The stud extends his hand, "I'm Sammy."

"Alexis," she replies with a blush as she shakes his hand hearing how Chloe clears her throat right beside her. "And this is Chloe."

"Nice to meet you too," he says and shakes Chloe's hand.

The bartender puts two mojitos by Alexis who waves her wrist and shows him her *"all inclusive"* bracelet and he walks away to serve more waiting passengers. "I love your accent," she remarks taking a step closer to Sammy. "You Brits have such a way with words."

"Thank you," he blushes. "Say, do you want to do something later?" he asks, feeling confident about himself.

"You mean, like a date?" asks Alexis feeling surprised. "But I hardly know you."

"I just got divorced," interrupts Chloe innocently, making Alexis sink her head in shame. "I am not looking for a date right now, besides, my dad would freak out if I told him I met a guy, so no thanks."

"Will you excuse me for one sec?" asks Alexis with a shy smile and quickly grabs hold of Chloe's arm and takes her a few steps away.

"Of course," he replies with a smile, patiently waiting and sipping his beer.

"Are you for real?" she whispers at Chloe. "What's wrong with hanging out with him for a while and getting wild? Have you seen his six pack? God, I haven't had abs like those in a long time, and honey, I have been around, let me tell yeah! Come on, it's a romantic ship, you get a bit of romance back in your life and who knows, maybe he's loaded! Set you up for life. Cut me some slack! I'm not getting any younger and by the way, neither are you."

"I just don't feel comfortable being with another man so soon after Michael." Chloe explains but sinks her head in regret.

Alexis now understands and nods her head. "How selfish was I? she hugs Chloe and they embrace reaffirming their sisterly bond.

Standing on the upper deck looking down at the top deck below, Morales slowly observes how Chloe and Alexis walk back to Sammy. Alexis engages him in a conversation while Chloe takes her mojito from the bar and sips it.

"I am all alone on this cruise taking a gap year from my studies in England, to explore your beautiful country," reveals Sammy as he gets closer to Alexis, finding her extremely attractive.

"You must have so many interesting and fascinating stories, and I see you are all alone, just like we are. What do you say you have dinner with us tonight? That way you can tell us all about yourself and I get a chance to hear more of that lovely accent of yours," says Alexis.

"Oh please, give me a break," mutters Chloe under her breath.

"Sorry Chloe, what was that?" asks Alexis knowingly with an impatient grin. "We didn't quite hear what you said!"

"I said, it sounds like a date," she replies with a smile.

"Yes, that definitely sounds like a date," he states.

"Great, it's settled then," Alexis says with an overwhelming smile. "Let's do this then. It's now five. Chloe and I have some girl stuff to take care of, so come round to our stateroom, that's 6505, on deck seven and pick us up at say, seven o'clock? Then we will have the whole evening to ourselves, will that work?"

"6505, seven sharp. I will be there," he replies confidently.

Alexis takes her mojito from the bar and grabs Chloe's arm. "Great, then see you in a few hours Sammy," she adds and pushes Chloe away, leaving Sammy all alone at the bar feeling happy.

"God, I'm in love!" whispers Alexis full of joy.

"You think it was wise giving him our room number?" Chloe questions.

"Will you relax already? You sound like your old man. Live a little, will yeah! Besides, what can possibly go wrong on a cruise ship?"

"How about you getting pregnant?" jokes Chloe, but then turns around to take one last look at Sammy's toned body. "I must admit, he is rather cute."

"Honey, cute is an understatement. He is, *hot*!" Alexis replies and sends a farewell wave at Sammy who promptly waves back.

Following them from the upper deck, Morales slowly walks along as he continues to observe Chloe. Suddenly, his pager beeps and this makes him angry. He quickly grabs the pager and turns it off.

***

"This is what I call heaven on Earth!" mutters Chloe in a relaxed tone as she and Alexis enjoy a full relaxing massage inside the luxurious Spa by two female crew masseurs, who sensuously rub oils over their backs. They lay on their chests on two massage tables situated one beside the other as the masseurs apply all sorts of professional pressure on their necks, backs and legs.

"You can put Sammy in front of me right now and I will completely ignore him, that's how good I feel," mutters Alexis in a relaxing tone.

"Are you sure you are getting waxed after this?" asks Chloe embarrassingly. "You know, down there?"

"You bet I am, and so are you."

"I am fine, really."

"The hell you are, girl. I've paid for the complete Spa package that includes a bikini line and you are going to get it done. The way you have it, you are more likely to scare away a guy with that wild and untreated scruffy bush of yours in desperate need of TLC!"

"I haven't had it waxed in, well, a long time."

"I rest my case. Now shut up and enjoy the rest of the massage."

The masseurs work their magic hands all over their bodies, making Chloe and Alexis totally relaxed.

3
The Monster Awakes

"Make sure you fill in the forms and sign here," explains a ship's nurse to a concerned mother as she calmly fills in a complex medical form by the reception desk of the ship's infirmary.

Stella, a 14-year-old girl in a bikini, sits patiently in tears having her back completely burned, as a result of too many hours in direct sunlight. She is a shy girl with long legs making her appear older than she really is. The freckles on her face trying to hide her anguish. "It hurts too much, mama," she cries softly.

"I know, sweetie, won't be much longer now," replies the concerned mother who now looks at the waiting nurse. "What's taking the doctor so long? We have been waiting for over thirty minutes."

"I have paged Doctor Morales and he should be arriving at any moment, madam."

The mother glances around at the spacious reception area noticing three connecting doors and one long corridor which is where they entered from: One door leads to the examination room. Another to an operating theatre and the third opened door leads to a ward where there are ten empty beds.

"It's a good thing we are the only patients, otherwise the doctor would have his work cut out," remarks the mother in frustration.

"We are fortunate to have doctor Morales on our staff," replies the dedicated nurse. "He is a brilliant doctor and skilful surgeon."

Footsteps are soon heard approaching from the long corridor and Morales walks into the reception area and stands by the desk.

"A boy tripped and fell by the pool. He will be fine but I got here as fast as I could," he says with a warm and innocent smile.

"Thank you, doctor," replies the mother with a sigh of relief.

"So, what seems to be the problem?"

"It's my daughter, Stella," explains the concerned mother. "She slept in the sun and burned her back."

Morales smiles at Stella and walks over to examine her back, noticing the extreme redness knowing she is in pain. "Eighty percent of all our patients aboard this ship are as a result of sunburn." He remarks as he tries to touch Stella's back, but she moves slightly and shouts, clearly in agony. "No sun cream I take it?" he asks the mother who lowers her head expressing guilt.

"I gave her the wrong one."

"Very common mistake but no need for alarm," he says confidently and helps Stella up. "Finish filling in the forms while I treat your daughter in the examination room," he says firmly and escorts Stella slowly into the connecting examination room.

"Should I assist you, doctor?" asks the nurse curiously.

"No, stay here and help poor mom with the paperwork. I got this covered," he replies with a warm smile and dominant tone.

"Thank you, doctor," replies the mother just as Morales and Stella walk into the examination room and he hesitates, glancing back at the reception desk, observing how the nurse is helping the mother fill in the forms in detail. Then he softly closes the door.

The examination room is spacious and has a large examining table in the centre, sophisticated monitors, large counters, locked up glass cabinets full of medication, two freezers, medical charts on a wall, several cupboards and shelves overflowing with medicines, medical books and lotions. A TV mounted on a wall is playing relaxing footage of travel destinations.

Morales locks the door firmly and turns to watch how Stella

remains standing timidly beside the examination table. He smiles and takes a few steps forward towards her. "I know it hurts but I am here to help you, Stella," he says softly and helps her onto the examination table where she tries to sit down as comfortable as possible. "How old are you?" he asks as he reaches into a cabinet and takes out a small medical bottle of lotion that is not clearly labelled.

"Fourteen, doctor," she replies innocently watching how Morales calmly applies lotion all over his hands and slowly walks impishly behind her to get a good look at her burned back.

"I would have thought you were at least eighteen."

"I get that a lot but I am fourteen."

"Fourteen is a good age," he remarks applying more lotion onto his now creamy wet hands. "I need you to be perfectly still. Can you do that for me?" He asks, raising his hands over her fragile back.

"I will try," she replies with a sniff, then wipes a tear from her eyes.

He rests his hands softly onto her tenuous neck and begins to rub the lotion sensuously over her shoulders, back and neck, making her moan repeatedly in pain, as with every stroke it feels like she is being stabbed by fiery lances. He continues touching her wounds, ignoring her suffering, as he is feeding on her pain, making himself sexually aroused. He moves his body closer against her back and leans his face against her cheek, caressing his lower lip with his tongue, clearly enjoying the sensation of power he has over her.

She can feel his heavy breathing becoming more erratic as he now begins to rub his hands under her bikini top and caress her small but soft tender breasts, making her feel very uncomfortable and confused.

"Do you like this?" he asks with an erratic tone and heavy breathing, trying to control his sexual desires.

"I want my mom to hold my hand," she replies crying, unable to endure the pain much longer.

He moves his mouth closer to her ear as he feels her nipples getting harder. "Girls don't need their mommies holding their hands."

"Please, stop," she cries in shock unable to move. But he ignores her and ruthlessly forces her flat on the table, resulting in more agonising and excruciating pain, as she now lays on her back, mercilessly trapped, forcing her to let out a blood curdling scream. She is clearly traumatised as to what is happening to her, helplessly watching how he carelessly sits on her legs, pinning her to the table and thrusts his entire body forward, trying to kiss her intimately on the mouth like a wild animal in heat.

Rejecting his malicious intentions she fights by moving her head from side to side while enduring the weight of his body, making it harder for her to breathe. "Please, stop!" she shouts gasping for air, clearly in shock as she suddenly feels his erect penis rubbing firmly against her leg, and she fears the worst.

A knock is suddenly heard at the door making Morales stop and cover her mouth with his creamy left hand as he quickly glances at the closed door, making sure it's locked.

"Is everything all right, doctor? We heard a scream," asks the nurse from the other side of the door.

"Just applying lotion to the burned areas," he replies calmly. "We will be out momentarily as she is still in a lot of pain," he adds, staring into Stella's petrified wide eyes that are clearly traumatised.

They soon hear the nurse walk away from the closed door and he touches Stella's forehead with his index finger, running it slowly down through her now quivering face. "I know who you are and I know your room number." He grins maliciously watching how tears pour down her petrified eyes making him more powerful. "Do you know what happens to stupid girls who tell their mommy or their friends fantasy tales about me?"

She shakes her head repeatedly, quivering with fear, while feeling the pressure of his dominant hand pressing harder against her mouth.

He continues moving his finger slowly to her heart where he then adds pressure, ensuring she remembers that pain. "I cut out the heart and watch them die!" he threatens putting his mouth closer to her face, feeling her vulnerability as he feeds on her overwhelming pain.

Morales licks her quivering face and now reaches his right hand down to his crotch where he impatiently unzips his trousers, taking out his erect penis. He begins to masturbate over her where he immediately ejaculates after a few quick strokes, moaning with pleasure as he drips semen all over her shivering chest, feeling how a large amount of warm semen ejects onto his hand while his penis's throbbing sensation lingers on.

He then raises his wet hand and smears semen all over her petrified face. "The monster will then come and eat her and her mommy alive!" He utters in a cold tone and she tries to talk but her words are muffled by his left hand still pressing hard against her mouth. He slowly removes his hand from her mouth where she hysterically gasps for air.

"I swear I won't tell anyone," she begs hysterically, in tears. "Please, I just want my mommy."

He grins maliciously knowing how frightened she is and stands up confidently, allowing her to sit up and adjust her bikini top while he straightens his uniform, cleans his penis, zips up his trousers and cleans his hands with a nearby towel. "You have been warned," he adds and then walks to the closed door where he looks back at her with a stone-cold stare. "Remember what I will do, Stella."

She wipes her tears, cleans some semen from her face and chest using the back of her hand and nods her head several times confirming her silence, as she stands on her feet and composes herself while waiting for the door to open.

He now faces the door and changes his demeanour, putting on a bright happy smile as he unlocks the door and opens it.

"Make sure you apply this lotion twice a day and keep her away from the sun for a week." He says fervently at the mother who is signing the forms and handing them over to the nurse.

A traumatised Stella runs past Morales and cries on her mother's shoulder seeking the comfort and support she so desperately needs.

"There now, it's all right baby, the pain will be gone soon, I promise." She says tenderly as she tries to comfort her daughter. "We will get your favourite ice cream now." She says and wipes some of the semen off from her shivering face believing it's lotion cream. "Looks like you still have some of that lotion on your face."

Morales walks up to the reception desk with the half empty bottle of lotion and hands it over to the mother who takes it. "If the symptoms persist, do be sure to call on me again. In the meantime, take aspirin for the pain."

"Thank you, doctor. May God protect you for all the good you do," replies the mother with gratitude and walks Stella towards the long corridor to exit the infirmary.

"He does every day," he replies happily and now turns to the nurse. "I will be inside cleaning up if you need me."

"Yes, doctor," she replies as she logs the patient's information from the forms into their computer system.

He walks back into the examination room, shuts the door, shoves his left fist into his mouth and bites hard, letting out continuous agonising screams that are muffled, so not to attract the nurse's attention outside. Expressing his outrage and disappoint he erratically punches the examination table repeatedly with his right fist, as if possessed by a demon, for a good twenty seconds until, just as soon as he started, he stops and gulps, controlling his adrenaline, taking a sequence of deep breaths to calm down.

"Breathe!" he tells himself trying to regain control while wiping a cold sweat from his forehead, giving the freezers a gruesome stare, allowing his thoughts to run wild in his deranged mind. He then slowly touches the small scar on his right eyebrow and mutters, "Focus," softly to himself and erratically glances at a small piece of paper on the desk that reads "*Urgent*." He composes himself and takes a long deep breath, he then slaps his hands several times and then slaps his face a few more times even harder, working himself up. "You can do this!" He tells himself and impulsively looks at the door with a malicious grin.

***

"She does not look like a virgin," remarks Pavlov as he stands beside Morales on the upper deck inconspicuously observing a 19-year-old Susan, sunbathing on a lounge bed by the pool in her sexy bikini on the top deck, exposing her tanned and bronzed athletic figure.

"Yet, she fits the description and that is all that matters." Replies Morales unmoved and with a cold grin on his face. "You positive she is alone?"

"She is staying by herself in stateroom 5645, has all her meals by herself and always sunbathes alone. Her booking was done online for just her, so yes, I am sure she is alone. Have I ever been wrong?"

Morales gives a mischievous smile and turns to Pavlov. "Never." He Replies coldly and glances back at Susan. "You know what to do."

***

"I'm not really hungry after everything we've eaten today," says an excited Chloe as she and Alexis are finishing the last touches of make up on their faces in the bathroom, both are wearing sexy cocktail dresses and high heels, ready to hit the town!

"I feel bloated too but tonight I intend to have a super large sausage, to blow my cobwebs away," replies a flirty Alexis and they giggle with anticipation.

"Maybe you end up having a micro cocktail sausage instead!" giggles Chloe and they break out in laughter.

"Well, as long as he knows how to use it, I'll forgive him."

A knock is then heard at the front door and they glance at each other with anticipation, they smile and take a deep breath.

"Are you sure about this?" asks Chloe expressing concern.

"Positive."

Chloe nods and they both put down their make up and walk to the front door where Alexis promptly opens it and they smile at a handsome Sammy, wearing an elegant suit and holding a box of chocolates, doused with a fragrance aftershave.

"We British are renowned for our punctuality," he says confidently and hands the chocolates to Alexis. "I hope you like chocolate?"

"They are my favourite," replies Alexis completely overwhelmed.

"The night is still young but I hope you're ready for a nice dinner, as they serve the juiciest sirloin steaks ever."

"Me!" Smiles Alexis unsurprised. "I'm famished, hell! I could eat a cow," she remarks smiling at Chloe not wanting to scare him away.

"Then, shall we?" Sammy asks extending his shoulder to Alexis who is clearly swept off her feet and quickly places her arm around his shoulder and throws the chocolates onto one of the beds.

"Lead the way," she says passionately and they walk away leaving Chloe standing all by herself.

"I'll lock up," says a disheartened Chloe knowing she is now the odd one out.

***

Walking along the many corridors making their way to the luxurious grand restaurant, Sammy is holding Alexis's arm with his right shoulder and Chloe's arm with his left shoulder, showing he is a true gentleman.

"I am honoured to have the company of two lovely ladies tonight for dinner."

"The honour is all ours, Sammy," replies Alexis, swooning.

"Oh brother, here we go again," mutters Chloe sarcastically under her breath.

"What was that?" asks a confused Sammy who didn't quite catch what she said, making Alexis nervous.

"Oh look!" shouts Alexis softy observing how some of the ship's photographers are taking professional portrait pictures of a few passengers waiting in line to enter the restaurant, in front of a beautiful Titanic grand staircase background. To get Sammy's attention, she says, "Let's take our picture together."

"Yes, that would be lovely," He says. "Wait here," he instructs and walks over to talk to one of the photographers.

"Are you deliberately trying to sabotage my chances with him?" asks a frustrated Alexis quietly so as not to attract attention.

"You're supposed to play hard to get, not throw yourself at his feet. No wonder your relationships never last. You never give them enough time to really know the person. It's not just one-night stands," Chloe responds.

"I think you are just jealous."

"Now you are this close to making me really angry. I already told you. I'm not looking for a relationship. It's too soon after Michael."

Alexis suddenly braves a wide smile as she spots Sammy returning. Chloe also braves a wide smile, acting as if nothing has happened.

"It's all arranged," reveals an overjoyed Sammy who stands by the girls. "We are next to have our pictures taken."

"What a guy," says Alexis with a confident and proud smile.

One of the ship's photographer's motions to Sammy and they all walk towards the background. The photographer professionally positions them correctly in front of the image. Alexis in a striking pose on the left, Sammy displaying a cool boss appearance in the centre and Chloe striking a pose on the right. A perfect picture that the photographer soon captures, taking several shots for good luck.

The photographer gives a thumbs up and Sammy nods with gratitude.

"The photographer told me the pictures will be ready for collection tomorrow morning," Sammy reveals as he escorts the girls towards the entrance of the restaurant where the maître d'hôtel greets them.

"Welcome to the Grand Restaurant."

"Thank you. Can we have the best table for three please, where we'll be undisturbed and away from the main entrance," asks Sammy and hands a twenty dollar bill to the maître d'hôtel who quickly accepts it and puts it into his pocket.

"Of course, sir," replies the maître d'hôtel and promptly glances behind him at a small army of ready waiters, nodding at the first one to his left. "Table two five one."

The waiter immediately steps forward and nods his head at Sammy. "Please follow me, sir and I will escort you to your table," the waiter says softly.

"Thank you," relies Sammy and smiles at a very surprised Chloe and Alexis who are speechless at the way in which Sammy has controlled the situation like a true gentleman.

The waiter walks slowly along the massive grand restaurant

followed by Sammy escorting Chloe and Alexis. They hear the soothing and relaxing sounds of a classical repertoire being elegantly played by a pianist in the centre of the room to the hundreds of dining passengers.

Chloe wanders her eyes in complete awe around the highly decorated restaurant, admiring the sparkling chandeliers, expensive paintings hanging on the walls, two staircases leading up to the second upper section of the packed restaurant, where hundreds of passengers are enjoying their sit-down meals, all being served professionally by an army of efficient waiters.

"Fancy, huh?" remarks Alexis with a secretive voice as they continue to walk further inwards, passing table upon table of conversing passengers. They finally arriving at an empty corner table at the very back where Sammy promptly gives the waiter a five dollar bill and helps the girls to sit down around a beautifully decorated table with fine china, polished cutlery, crystal wine glasses and fresh flowers placed in the centre of the table beside a lit candle.

"Your waiter will be here momentarily to take your order. Enjoy," says the waiter with a confident smile and walks away.

Chloe and Alexis are super impressed as they have rarely been in such a fancy restaurant before, being more familiar with the inexpensive restaurants or fast-food places located around town.

A head waiter promptly arrives holding three "*A la carte*" menus, handing them over to Sammy, Chloe and Alexis who impulsively open them to glance inside. "My name is Hans and I will be your head waiter for tonight," he says with a German accent while keeping a firm posture.

"Thank you," they all reply and now observe a sommelier holding two bottles of wine: one red and one white. He walks towards their table and stands beside the head waiter.

"My name is Francesco and I will be your sommelier for tonight," he says smartly with an Italian accent as he proudly shows them the wine bottles. "As per your reservation, sir, we will offer the Chateau La Mission Haut-Brion 2015 and the Rene et Vincent Dauvissat-Camus Les Clos, Chablis Grand Cru."

"You had this all arranged?" asks an impressed Alexis with an obvious blush on her face.

"I figured while you were doing your girl things, I would use that time in a productive manner, so I went through the restaurant's wine list and found these which are amongst the best," replies a confident Sammy with a wink making Alexis blush even more. "So, the question Francesco is asking is, would you like red or white wine?"

"Red for me please," replies Alexis, overwhelmed.

"White, please," replies Chloe, feeling spoiled.

"White for me please," Sammy says.

The sommelier immediately begins to fill up their glasses, respectively. Alexis and Chloe share a secret smile of acceptance and hold their hands under the table clearly supporting one another.

A new waiter now arrives with two wine buckets full of ice and places them beside their table. The sommelier professionally covers each wine bottle and securely places them inside their own wine bucket, and then he walks away with a confident smile.

"I shall send over one of my best waiters to take your orders so your night can be as perfect and memorable as can be," says the smiling head waiter who walks away leaving Sammy and the girls alone.

"So you had all this arranged, huh?" says Chloe feeling more confident about Sammy. "I bet those bottles set you back a bit."

"If you are referring to their price, that is something I am more than happy to pay, in order to make sure we all enjoy the night and more importantly, the company."

"What is it you do exactly, Sammy?" asks a concerned Chloe.

"I am studying at my father's law practice in London. I have another year to complete before getting called to the Bar but I want to live a bit more before relinquishing my freedom and dedicating my life to the practice."

"A lawyer," remarks a contented Alexis as she sensuously passes her fingers down his arm making him blush. "Nice."

"How about you two?"

"I always wanted to be a fashion designer," reveals a joyful Alexis. "I want to create my own label and have my clothes worn by the rich and famous all over the world."

"An up-market fashion designer, excellent," he compliments and now glances at Chloe. "And you, Chloe?"

"My dream was always wanting to open my own accountancy firm," she replies timidly, afraid of what people might think of her ideas, "as it was something I could never do while I was married."

"Why not?" asks a curious Sammy.

"Let's just say, Michael, my ex, had other plans for me and running a business was not on his agenda," she replies bravely and flicks some hair from her head feeling a bit uncomfortable.

"I see," he replies softly perceiving she had a rough time in her marriage. "Well, a good label will always need an equally good accountant," he says trying to combine their dreams together.

"I'll drink to that," says a surprised Alexis for not thinking about that before. She raises her glass for a toast.

"A partnership with good friends," remarks Chloe raising her glass for the toast.

"And a good partnership will need an equally great lawyer to represent them," he adds with an optimistic smile. "To making dreams come true," he says raising his glass and they all clink their glasses together and drink up, savouring the rich texture and taste of their fine wines.

"That was so good," says a satisfied Alexis in astonishment as she has never tasted a wine like that before.

"Oh yeah," mutters Chloe in awe as she too has never tasted such a great wine before and is totally lost for words.

"Exquisite, as always," he says in a soft tone clearly accustomed to drinking these fine wines frequently, and looks at his menu. "So, I hope you're famished as they serve the most tender salmon that will make your mouths water," he adds raising his hand to get the waiter's attention.

***

As the night lingers on, Sammy, Chloe and Alexis are blissfully enjoying a West End show at the Grand Theatre, rivalling any top theatre production in New York. The professional dancers give a stunning performance on the spacious stage, dancing to the live music being performed by the ship's twenty-piece orchestra playing beautifully in the foreground.

Chloe feels alive as she takes everything in around this luxuriously decorated auditorium, along with the nearly one thousand other passengers, all enjoying the memorable show. She is clearly having fun and loves this particular dance routine. She cannot help noticing how Alexis snuggles up to Sammy, and they kiss intimately on the lips making Chloe feel happy for her friend.

***

A seasoned professional entertainer plays an electric piano in this crowded and popular Schooner bar where nearly one hundred passengers, including Chloe, Alexis and Sammy, sit comfortably, singing-along to the popular song. Everyone is having a great time and it shows, even the bartender sings as he continues to serve countless drinks to waiting passengers.

"This is one of the best nights of my life!" shouts tipsy Chloe at the top of her voice at Alexis who can barely hear her with so much noise. "I can't remember the last time I felt this good!"

Alexis gives Chloe a much-needed supportive hug and they

embrace for what feels like an eternity. "I am happy for you!" she shouts into Chloe's ear, also feeling a bit tipsy. "You know what you need?"

"What?"

"Being transported back in time to the seventies!"

"How can we do that?"

"I saw on the ship's entertainment brochure, there's a disco night at one of the other bars two decks up," reveals Alexis with an impish grin on her face making Chloe smile brighter.

***

"I'll get the next round!" shouts an excited Chloe as she gets up from a corner booth trying not to knock over a small table littered with empty cocktail glasses. Alexis and Sammy are finishing their drinks. They are all in one of the three ample disco bars the ship offers, and as the music is so loud they can feel the constant beat of the bass penetrating through their bodies, not allowing them to think straight. Dozens of passengers dance the night away on the dance floor to classic seventies disco music blasting away. The atmosphere is electrifying with reflecting disco balls, fog smoke and colourful flashing lights giving you a sensation of being transported back in time to the seventies.

"Make them doubles this time!" shouts an elated Alexis as Sammy ushers her to the dance floor and they begin to dance to the groovy music.

"Double!" mutters Chloe sarcastically to herself while avoiding getting bumped by so many people dancing everywhere as she negotiates a safe route to the bar. "Why not make them a triple instead? That way I won't have to wait in line at the bar all night." She comments as she finally reaches the small line of waiting passengers at the bar, patiently waiting her turn, tapping her foot on the floor to the rhythm of the addictive beat of the popular music track. She begins to hum the tune, turns around and smiles at Alexis and Sammy dancing on the dance floor watching how they clearly have chemistry between them, observing how they embrace and kiss like two wild teenagers on their first date while swaying to the music. "Good on you, Alexis," she says with a warm smile on her face, clearly happy for her best friend.

***

Slightly drunk and trying to walk straight, Chloe, Alexis and Sammy sing loudly as they make their way along the labyrinth of corridors trying to find Sammy's stateroom.

"I think it's over there," he says trying to keep a straight face as the alcohol has clearly kicked in, motioning to one of the doors at the end of the corridor. They eventually reach it and he takes out his boarding card from his pocket and smiles as he hesitates to focus, and then successfully swipes the card on the keypad. The door clicks open. "Well, this is me," he adds trying to keep straight and then leans back against the wall so as not to fall over.

"It has been fun, Sammy, thank you for an unforgettable night," says Chloe also trying to stand up straight with a bright smile on her face.

"I can go all night long!" shouts Alexis seductively and puts her arm around Sammy's waist leaning against his body.

"Oh, where are my manners?" he asks himself, feeling guilty. "Would you girls like to come in for a night cap?"

"I thought you would never ask," replies Alexis excitedly and winks at Chloe with anticipation.

"You guys go on without me," replies Chloe knowing this is what Alexis was waiting for and she doesn't want to ruin the moment for her.

"You sure? It's a big room and I can order more drinks," he insists grabbing Alexis firmly by her waist.

"I'm fine. In fact, too fine! You guys enjoy yourselves. It's a lovely night for a stroll around the deck and the fresh air will do me good."

"In that case," replies Sammy offering his right hand at Chloe, "it was a pleasure meeting you, Chloe."

"It was a pleasure meeting you also Sammy," replies Chloe politely shaking his hand. "Well, good night then," she adds, giving a mischievous smile at her friend.

Alexis opens her mouth in excitement, mimicking the words, "Thank you," with her lips.

Sammy gives the door a gentle kick and it swings open, he then escorts Alexis into his room and the door is softly closed behind them, leaving Chloe standing all alone in the corridor, again feeling happy for her best friend but somewhat lonely.

"The story of my life," she mutters to herself and walks down the corridor humming a happy tune until she soon reaches a junction and looks at three sets of corridors: one leading to the left, one forward and to the right. "Must be this way," she whispers confused and walks down the corridor to the left. Eventually, she reaches a door that has a sign *"Top Deck"* and swings it open, walking outside to the top deck where a sudden gust of cold air hits her face and it freshens her up. She takes a moment to breathe the fresh air and closes her eyes feeling alive and free.

Chloe looks up at the spectacular night sky surrounded by thousands of tiny stars and walks slowly to the railing where she stands overlooking the dark sea, enjoying the cool breeze on her face. In the distance she hears a number of romantic couples strolling past her while other couples lounge on the scattered deck chairs enjoying their drinks, some passengers can even be heard splashing into the pool, watching the impressive TV screen that is showing travel videos of tomorrow's port of call at Jamaica's *"Ocho Rios"*. She curiously leans forward to try and see the hull of the ship skimming through the sea but the deck is over one hundred feet high making it virtually impossible to see the water at night.

"I would not lean forward so close, unless you intend to jump," says Morales as he walks towards a now startled Chloe who promptly composes herself clearing her throat. She turns around, leaning her back against the railing while watching him walk closer. "This deck is over one hundred feet above the waterline and if you fall from this height, it will be like landing on concrete."

"I just wanted to see the waves."

"Best to see them in the daytime, not at night," he replies standing opposite a now shy Chloe. "Night is to see the stars," he adds romantically glancing up at the night sky. "They are beautiful, are they not?" he asks softly at a now relaxed Chloe who gazes up at the night sky admiring their splendour.

"They say each star represents a soul, looking down over their loved ones and guiding them safely in this cruel, yet, evolving world." She says and turns to face him, observing the sad expression on his face.

"In all my years at sea, I have never heard such a quote, that is as beautiful, as you are," he remarks with an impish grin. "I am the ship's doctor, Hugo Morales, at your service."

She is captivated by his charm and blushes, staring at his smart appearance and perfectly ironed uniform. "Chloe Moore."

"Un gusto conocerte, señorita Moore," he says softly, lowering his head out of respect.

"You are Spanish?"

"Actually I am from the Dominican Republic."

"As you might have guessed, I am from the good old U.S. of A."

"I assumed that by your accent. Tell me, señorita Moore, why would such an attractive woman like yourself be out here all alone on such a beautiful night like this?"

"I am travelling with my best friend but she is resting now. So here I am, taking in a midnight stroll to get some fresh air."

Morales touches his scar on his eyebrow and impulsively puts his hand on Chloe's right cheek, taking a step closer, making her startled and feeling rather uncomfortable.

"What are you doing?" she asks leaning as far back against the railing as she possibly can without going overboard.

"Forgive me," he replies staring into her now scared eyes, "but do you have a temperature?"

"A temperature?" she replies, feeling utterly perplexed noticing how he takes another step closer and he now has her pinned against the railing making her extremely nervous. "This isn't funny."

"It was not meant to be funny," he remarks emotionlessly and touches her now shivering left cheek with the back of his right hand, feeling her vulnerability and obvious fear.

"It's kinda late," she replies giving him a subtle push enough to slide to one side and break free. "And I should be getting back to my friend right about now," she adds while composing herself.

"Why are you frightened?"

"Excuse me?" she shouts crossing her arms indignantly. "Maybe in the Dominican Republic women fall for those seductive methods but where I come from, we don't. You scared me, doctor, and believe me, after what I have been through, it takes a lot for me to be afraid."

"I just wanted to make sure you did not have a fever."

"Why would you want to know that anyway?" she asks and starts to walk away. "I can assure you," she stops and turns back to face him, "that I am perfectly healthy and don't have a temperature. Thank you for your concern. I would like to think that maybe you meant well and your approach was the wrong one. Either way, I am not interested in a one-night stand, so good night." She walks away feeling an uncomfortable sensation in the pit of her stomach. "Weeee'errrrrrd!" She tells herself heading as far away as possible, not realising he continues to watch her with angry eyes, clutching his fists in disappointment.

4
Ocho Rios

The ship is berthed at this popular lively Caribbean Port Town that the locals call *"The Garden Parish"* located on the north coast of Jamaica. The Ocho Rios harbour is small and has two docking piers for cruise ships: *"The Reynolds bauxite mine Pier,"* also known locally as the *"James Bond Pier"* after it was used as a background in the film version of Dr. No, and emblematic *"Turtle Bay Pier."* Both conveniently located between a ten-to-fifteen-minute walk from the town and offering stunning views across the bay of the town's largest beach *"Ocho Rios Bay Beach"* also known as *"Turtle Beach."*

Hundreds of passengers disembark from the ship and walk along the narrow pier towards the cruise terminal exit to enjoy their day in this beautiful little paradise in the Caribbean. Amongst them are Chloe, Alexis and Sammy who are walking blissfully towards the small wooden terminal building, following directional signs that read *"excursions - buses, taxis"*, where dozens of local guides and drivers are gathered hoping for the arriving tourists to hire them for tours.

"I'll get us a guide," says Sammy and walks at a faster pace towards the local guides, leaving Chloe and Alexis walking at a slower pace behind.

"Well?" asks an excited Chloe observing how Alexis is bursting to tell what happened last night when she left them alone in his stateroom. "So, was it a jumbo or a cocktail sausage?"

Alexis makes a large gesture with her hands in astonishment. "Massive! I hardly slept. That boy has moves, God! The cobwebs are officially gone!" She jokes and they hug and giggle.

"Slut," whispers Chloe into Alexis's ear as they continue hugging.

"I love you too, Chloe."

"I know you do."

"Enough about me, what about you? How was *your* night? Did you go to a bar and get lucky?"

"Believe me, getting lucky is the last thing on my mind."

"How sad, especially after getting you waxed and all," says Alexis loudly, making Chloe embarrassed as many passengers overhear as they continue to walk past.

"Will you lower your voice?" asks a timid Chloe. "Last night I just went out for some fresh air before going to our room where I then slept alone *and* like a baby."

"At least one of us did," giggles Alexis mischievously.

"Mind you," remarks Chloe with a sense of apprehension. "I did meet the ship's doctor last night."

"Oh, a doctor. Nice! I always love a man in uniform, or without it, preferably."

"This one was anything *but* nice."

"What do you mean?"

"There was something strange about him. I felt uncomfortable. "

"Uncomfortable in what way?"

"Without asking me, he leaned forward and placed his hand on my face to see if I had a cold. It was just weird."

"Maybe he saw your sorry expression and thought you were ill?"

"No. I perceived doctor Morales had other intentions."

Alexis takes a firm grip of Chloe's arms and looks straight into her eyes. "Chloe, you are my best friend and the sister I never had but I think that Michael has fucked up that head of yours, big time! That doctor was probably out to have a good time and maybe you're just over reacting to his intentions. After all, he is a doctor who gave an oath to save lives, right?"

Chloe takes a moment to digest Alexis's comment and then smiles feeling rather stupid. "Right," she admits feeling guilty for the way in which she handled the situation last night.

"You were on a moving ship in the dead of night. I mean, what were you afraid of? What possibly could go wrong?"

"I don't know what I was thinking. Blame the ordeal of the divorce combined with the alcohol, come to think about it, maybe I did over react."

"Not maybe, Chloe. You did, and the best thing you can do is contact that doctor when we return to the ship and apologise for your dumb ass behaviour," suggests a concerned Alexis who then smiles. "With any luck he can touch something else and get your batteries re-charged!"

"Is there anything else you think about, besides, sex?"

"Let me think." Replies Alexis with a degree of hesitation. "No."

"Okay," shouts a contented Sammy who is rushing towards the girls being followed by a local guide, "we got our guide and I have negotiated a great price for us."

Watching from the top deck, Morales grips the railing firmly as he observes how Chloe, Alexis and Sammy are greeted by a local guide who gestures for them to follow him to a waiting vehicle.

"It's confirmed," says Pavlov softly standing behind Morales holding a large empty Tupperware container with a blue lid, passing it to him. They then exchange a cold glare and Pavlov walks away, leaving Morales staring down at the Tupperware in his hand.

***

Morales walks into the infirmary's examination room carrying the empty Tupperware in his hand, opens one of the freezers and shoves the container inside slamming the freezer's door shut. He then takes a key from his pocket and unlocks a drawer where he soon takes out a large envelope hidden inside the drawer. He removes a large selection of photographs from the envelope which he closely studies with his cold dark eyes, making his breathing become heavier.

***

As the afternoon continues, Chloe and Alexis, wearing bikinis, and Sammy, wearing bathing shorts, happily enjoy the stunning *"Blue Hole Secret Fall"*: a breath-taking waterfall lagoon situated about a twenty-minute drive from the port. It's not a mainstream tourist attraction but it is clearly a hidden gem surrounded by a lavish green jungle and exotic flowers. Their guide waves at them as he patiently lounges on a rock. Many people are walking from one natural pool to another which have been created by the rivers throughout the years.

Alexis uses her camera to take many selfies, capturing the memorable moments as they explore their surroundings and dive into the warm tranquil crystal blue waters to cool off from the intense heat. Sammy swings from one of the many ropes at the foot of a high waterfall and dives into the water, getting smothered by the cool water spray created by the waterfall.

"That was great!" he shouts at the girls.

"I'm going to dive from the rocks up there!" shouts Chloe confidently, and she begins climbing the rocks near the waterfall.

"Be careful!" shouts Alexis aiming her camera and recording a video of Chloe skilfully climbing and then diving, in a leap of faith, from the waterfall. "Yes!"

Sammy swims over and kisses Alexis passionately while Chloe continues to swim feeling alive. "The guide sure did pick the right place for us."

"It's beautiful, Sammy," replies a happy Alexis. "Thank you," she adds and they continue to kiss, caressing their bodies in the water.

***

After a visit to the Blue Hole, the local guide has now driven them to *"The Bamboo Blu Restaurant"* situated in the iconic *"mammee bay"* which is one of the best restaurants by the beach front offering a superb menu by the beach.

Chloe, Alexis and Sammy have just finished their amazing seafood lunch and they run to the clear sands of the beach where another local guide is waiting for them with snorkelling gear. They all quickly put their underwater goggles over their eyes and flippers on their feet.

"Come on!" shouts an excited Sammy, and they all dive into the turquoise water swimming together into the open sea. "The water is amazing!" he shouts at the girls beside him. He then dives under the water to experience swimming with a large variety of tropical fish. Alexis and Chloe also dive under the water and the three are amazed at so much beauty beneath them. After holding their breaths for a while, they all surface and smile.

"It's so beautiful here, I love it!" shouts Chloe making Alexis swim closer to her and hug her.

"I am so happy for you, Chloe."

"This has been, by far, one of the best days of my life," reveals Chloe and she dives once again under the water.

Sammy grabs Alexis firmly and kisses her once again passionately on the lips. "And going on this cruise has been the best decision I have ever made, for it has given me the opportunity of finding you," he adds romantically, making Alexis fall for him even more.

5
The Monster's Wrath

"I can spend the whole week in here," says a relaxed Chloe soaking her body in one of the many Jacuzzis on the Top Deck, sipping a cocktail while admiring the spectacular sunset, as the ship slowly sails into the horizon, leaving Ocho Rios behind.

Alexis and Sammy sip their cocktails cuddling together like old lovers, their eyes gazing at the bright sunset in the horizon behind a red and orange beautiful coloured sky, oblivious to the other passengers around them in the pool, deck chairs, other Jacuzzi's, the bar or just walking around.

"I wish we could stay like this forever," dreams a romantic Alexis emotionally smiling at Sammy.

"You know what they say," remarks Chloe knowingly.

"All good things come to an end," replies Sammy understanding the possibility that when the cruise ends, he may not see Alexis anymore but desperately wanting to stop time, so that day never arrives.

"That's right. It certainly does," remarks Chloe feeling overjoyed.

"We still have a few more days left so make the best of it, I say!" remarks a happy Alexis and she kisses Sammy passionately on the lips.

"I remember that feeling vividly," mutters Chloe watching the lovers with a nostalgic frown, "shame though it ended in divorce."

"Chloe," says a worried Alexis and leans over to get closer to her. "Please don't be mad at me."

"Why would I be?"

"Sammy and I," adds a guilty Alexis with a timid tone in her voice, "well, as we don't have much time…"

"You want to spend the time you have with him," interrupts Chloe understandingly, "even though the whole idea of this cruise was to spend time with me."

"You always were the clever one," mentions Alexis and then hesitates feeling guilty, "I was thinking of staying at his stateroom again tonight and have room service," she adds and holds Chloe feeling sad. "Please understand. What we have is just," she pauses as she cannot find the right words, her eyes glittering with passion.

"I understand, really I do," replies a supportive Chloe who flicks some of Alexis's hair from her eyes observing how guilty Alexis is, "and I would have expected the same from you, if the circumstance were reversed. Just promise me one thing."

"Anything."

"You've just met him so try not to get pregnant."

"He uses protection and I don't leave home without the magic pill, so we got that covered."

"I envy you sometimes," chuckles Chloe expecting that reply from her wild best friend.

"Come on," encourages Alexis holding Chloe's hands, "the ship's full of studs. Choose one and move on with your life. Live the moment with no regrets. It will do you good to clear your cobwebs."

"My father would kill me if he found out I had a one-night stand."

"Then don't tell him," she replies candidly. "You are a grown woman, married for just over two years and recently divorced, trust me, you don't need his permission to have a good time anymore. Besides, I won't tell if you don't," says a mischievous Alexis with an impish grin on her face.

"You just focus on you for the duration of the cruise and then I will have you all to myself again when we return. I will stay a while longer and then get a bite to eat," says a compassionate Chloe and smiles at Sammy who is patiently waiting for her approval, "you two go now and don't worry about me."

Alexis gives a tender kiss on Chloe's cheek. "You're the best," she adds and then stands up and takes Sammy's hand, as he too stands up and they jump out from the Jacuzzi, leaving Chloe alone. "Let's meet up in the morning for breakfast, okay?" asks a much happier Alexis. Chloe nods her head in agreement but doesn't reply. Alexis then grabs Sammy by the waist and they walk away.

"The story of my life," mutters Chloe under her breath leaning back to continue admiring the amazing views in the horizon. "Are you going to feel sorry for the rest of your life?" she asks herself quietly and looks at her half empty cocktail glass in her hand. "Who am I trying to kid? What am I a freaking nun?" she adds observing a number of romantic couples walking and lounging around. "To hell with it!" She downs her cocktail in one go. "And to hell with you Michael!"

***

Wearing a short but sexy dress, Chloe is dancing alone on the disco's dance floor holding a cocktail in her hand, swaying to the vibrating sounds of the eighties music blasting away inside the crowded bar, unaware she is being observed by Alex, a handsome young man in his twenties, wearing an elegant suit. He finally gathers enough courage to ask her for a dance, so he downs his beer and walks confidently towards her, swaying with the rhythm of the music while avoiding many passengers dancing in all directions.

"Hi!" shouts a nervous Alex at Chloe who looks at him from head to toe, sipping her cocktail finding him attractive. "I'm Alex!"

"Chloe!" she replies shouting at the top of her voice while

continuing to dance.

"Do you mind if I dance with you?"

"It's a free country," she replies anticipating where this is leading and he quickly moves closer and holds her tight, dancing in a synchronised routine which makes her feel at ease and completely comfortable with his gentle touch and handsome appearance. "You are a good dancer," she acknowledges with a smile.

"Thank you, so are you," he replies and gets closer, rubbing his body sensuously against hers, swaying from side to side, up and down making her feel excited.

"It's hot in here," she says pushing him aside, losing the nerve to go through with it, "I'm sorry," she adds and rushes to the exit.

"Wait!" he shouts at the top of his voice and follows her.

Chloe walks out of the disco bar and stands near the foyer where there is an amazing aerobatic show being performed by a number of professional performers who fly around secured by wires, being watched by hundreds of passengers in awe. She soon feels Alex's hand grabbing hers tenderly as he stands beside her.

"It was not my intention to make you run," he says, feeling worried without taking his penetrating eyes from hers.

"It's not you."

"Then what are you afraid of?"

"My emotions," she replies and impulsively kisses him passionately on the lips and they embrace, oblivious to the aerobatic show and the people around them. "I haven't done this in a long time."

"Neither have I," he confesses shyly, "but I will be gentle." He adds and they kiss.

***

Inside stateroom 6505, Chloe and Alex are wildly making love under the clean white sheets of her bed. Their combined clothes scattered along the floor and an open bottle of champagne with two half-filled glasses are resting on the night table. It has been too long and Chloe has almost forgotten what it feels like to make real love, to be caressed and tenderly kissed all over her body without trying to establish a new record for the fastest lay in the town.

Enjoying every stroke and second of what would be a long but pleasant night, feeling his heartbeat against hers, losing her troubles and fears, clutching his hands tight as he slowly kisses her neck and works his way slowly down her chest with his warm sensuous lips which soon reaches her waxed vagina where he begins to perform oral sex, gently rubbing his tongue all over her wet and throbbing labia majora and labia minora and deeper into her wet orifice, making the climatic anticipation even greater, as she groans and moans with a pleasure she has not experienced in years and clearly forgotten, as oral sex was not something that Michael practised during their nearly three years together: six months as fiancées and the two and a half years as a married couple.

"There, Alex, yes, there," she moans ready to explode trying to crawl upwards, "don't stop." She pleads as she continues working his magic on her making her move her head violently from side to side with every pleasurable moan getting louder by the second.

***

"Shall I make you another? Asks a bartender to Susan, the 19-year-old who is sitting alone at a not so crowded bar with a few empty margarita glasses in front of her, wearing a lovely green cocktail dress.

"I have reached my limit, thank you," she replies and carefully gets off the bar stool trying not to fall over, as the alcohol has clearly gotten to her head. "Good night," she says, waving to the bartender as she walks gingerly to the exit, unaware that Pavlov has been patiently sitting on a corner table for the past twenty minutes observing her.

***

"Why must they all look the same?" asks a confused but happy Susan as she negotiates the labyrinth of corridors feeling woozy from the alcohol, trying to keep her balance, as she tries to find her stateroom, not realising that Pavlov is silently following her, keeping his distance so as not to alarm her.

She eventually reaches stateroom 6156 and opens her small purse, trying to find her boarding pass. "Where are you?" she mutters under her breath and grins as she finds it. "Gotcha!" She yells and after two attempts she manages to swipe the card correctly over the keypad, the door clicks open and she walks safely into her room, closing the door shut behind her.

Pavlov soon reaches the now closed stateroom 6156 door and clenches his fists, glancing around to make sure no one is watching, he then stands guard at the door glancing at his wristwatch and waits.

***

Fifteen minutes have now passed and Susan is fast asleep on her bed under the sheets. A dimmed night lamp has been left on partially illuminating the room. The front door suddenly clicks and Pavlov swings the door slightly open with his left hand holding a passkey, as he plays it safe and checks the room before entering, noticing Susan is fast asleep. He takes one last glance outside to make sure no one is around and then leaps quickly inside the room and softly closes the door, trying not to make any sound that might wake her up.

He slowly approaches the bed stepping over her dress lying on the floor, taking a small bottle of chloroform and a cloth from his pocket and soon stands beside her, staring down with a menacing frown. He tilts his head to the right observing her sweet face and then takes a deep breath. He opens the bottle's cap, soaks the cloth entirely with chloroform and without any warning he mercilessly shoves the now wet cloth against Susan's nose and mouth with his right hand while holding the back of her head firmly with his left hand and simultaneously sits on her legs so she doesn't escape, waking her up in a frenzied state of panic, feeling how this stranger has her pinned defencelessly to the bed she tries to scream, her eyes opening wider with horror not being able to move or comprehend what is happening but her muffled cries for help are slowly reduced to a whimper until she finally loses the battle and goes unconscious.

He waits for a few more seconds and then steps back and removes the bed sheets, observing her naked body with lustful eyes. He then proceeds to remove his clothes revealing his erect penis and savagely rapes her, pounding and penetrating her repeatedly without getting any reaction from her but he doesn't care, he just continues to grunt with pleasure, using her body like a sex doll.

***

Inside a large utility room located deep below the hull of the ship with no porthole or windows and filled with shelves containing miscellaneous construction items and hardware, Pavlov firmly secures handcuffs onto Susan's wrists and chains on her ankles, as she is tied to a post and still unconscious, wearing a tee shirt and shorts.

He ensures the cuffs and chains are secured and then takes two steps back, again tilts his head to the right as he takes one last look at her innocent face before walking to the only door in the room, flicks off the light switch and exits, leaving her completely alone and in the dark. Pavlov locks the door which has a sign *"Utility 125"* and walks down a long solitude narrow corridor.

***

Eating a large variety of buffet breakfast choices on one of the tables in this extremely busy restaurant, Chloe eats alone completely lost in happy thoughts which is evident on her bright face when suddenly she gets woken up from her daydream as Alexis and Sammy join her and place their breakfast plates on the table.

"I didn't hear you arrive," says a content Chloe making Alexis smile as she hasn't seen Chloe's happy face in years.

"Oh my God!" shouts an excited Alexis in anticipation. "I know that face, you got laid last night, didn't you?"

"I did," replies an excited Chloe without caring who might be listening anymore.

"I'll fetch the coffees," says a shy Sammy as he quickly walks away leaving the girls to talk in private.

"Who was he?" she replies looking around the restaurant, "is he here?"

"It all happened so fast I honestly never got his name."

"You slut," she says with a sensuous tone.

"I didn't sleep a wink."

"Neither did I."

"I guess we might just need a vacation after this vacation," remarks a dazed Chloe who is seriously lost in happy thoughts and they break out in giggles and embrace.

Sammy returns with three cups of coffee and sets them down on the table glancing out the windows at "George Town" where the ship docked a few hours ago at their next port of call in the Grand Cayman Islands. "George Town in Grand Cayman Island. God, I never thought I would see it."

"It is beautiful," concurs Chloe as she takes a closer look, noticing how a small fleet of the ship's tender boats are shuttling passengers to the "South Terminal" at the land port as they are anchored in a safe area outside the port.

***

Feeling the gentle sea breeze, Morales cautiously walks along the entire length of Deck D passing a number of passengers as he makes his way towards a seemingly unused area which has a blind spot for the many CCTV cameras around the deck. He casually strolls towards a particular corner beside a door leading into the ship, an area which he knows all too well, as he approaches a railing where he firmly holds onto and leans his upper body over it to observe the impressive sheer over one-hundred-foot undisturbed drop down to the sea below. He then composes himself and stands straight where he takes a deep breath and observes the tender boats shuttling the passengers to the land port.

***

"What about this one?" asks Alexis as she holds a local dress against her body and makes a funny pose, making Chloe and Sammy laugh. They are exploring a busy street market in town offering cheap local products, souvenirs and plenty of locally distilled rum.

"Maybe not," replies a candid Chloe who promptly takes the dress and hands it back to the street vendor while Alexis continues to take many selfies and pictures of everything she finds of interest.

Sammy walks to a local ice cream street vendor and buys three ice creams, pays for them and catches up with the girls.

"Thank you, Sammy," says Chloe as she accepts one of the ice creams and starts licking it, enjoying its unique local taste. "With this heat, the ice cream is a breath of fresh air."

Alexis and Sammy lick their ice creams and nod their heads in agreement, as they also enjoy its original taste.

"Let's get a guide to take us around the island," says Chloe.

"I shall arrange that," Sammy replies and promptly walks

around to find one of the many local guides in the area.

***

Morales walks slowly along a sequence of corridors passing a number of passengers, discretely glancing around checking to see if there are any hidden or visible CCTV cameras but cannot find any new ones.

He soon arrives at a junction of corridors where he does find a small CCTV camera pointing to the corridor leading on the left but there are no cameras pointing at the corridor to the right. He grins mischievously and glances back at the long corridor realising he now has all the information he needs for his malicious plan.

***

A 43-year-old ship's engineer, wearing his work overalls, whistles a tune as he walks in solitude along the quiet and narrow corridor holding a clipboard in his hand. He suddenly stops and listens, as he faintly hears a woman crying for help, which grabs his attention. Glancing down the long corridor and back from where he came he tries to pinpoint where the cries are coming from.

"Hello?" he shouts anxiously and waits for a reply. Soon Susan's faint yells can be heard. *"In here! Help me!"* she calls, and the engineer frantically runs down the corridor noticing the cries getting louder until he can hear them coming from behind the *"Utility door 125,"* which he quickly tries to open.

"I hear you, hold on!" he shouts as he nervously tries to find his passkey to unlock the closed door, while Susan continues yelling for help from inside.

***

Inside the impressive state of the art kitchen, Pavlov fills a tray with a small bowl of green salad, several fruits and a glass of orange juice, while over fifty cooks and assistants are busy preparing enough food to feed an entire army.

"Here," says a sous chef handing Pavlov a freshly prepared meat roll. "She will need some strength to last her till the afternoon."

"Thank you," he replies placing the roll on the tray. Then he walks towards one of the many exits with a cold expression on his face.

***

"Help me!" cries a distraught Susan trying to escape from her handcuffs and chains, which are bruising her wrists and ankles as she frenetically fidgets in tears unable to break free. "In here!" She shouts, gasping for air just as the door is unlocked and swings wide open, revealing the silhouette of the concerned engineer standing in the light outside.

"Oh, God!" She cries believing this is her attacker. He quickly flips on the light switch by the door and the dimmed light inside the utility room shines enough to reveal a totally confused and shocked man wondering why she has been tied up in here. "Please, don't hurt me!" She begs breaking down into more cries and tears.

"I won't!" he replies as he quickly runs to her aid and tries to release her from her restraints.

"You promise?"

"Cross my heart and swear to die," he replies totally in disbelief as he is unable to break away the chains or the handcuffs. "Who did this to you?" He asks in frustration as he continues to fight the chains.

"I don't know but it hurts. Please, I just want to go home. Get me out of here."

"I need something to cut these off," he says glancing at the shelves inside the room hoping to find something. In his desperate attempt ransacking the shelves, he drops numerous construction hardware all over the floor. "This should do it," says the extremely nervous engineer picking up a hacksaw and rushing back to Susan where he looks into her petrified eyes. "I don't want to cut you, so I need you to remain perfectly still now, you understand?"

"Yes, please hurry," she replies nodding her head frantically and sniffing to try and relax. When he smiles at her she notices a gold tooth in his dentures, which catches her attention. Then he concentrates, resting the hacksaw blade firmly against the right ankle chain and carefully begins to saw, trying not to cut her flesh. After a few moments the chain snaps and breaks loose.

"Now the next one," she pleads impatiently, noticing how he smiles again to try to reassure her that everything will be fine, showing his gold tooth. "You will be out of here in no time."

***

Inside the examination room, Morales is meticulously preparing a liquid solution from a number of small medical bottles he has grouped together on the counter, some labelled: *"Barbiturates," "Benzodiazepines," "Clonazepam," "Bamma-hydroxybutyrate (GHB),"* opioids and sleep-inducing drugs such as *"Zolpidem (Ambien)" "Fentanyl,"* and *"Eszopiclone (Lunesta)"* as well as many other unlabelled bottles containing liquid sedatives. "Where was it?" He mutters to himself glancing around. Then he opens a drawer where he soon picks up a medical chart from inside and studies it briefly, trying to calculate the right dosage, depending on the weight and height of the patient. "Okay." he mutters throwing the chart back into the drawer. Then he takes a few tablets from some of the bottles, slices them in half, puts half back into the bottles and grinds the remaining halves together into a fine powder on the counter. Once that is done, he takes a small glass beaker from a shelf and pours the powder inside.

He now picks up the first liquid bottle and carefully adds twenty-five drops into the beaker, then jumps to the third bottle and adds thirty drops into the beaker. He now jumps to the fifth bottle and adds sixty-two drops into the beaker, then stirs everything together dissolving the powder and creating a pink liquid, custom-made sedative, which he admires.

"Beautiful," he remarks to himself softly as he now picks up a small syringe from a drawer. He clicks a needle onto it, then inserts the needle into the beaker and begins to fill the syringe with the pink liquid. Then he raises the now filled syringe up against the light, admiring his malicious creation. He softly presses the plunger and observes a small squirt of liquid ejecting from the tip of the needle into the air. He glances at the desk, picks up a tiny needle cap and places it over the tip of the needle.

***

The engineer carefully hacks the chains on Susan's left ankle which soon snaps and breaks loose. He quickly stands up and positions the blade firmly against the right handcuff and begins to carefully saw it, unaware that behind him Pavlov is slowly creeping into the room setting the tray down on the floor, noticing how Susan is so focussed on the handcuff she doesn't notice him entering.

"Nearly finished," says the engineer watching how the handcuff is nearly cut, unaware that Pavlov is silently taking out a switchblade from his pocket as he continues to creep towards him. Suddenly a faint squeaking noise is heard as Pavlov steps on the wooden floor, forcing Susan to glance up and spot him now only a few steps away from the engineer.

"Behind you!" she shouts just as the handcuff snaps loose. He quickly turns around and is shocked to find Pavlov standing just one step away from him, plunging the sharp switchblade mercilessly and repeatedly into his heart in a violent spree. The force causes the engineer's lifeless body to fall to his knees and roll over in a pool of blood.

Susan screams hysterically, witnessing the man who was trying to save her, being murdered in front of her. She feels it was her fault, as she frantically tries to break free but is still trapped by the left handcuff and is unable to escape.

"Look what you made me do," says an angry Pavlov and then slaps her face to shut her up.

"What the hell is going on in here?" shouts Morales barging into the room seeing the body on the floor.

"Please, help me!" whimpers a distraught Susan.

"He was cutting her loose!" replies a cold Pavlov wiping the blood from his switchblade on Susan's tee shirt.

"Please, let me go," she begs in tears, "I promise I won't tell anyone."

Morales closes the open door to prevent any further surprises and then walks back to Susan taking out the prepared syringe from his pocket; he shows it to her. "I know you won't, querida." He says knowingly as he removes the cap from the tip of the sharp needle.

Susan lets out a continuous blood curdling scream as Morales brutally stabs the syringe's needle into her chest and rams the plunger down hard, forcing the entire pink liquid to be injected into her body which immediately makes her convulse and fidget uncontrollably. Soon her cries for help are reduced to a vague whimper as she desperately fights to remain conscious but is unable to move although she is still able to listen and observe with difficulty.

"What do we do with him?" asks Pavlov, staring at the body.

"We cannot afford the luxury of keeping the body in here for someone to find it," replies a frustrated Morales, "and you cannot take it topside to throw it overboard in the daylight. So, I suggest you dispose of it like in the old days. After all, it is your mess, so you clean it up." He adds cold-heartedly, and then walks to the closed door and starts to open it. "The transport leaves in exactly two hours, so you have until then to make him disappear and get her ready." The doctor walks out slamming the door shut.

Pavlov stares at Susan and hears her slight whimpering. He

grunts, then walks to one of the shelves where he collects a large sheet of plastic and carefully covers the entire floor with it. Positioning the body over the plastic, he then stands opposite Susan where he begins to undress while staring into her eyes. "You are going to love what I am going to do next," he says in a frosty tone. He sets his clothes carefully on a top shelf, then walks back to the body and begins to remove all of the man's clothes, leaving the body completely naked. He throws the clothes to the back of the room, keeping her guessing as she watches petrified not knowing or understanding what is happening. Susan's eyes try to focus as they now follow him walking to the back of the room where he disappears amongst the numerous shelves. She blinks anxiously as she cannot see him.

Moments later, a horrifying sound of a small engine revving up is heard, making her feel even more afraid as he walks back to the body holding a chainsaw in his hands. Her delirious eyes open as wide in complete horror as he repeatedly revs the chainsaw to maximum power, taunting her, until he soon bends down, rests the chainsaw's menacing blade against the bodies' left hand and cuts it clean off.

Susan is in shock as he continues to mutilate the engineers' body and she vomits in disgust, as he cuts off his hands, arms, legs, head and limbs into small chunks, cutting through tissue and bone, splattering blood everywhere. The girl cannot hold on much longer and goes unconscious while he continues with the savage carnage.

***

A now showered and cleaned up Pavlov is pushing a trolley filled with sealed plastic bags containing the mutilated remains along the busy kitchen where a small army of chefs and assistant chefs are continuously preparing many tons of food for the passengers in this hectic but organised environment. He soon spots his cohort sous chef waving at him on the corner of the kitchen beside an industrial mincer machine. He nods his head as he walks towards him.

"Next time give me a bit more warning, Viktor," mutters the sous chef as he inconspicuously picks up one of the bags and glances around, ensuring no one is watching, then he rips the bag open.

"He wants this dealt with straight away, so get to it," he replies emotionally. He turns on the mincer machine and the sous chef discretely throws the mutilated pieces of flesh from the bag into the mincer and the empty plastic bags into the trash, hearing how the machine eats through the flesh and bones grinding them into mincemeat within seconds. They open more bags and throw the contents into the machine without losing a heartbeat, as this is something they have done before many times. They calmly watch as all the body parts are reduced to a large pile of minced meat. It is a bloody and gory mess but they continue with complete discipline, undisturbed by the carnage.

Once the last body part is thrown into the machine Pavlov takes out a stack of one hundred dollar bills and shoves them into the sous chef's upper pocket, with a gratitude pat on the back for a job well done. "Remember no trace," he adds and walks away leaving the sous chef perplexed as to what to do with so much mincemeat now.

***

Standing by the embankment area at the pier, Chloe, Alexis and Sammy are waiting near the front of a small line for the next tender boat to arrive so they can all return back to the ship. Hendreick, one of the ship's junior officers in his thirties, is conversing with a few of the passengers.

"What a day. It's been awesome!" remarks a content Chloe.

"And the afternoon is still young," replies a satisfied Alexis.

"We will most likely get on this one," says Sammy, watching a tender boat dock near them.

Inside the arrived tender boat, Morales nods at the helmsman who nods back at him with a cold expression on his face. "Get her up," he says to Pavlov who is patiently sitting beside an unconscious Susan, who is now wearing a nice summer dress, hat and sunglasses.

"Hendreick has everything arranged as planned," says the helmsman with a Scandinavian accent.

Pavlov helps Susan stand up, firmly holding her tight, as she softly moans. The sedative is beginning to wear off. "She is waking up."

"We still have plenty of time," replies a confident Morales, noticing Hendreick outside waiting with the passengers, "just stick to the plan like we always do," he adds and gives Hendreick a stern nod.

"Can we stand back please," shouts Hendreick to the waiting passengers in line, "and make way for one of the visitors to the ship who is feeling unwell, thank you." He adds and the passengers immediately take some steps back as Morales and Pavlov help a now drowsy Susan walk out from the tender boat and onto the pier.

"Oh my God," says an excited Chloe holding Alexis's hand, "that's the ship's doctor I was telling you about."

"OMG girl," remarks a stunned Alexis, "he is *hot*!"

"What happened?" asks a curious and concerned passenger.

"She has had one too many piña coladas during her visit," replies a happy Henderick as Morales and Pavlov walk an apparently drunk Susan swiftly away. "They are just taking her home," he adds and now waves his hands in the air, "so we shall begin boarding the tender, please watch your step as you board, thank you." The passengers soon begin to board one by one, being assisted by Hendreick and the helmsman.

"I hope she'll be okay?" says a concerned Chloe watching how they usher Susan away into the town.

"Now there goes a girl who can't hold her drink," replies

Alexis, sarcastically.

"We're up," says Sammy as they are next to board the tender.

Morales, Pavlov and Susan continue to walk away from the busy town and turn a corner into a quieter area. They soon see an emotionless man, in his forties and wearing casual clothes, waiting patiently beside a parked car.

"There he is," says a cold Morales as they approach the parked car. The man quickly glances around, ensuring there is no one watching. He opens the back door and helps them carefully place Susan on the back seat, allowing her to lie down comfortably. The man then ties her arms and legs with prepared ropes while Morales tapes her mouth with duct tape. "She's nineteen," he adds staring at the man's cold eyes, "just as Mister Hakim requested."

"Mister Hakim asked me to convey his personal gratitude," replies the man with an Eastern European accent as he opens the passenger door and takes out a heavy sports bag. "And to give you this." He adds, throwing the bag at Pavlov who quickly grabs it with his sharp reflexes.

"The sedative should wear off completely within the next thirty minutes," says Morales.

"Plenty of time," replies the man as he shuts both the back and passenger doors. He opens the driver's door, gets in, starts the car and drives off, leaving Morales and Pavlov in a small cloud of smoke.

"We should have counted it before he left," says a bemused Pavlov staring at the bag in his hands. He unzips it to reveal its full with fifty and one hundred dollar bills.

"We never had any problems with Hakim before," replies a positive Morales as he quickly zips the bag closed. "We build our network over the years based on trust."

"What about the passengers who saw us arriving at the pier?"

"The mind is a mysterious thing," replies Morales with an

impish grin on his face and touches the scar on his eyebrow, "it only sees what it wants to believe."

***

Having left the port an hour ago, and now resting on their deck beds by the pool on the crowded Top Deck, Chloe, Alexis and Sammy are amongst other passengers sleeping while soaking in the sun, snoring softly as the ship sails graciously into the horizon. Alexis coughs and wakes up, noticing how Chloe and Sammy are snoring. Giggling she grabs for her cell phone and promptly takes a number of pictures of them sleeping, then several selfies with her friends fast asleep, completely unaware that Morales is gingerly lurking in the background close by, hiding behind a white post watching them.

***

Enjoying a wonderful evening at the ship's karaoke bar, Chloe and Alexis are singing their hearts out to a popular music track as they stand centre stage, showing off their spectacular pink dresses. Nearly sixty passengers, enjoying their drinks, watch the performance. Sitting on a corner table, Sammy cheers the girls on as he sips a beer, until the song ends and the bar erupts with overwhelming applause. The girls bow and quickly shoot off to their table and sit down beside Sammy.

"A few more songs and you can start your own group," says a content Sammy giving Alexis an encouraging kiss on the lips.

"Oh, that's sweet," replies Alexis completely in love with Sammy.

A new passenger now stands centre stage and begins to sing another popular track.

"I must confess," says a happy Chloe reaching out for her cocktail at their table, "we were good!"

"We definitely were," concurs a happy Alexis and she takes her cocktail from the table, raising it for a toast. "To us!"

Chloe and Sammy raise their glasses and clink their drinks together.

"To best friends," replies Chloe with a wide smile on her face.

"And to an unforgettable cruise," replies a proud Sammy and they all sip their drinks and get comfortable watching the passenger sing.

***

The promenade snack bar situated at the back of the ship is busy with many families and couples who are enjoying late snacks such as pizzas, hotdogs and burgers, as it remains open all night.

At one of the large tables crowded with warm pizzas and ice-cold beers, sits John who is 41 and his wife Sofia who is 36. They are enjoying their pizzas. "These are undoubtedly the best pizzas ever," says John.

Their two obese sons, Mike who is 14 and his younger brother Frank who is 12, arrive at the table carrying a platter with twelve hamburgers, fries and two large ice-cold sodas. "They have all types of fillings for burgers, dad," says an amazed Mike as he gets comfortable and begins to eat one of the burgers.

"Enjoy it while you can," replies a concerned John, "because when the cruise ends you two are going on a strict diet."

"Yeah, dad," replies a happy Frank who takes a burger and admires its perfection, "but until then, we can't just ignore all of this free food," he takes a massive bite, enjoying its wonderful taste.

"Let the boys have their fun so we can have ours," says Sofia cuddling closer to her husband and putting her hand sensuously on his crotch.

"We gotta come here more often, these burgers are the bomb!" says a content Frank as he continues to stuff his mouth.

"They are the best yet," confirms Mike as he continues to eat.

Suddenly, just as Frank takes another bite of his burger, he bites into something hard making his teeth hurt resulting in a sharp pain and he shouts in agony.

"What's wrong?" asks John, concerned.

"I think I bit a stone or something," explains Frank reaching his fingers into his mouth and soon takes out the engineer's gold tooth. They all watch in horror, wondering how did that get there, not realising what meat the sous chef used to make the burgers.

***

Inside Sammy's stateroom, Alexis and Sammy are passionately making love in his bed. She moans with pleasure as he takes his time kissing every inch of her naked body in what will be another long and sleepless night for the young lovers.

***

On the ship's busy guest area where many passengers are calling from many specially arranged landline phones, Chloe has finally got through to her father. Cell phones have no coverage at sea and anyone wishing to make calls must go through the ship's telephone service which is rather expensive. Chloe and Ethan have been talking for a while as she explains their adventures in detail.

"I am happy you are having such a nice time, pumpkin," says an elated Ethan, glad to hear his daughter's voice and learn how much fun they have been having, something he knows she desperately needed after the over two years of hardship with Michael.

"It's just gone by so fast," says a much happier Chloe as she holds the telephone's receiver closer to her ear, "tomorrow will be our last day at sea and then back in Miami the day after."

"You just enjoy the rest of the cruise honey and recharge your batteries. I can't wait to see you. I miss having you around."

"I miss you too dad."

"How's Alexis behaving?"

"Oh, you know Alexis."

"That's precisely why I am asking."

"She's good dad, we are having a blast and the food is to die for."

Chloe hears a faint beeping on her phone.

"I will cook your favourite lasagne for dinner when you arrive."

"Thanks, dad. I only have another ten seconds of credit left."

"Call me again tomorrow when you get a chance, okay?"

"I will. I love you."

"Love you too, baby. Sleep well and good night." The line is disconnected and she puts the receiver down.

***

Hundreds of passengers are enjoying their buffet breakfast at the Windjammer restaurant. Chloe, Alexis and Sammy eat their pancakes, fruits, bread, croissant, cheeses, pate with hot cups of coffee while overlooking the open ocean on this beautiful sunny morning.

"Why is this food so delicious?" asks Alexis as she eats without caring for her waist line. "I haven't stopped eating since we started the cruise."

"The good thing is," replies Sammy holding firmly to Alexis, "later we burn off all those calories together."

"That we do," replies Alexis with a giggle and they kiss.

"As for me," explains Chloe stuffing her face with cheese, "when I get back it's straight to the gym. Until then, I'm eating like a pig."

Alexis laughs and oinks at Chloe who happily oinks back at her clearly enjoying every moment of their company.

***

At midday many of the ship's crew are proudly carrying the national flags from their countries as they perform a parade while all passengers, wearing their bathing suits and bikinis, clap and cheer. Many other crew members are preparing a large BBQ buffet next to the pool, a tradition on board this ship for the last day at sea.

Chloe, Alexis and Sammy are clearly enjoying the show clapping their hands along with the rest of the passengers crowding the Top Deck. Its impressive observing all countries being represented, evidence of an International crew. Alexis takes out her cell phone and snaps many pictures and selfies.

Moments later the BBQ is ready with sizzling meats and Spanish paella, enticingly laid out along many tables. Chloe, Alexis, Sammy and the other passengers walk along the buffet line with plates as the cooks fill them up with everything: pork, beef, chicken, corn, salads and paella.

"It smells lovely," remarks Chloe, excitedly, as she makes her way to her deck chair with a filled plate. She's followed by Alexis and Sammy, and they all sit on their chairs and begin to eat their irresistible meals while watching the ongoing parade of flags.

"As this will be our last night on this ship, I would like to invite you both to dinner, my treat," says Sammy, confidently. Alexis kisses him on the lips holding her tears as she knows they will go their separate ways tomorrow when they arrive back in Miami. "Hey, why are you crying?" he asks expressing concern and wiping away some of her tears from her eyes.

"The cruise ends tomorrow," she replies with a painful smile, trying to stay brave.

Chloe understands Alexis's emotions, puts her plate down and comforts her with a much-needed hug. "Tonight will be the best night ever," she whispers into Alexis's ear as they continue to embrace.

6
The Devil's Call

The majestic ship sails gracefully along the calm seas in the romantic back-drop of a breath-taking sunset. There's nothing but open blue ocean and orange skies all the way to the horizon.

At one of the most luxurious and expensive *"A La Carte"* restaurants on board, Chloe, Alexis and Sammy are sitting by the terrace enjoying the beautiful sunset, wearing formal attire. They sip champagne from fine crystal champagne classes savouring luxurious starters such as: duck pate, oysters and lobsters.

"What else could a girl dream of?" asks a romantic Alexis in this perfect evening, enjoying the amazing sunset.

"Magnificent. That's all I can say," sighs an overwhelmed Chloe.

"Alexis," Sammy impulsively says after gathering the strength to look into her eyes and hold her hands, "you have stolen my heart and tomorrow we shall depart," he confesses watching how she emotionally holds back her tears and caresses his face with her palm.

"And you have stolen mine, Sammy," she confesses and they passionately kiss on the lips, making Chloe cry with joy, happy for her friend who seems to have finally found true love.

***

Sitting on a corner table sipping cocktails in the Grand foyer, Chloe, Alexis and Sammy are enjoying a spectacular live show along with the rest of the passengers. When the show ends, everyone applauds. Then a three person band performs relaxing music on a small stage beside the foot of the staircase.

"They sure do have the best performers on these ships," remarks Chloe downing her drink in one shot. She can't help noticing how Alexis is all over Sammy, completely ignoring her. "Well, it's late and I am going to turn in," she stands up getting their attention.

"Stay a while longer, it's our last night," says Alexis.

"Precisely," replies Chloe knowingly with a bright smile and hugs her, "cherish every last second of it. I will meet you tomorrow at nine for breakfast as usual."

"Thank you," whispers Alexis knowing how Chloe is sacrificing her last night so she and Sammy can be alone.

Sammy stands up and shakes Chloe's hand. "Good night, Chloe and thank you."

"No need to thank me," she replies with a positive wink. "See you in the morning." She turns around only to accidentally bump into Morales who is walking behind her at that very moment.

"I am so sorry," says Morales holding Chloe by her arms. "I hope I haven't hurt you."

"I am fine, thank you, doctor," she replies with a shy blush and smiles at him. Alexis and Sammy grin at each other as they see how Chloe with Morales seem to have a connection.

"Maybe she will get lucky too!" mutters Sammy softly into Alexis's ear, then kisses her passionately on the lips.

"I was just leaving," says Chloe as Morales takes a step back.

"Please, I just wanted to apologize for the other night."

"After thinking about it," replies a timid Chloe, "I feel it is I who owes you an apology, as you were just doing your job ensuring I was okay. You just caught me off guard, that's all."

"Let me make it up to you."

"There is no need, really."

"Please, I insist."

"All right then," replies Chloe, feeling comfortable.

"Doctor, how is the girl from this afternoon?" asks Alexis.

Morales looks at Alexis with a mischievous smile, "Oh, I don't think she will drink so much after today but she will survive," he replies and extends his elbow to Chloe like a true gentleman. "Please, just one drink. I don't want you to leave this ship with a bad impression about me," he tells Chloe with a guilty frown.

"Well, it is the last night so one drink won't hurt I suppose," replies Chloe with a bright smile as she puts her arm around his elbow. Morales escorts her away leaving Alexis and Sammy kissing.

"We will go to the Schooner bar," says Morales confidently as they enter the nearby crowded bar and make their way to a corner table at the back. They negotiate around many passengers shuffling in all directions with drinks while listening to a professional performer sing and play a piano. "What will you have?" he asks as he makes sure she is comfortable in her seat.

"How about a bloody Mary?" she replies with a blush.

"Coming right up," he says with a warm smile.

He walks towards the bar where a bartender just finishes serving drinks to a waiting passenger. "One bloody Mary and one vodka, please," he tells the bartender with a cold expression on his face.

"You got it, Doc," replies the young 23-year-old who promptly begins to prepare the drinks.

Moments later the bartender puts a bloody Mary in front of Morales and turns around to prepare a shot of vodka. Morales casually looks around to see if anyone is watching and carefully takes out a small envelope from his pocket then cleverly empties a while powder substance into the bloody Mary, without attracting any attention to himself. He mixes the powder in the drink and smiles as the bar tender now puts a glass of vodka beside the bloody Mary. "There you go," he says swiftly turning to attend another passenger waiting at the other end of the bar.

Morales takes a deep breath and smiles, grabbing both drinks and walks back to the corner table where Chloe smiles at him, unaware. "To a fresh start," he says joyfully as he offers the bloody Mary to her with a smile and sits down beside her.

"I will definitely drink to that," she replies and sips her drink to find it very refreshing. "Now that's what I call a bloody Mary."

"To get the full effect you need to down it in one go. Like this," he says and downs his vodka as a shot and slams the empty glass onto the table.

"All right." She says and downs the rest of her drink also in one shot, slamming her empty glass onto the table beside his empty glass. "There," she giggles with a bright smile.

"Well done." He smirks proudly, clapping his hands and glancing at his wristwatch.

"So what exactly does a ship's doctor treat most on board?"

"We treat many cases of sunburn," he replies with a funny smile on his face, "but someone's gotta do it."

"Sunburn, huh?"

"And the occasional sea sickness, of course," he replies noticing how her pupils are beginning to dilate and she has trouble focussing.

"I must have underestimated that drink," she says feeling dizzy, putting her hand to her head.

"The fresh air will do you good," he replies calmly. Glancing again at his watch he erratically stands up, "Let's go for a walk. It's such a lovely night it's a shame to allow it to just simply slip away."

"Yes," she mumbles, trying to be rational, "fresh air."

Morales helps her to stand up and holds her tight, as he walks her casually out of the bar towards one of the elevators in the grand foyer. He glances over to see if her friends are watching, but Alexis and Sammy continue kissing at their table, not noticing his malicious intentions. They reach the elevator and he walks Chloe inside where he presses a button.

"Where are we going?" asks a curious Chloe trying to focus.

"The Top Deck. We can see the stars better from there."

"Stars, yes," she replies and clears her throat.

***

Morales and Chloe stroll along the not so busy Top Deck, staring up at the stars illuminating the night sky.

"Fresh air is doing me good," she says feeling slightly better with a smile. "Maybe I was wrong about you."

"Oh?"

"Let's face it, you didn't really make a great first impression on me," she confesses, holding onto Morales with fear of falling.

"Are you all right?"

"It must be the alcohol. I feel a bit woozy."

"Alcohol and fresh air don't mix very well sometimes," he replies glancing at his wristwatch, he then takes a closer look at her pupils that are now fully-dilated.

"I don't feel very well."

"Let's go to the infirmary. I will give you something that will make you feel better," he replies and holds Chloe tighter as she's having trouble keeping her balance.

"Now I know what that girl must have felt like," she says feeling nauseous as he walks her towards one of the entrances back into the ship.

***

Morales helps a now delirious and semi-unconscious Chloe onto the examining table. He lays her down as she tries to open her eyes.

"Don't fight it," he says walking to the door, which he securely locks.

"I, feeeeeeel, straaaaaaangeeeee!" she mumbles trying to focus.

"You won't feel a thing," he tells her as he walks back to the examining table and stares at her, "I promise." He sees that she is nearly unconscious and he begins to remove her dress, revealing her firm breasts, then he undresses himself.

"Whaaaaaaaat, rrrrrrrrr, uuuuuuuu, dooooooooooooooing?" She asks trying to comprehend what is happening to her. Then he brutally rips off her panties and climbs on top of her naked body, rubbing his hands all over her breasts and begins to masturbate his erect penis over her body until she loses consciousness and closes her eyes.

***

Inside Sammy's stateroom, Alexis and Sammy are anxiously undressing each other while they passionately kiss.

"This will be a night to remember," he tells her with anticipation.

"You got that right," she says, pushing him onto the bed. Then she cunningly climbing on top of him, guides his erect penis with her hand into her wet vagina and sits on it, feeling how the penetration goes deep into her womb. They both moan with pleasure while she moves from side to side, until suddenly, she stops and looks at the closed door with a concerned expression.

"Why have you stopped?"

"I got a terrible feeling about Chloe," she replies, feeling a bad sensation.

"She's probably getting laid right about now," he says moving his hips, feeling his penis swelling in her wet vagina, "you can ask her tomorrow, now come here," he adds, holding her firmly and pushing her on her back. He kisses her passionately on the lips as he tenderly penetrates her, hearing her moans as they continue to make love.

***

Covered in sweat, Morales stands naked by a glass cabinet and puts latex gloves on his hands, glancing over at Chloe's naked and raped body with traces of his semen still on her chest. He wipes sweat from his forehead as he opens the cabinet doors.

***

Sammy is thrusting wildly as he penetrates Alexis repeatedly until she soon reaches a climactic orgasm but he continues pounding deeper into her grunting like a wild animal.

"Oh yes, don't stop! Yes! Yes!" she cries in ecstasy, scratching her nails deep into his back not wanting him to stop.

***

Morales takes a specially prepared syringe from the cabinet and admires it as he removes the needle's cap and walks over to the examining table. He holds Chloe's forearm, feeling her pulse and professionally injects the needle into her arm, pressing hard on its plunger, watching how the entire liquid enters her bloodstream. He then takes one step back to admire her and touches the scar on his eyebrow, tilting his head sideways like a stray puppy.

***

"I'm coming!" shouts an aroused Sammy as he continues to pound harder into Alexis who is shouting in utter ecstasy.

"Yes, baby, don't stop!"

***

Morales walks to a closed drawer, opens it and frowns at a shiny scalpel resting inside. "Come to daddy," he mutters as he picks up the scalpel and admires his own reflection on its razor sharp blade. He then walks to the freezer, opens it and takes out the Tupperware container with the blue lid. He glances back at Chloe with a malicious grin. "Not long now," he mutters to her as he removes the lid and sets the scalpel down on the counter.

He then walks to a cabinet and takes out a large medical bottle labelled *"UW solution - formalin."* He opens the cap and pours the liquid solution from the bottle into the Tupperware, filling the container three quarters full.

***

Sammy thrusts with all his might until he ejaculates inside her and continues to penetrate, making her scream with pleasure; not thinking of the unprotected sex they are having.

***

Morales stands over Chloe's limp body and rests the tip of the scalpel onto her lower abdomen, then he glances at a digital clock on a corner that reads *"03:25"*. He hesitates wiping sweat from his forehead and takes a deep breath. "You can do this," he tells himself confidently, "you've done it hundreds of times before." He then makes a series of precise multiple incisions, opening her abdomen as if he were peeling an orange, splattering the table, floor and his own naked body with her blood.

***

Covered with sweat, Alexis and Sammy rest in each other's arms on the bed. "My heart will break tomorrow after we leave," she says feeling sad.

"I will rip my heart out and give it to you so you can carry it with you," he says romantically and kisses her lips.

"God, I love you."

"I love you too, Alexis," he replies and kisses her.

***

The digital clock now reads *"05:54"* as Morales carefully removes Chloe's second kidney, placing it with great care, beside her other one in the Tupperware container, ensuring they are both fully submerged in the liquid solution. Once satisfied, he seals the lid back on and stows the container carefully inside the freezer, then he shuts the freezer door. He looks back at Chloe's mutilated body and stares down at the blood on his gloves, knowing the monster has mercilessly struck again.

***

Acting like she has passed out, Morales walks Chloe, who is now fully dressed, down a sequence of corridors until he reaches the junction he saw the other day and notices the CCTV camera pointing to the corridor on the left. Glancing around to ensure they are alone, he walks her into the corridor to the right and continues towards a door leading to *"Deck D"* which he soon reaches. He opens the door and steps out onto the deck, allowing the cold sea breeze to blow in his face as they walk towards the corner blind spot. He leans Chloe against the railings, looking carefully around, ensuring there is no one watching.

"What have you done?" asks a delirious Chloe who is beginning to wake up in complete agony feeling sharp pains in her stomach.

"What I have to do in order to survive," he maliciously replies and mercilessly lifts her body up over the railing staring into her now petrified, opened eyes. She stares back at him crying and pleading for mercy. But he is determined to go through with his malicious act and her pleas fall onto deaf ears as he cruelly throws her overboard.

Morales quickly leans over the railing, observing how she plummets and splashes hard, legs first, into the dark cold waters below. Her body bobs on the surface and she moans and cries out in utter agony as both her legs were broken by the sudden impact of the fall, only adding to her unbearable pain.

"Help me!" she yells opening her eyes in terror, watching the ship sail away into the dark horizon and realizing no one will come to her rescue.

Fear quickly sets in and it shows on her petrified face as she now cannot move due to the sedative Morales gave her, paralysing her body. She screams vaguely while trying to remain afloat, but soon begins to sink below the surface, fighting with all her might to remain above water. But it's futile, as she hasn't got the power or the energy to swim. She starts to drown, swallowing the cold salty water, frantically gasping for air, fighting for her life with every ounce of strength she has left. But she knows deep down she cannot sustain this indefinitely as she is too weak. So against her darkest fears she begins to drown as taking in the salty water is just too much to bear. After a minute of panic she dies.

Chloe's lifeless body floats motionless above the water until it soon sinks and disappears under the sea forever, taking Morales's secrets with her.

***

Morales meticulously cleans the entire examination room like a mad man, removing any evidence of foul play from the examination table and the floor. He wipes all the blood away with a special liquid until he is satisfied everything is clean.

***

Morales takes a long warm shower and removes all the blood stains from his body, scrubbing like crazy to get Chloe's blood and smell from him. He allows the steam to cleanse his guilt, while her blood mixes with the soap and water being washed down the drain.

7
The Search

In the early hours of the morning, just as the sun is about to rise, the ship has docked by its pier and an army of workers are shuffling in all directions unloading thousands of luggage and tons of trash in special containers from the vessel. Another army of workers are simultaneously loading tons of fresh supplies, food, beverage, provisions and diesel on board for the afternoon's cruise. The atmosphere is electrifying as they have a tight schedule to maintain.

Standing at the pier, Pavlov waits as he patiently observes how one of the trash containers, clearly marked with a small red letter "X" on the side, is placed by a forklift on the pier beside many other containers.

Standing by a railing on one of the ship's decks looking down, Morales observes the trash containers and closely watches how Pavlov walks cautiously to the marked container. He soon removes a large brown bulgy bag from inside.

A man in his forties, wearing a suit, smokes as he patiently waits beside a black SUV near the terminus building. It is evident this man has been waiting for a few hours, as he has thrown about a dozen cigarette buds on the ground in that time.

Suddenly, he hears footsteps approaching and he smiles as Pavlov walks towards him carrying the brown bag in his right hand. The man tosses the cigarette bud and pops open the trunk of his SUV where there is an electronic medical machine running on batteries inside beside a brown paper bag.

"You are late," he says with an Eastern European accent as Pavlov reaches the SUV and stands beside him. "Did you bring them?"

"Two," he replies, extending the brown bag, "as requested."

"What time frame are they?"

"They were extracted just under four hours ago and preserved like always."

"Good," replies the man as Pavlov sets the bag next to the machine and shows the filled Tupperware container inside with Chloe's kidneys, making the man happy.

"It's all there," replies the man watching how Pavlov leaves his bag and now picks up the other bag inside the truck and opens it revealing stacks of hundred dollar bills inside.

"It's been a pleasure doing business as usual with you," says Pavlov clutching tight to the money bag, then starts to walk away.

"My client has another order for next week, a heart and lung," says the man forcing Pavlov to stop. "Will this be problem?" he asks with a cold tone.

Pavlov slowly turns around and faces the man. "It is never a problem. You will have them. Just have the money ready," he replies and walks away leaving the man staring at the Tupperware with a malicious grin.

Morales observes how Pavlov walks to one of the workers on the pier loading up a container of provisions and discreetly hands the brown bag containing the money over to him. The worker cautiously hides the bag in the container and they all watch it slowly being lifted on board.

Pavlov shakes the worker's hand and secretly passes him a few hundred dollar bills. He quickly shoves them into his pocket and nods at Pavlov. They have conveniently devised this controlled method to smuggle things in and out from the ship. For it would be impossible for Pavlov to return on board with that amount of money as he would be questioned by the ship's strict security.

***

A small army of workers are busy stowing away the tons of provisions arriving by the minute in the galley. Pavlov walks in and approaches a young steward. They stare at one another until the steward nods his head gesturing to Pavlov to follow him. They move towards one of the containers where he cautiously removes the brown money bag and hands it to him. Pavlov ensures no one is watching, takes a few hundred dollar bills and gives it to the steward who quickly shoves them into his pocket and walks away.

***

At the busy Windjammer restaurant, the passengers are all enjoying their last breakfast aboard before disembarking from the ship. Alexis and Sammy walk into the busy restaurant holding hands, looking around for Chloe. "I'll get us the coffees," he says with a smile.

"I'll find Chloe," she replies. Sammy walks to the coffee station while Alexis happily walks around scanning the tables for her friend, occasionally glancing at the rich food on offer along the counters.

***

On the deck, Morales observes how the workers continue with their arduous work as he leans confidently on the railings. Pavlov soon stands beside him empty-handed but with a confident smile.

"Any problems?" asks Morales staring out to the terminus building.

"Like clockwork."

"Make sure my share reaches my account as usual."

"They have another order for next week," he says cautiously glancing around ensuring no one is watching or hearing their conversation, "a heart and lung."

"Business is picking up," replies a much happier Morales,

"good."

"Let's get two more kidneys," replies Pavlov with a stern expression, "I have a new buyer who will pay double for them."

"I love America," replies Morales.

***

Alexis and Sammy are eating their breakfast glancing at the main door, hoping that Chloe will arrive at any moment.

"It isn't like her to be so late," explains a now concerned Alexis.

"Will you relax already? She's probably saying her goodbyes to her date from last night."

Alexis stands up with a bad sensation.

"Where are you going?" he asks, feeling concerned.

"To our stateroom," she replies and walks away.

"I'll come with you," he shouts and they walk quickly away, leaving their unfinished breakfast on the table.

***

Alexis and Sammy enter the stateroom only to find the bed has not been slept in and all the clothes still in the wardrobes.

"Something's definitely not right," she remarks while checking the connecting restroom perceiving something bad must have happened to her best friend, "she would have been packed by now."

"Maybe she had a one-night stand and is still sleeping in the guy's room?"

"You don't know Chloe like I do," replies a worried Alexis, "she is meticulous and knowing we have to disembark in," she adds glancing at her watch, "about an hour from now, she would have already been packed and out of this room." She glances around at the untouched personal items everywhere. "Yet, it's like as if she has never been here."

"Maybe you're right," replies a now more concerned Sammy, "if anything has happened to her, I am sure the ship's security must know," he adds and takes her hand. "Come on."

***

"It's just not like her," confirms a distraught Alexis to the ship's "*SECO*" Chief Security Officer, Lieutenant Martin, a seasoned officer in his fifties who has been working aboard a spectrum of cruise ships throughout a twenty-three year career within the security industry. He listens attentively at Alexis's missing person report, taking detailed notes in his black notebook as he stands beside two junior ship's security officers inside a waiting area. He glances at Sammy who constantly comforts Alexis by tenderly squeezing her hand.

"I can assure you, Miss Young, my security team who man the gangways, and any possible exits from this ship, have confirmed that Miss Moore has not walked off the ship since we docked this morning," confirms a shrewd Martin.

"So she must still be somewhere on board. That is what you are saying, right?" asks a worried Sammy holding Alexis's hand.

"My men are searching the ship as we speak. If she is on board, we will find her."

"I'm sorry," interrupts a now confused Alexis, "but what do you mean, *if*, she is still on board? You just told us she hasn't walked off the ship, so she must then be somewhere *on* this ship."

"Not necessarily," replies Martin firmly, "there have been similar reports from missing persons in the past who have jumped ship to end their lives," adds a candid Martin without showing remorse.

"You don't seriously expect me to believe that my best friend has resorted to taking her own life now, do you?" she shouts, raising her voice but keeping her composure.

"At this moment in time I can only go with the facts, which are, your friend is currently missing, she has not left the ship through the normal exit points and we are conducting a search which at this time has resulted in no sightings of her."

"So the suicide you mentioned is just speculation?" asks Sammy sharply.

"It is," replies Martin abruptly, "but we are leaving all options open and not ruling anything out at this time." Martin glances at his notebook. "And with regards to doctor Morales, we have spoken with him and he does confirm that he met with Miss Moore last night, just as you have mentioned to me on your statement. After having a quick drink with her, he was called to an emergency moments later where, he left her at the Schooner bar, not seeing or hearing from her again."

"What am I going to tell her father?" asks an emotional Alexis.

***

Waiting patiently inside the cruise terminal building watching a continuous row of passengers disembarking from the ship's gangway, Ethan anticipates Chloe and Alexis will be soon be walking out and hugging him. He watches with a bright smile on his face and glances at the new line of passengers waiting to check in for the afternoon departure.

"Ethan," shouts Alexis running down the gangway in tears making his bright smile quickly fade away expressing concern as she reaches and hugs him.

"What's happened? Where's Chloe?" asks an anxious Ethan, glancing around not finding his daughter anywhere.

"We can't find her," she cries on his shoulder bursting into tears.

"What do you mean you can't find her?" asks Ethan holding

her tight by the shoulders at arm's length to look into her eyes. "Where is she?"

***

Inside one of the ship's VIP lounges, Ethan, Alexis, Sammy, Martin and Captain Jones, a stern man in his late fifties, are talking in private over coffees.

"We don't know," answers Martin candidly.

"I'm sorry but that is just unacceptable," replies Ethan in frustration. "This is my only daughter we are talking about and right now no one seems to know where she is. How difficult can it be to form a search party and comb this ship for Christ's sake?"

"Mister Moore, sir, you must understand, we will set sail in less than two hours. That is the window we have, not a second more," replies the ship's Captain bluntly. "I have been updated about this incident and all we can do is try to find her before we sail."

"What?" asks a bewildered Alexis.

"You can't be serious, Captain!?" cries a concerned Ethan.

"I can assure you, Mister Moore, I am very serious."

"My men continue searching high and low for the next two hours," replies Martin professionally, and he closes his notebook.

Ethan angrily takes out his detective's badge and waves it at them trying to hold his composure. "You are not sailing anywhere until my daughter is found, you hear?"

"I am afraid you have no jurisdiction aboard this ship, sir," says a stringent Captain taking offense to Ethan's threat.

"Captain, sir, with all due respect," he replies trying to maintain a rational tone, "my daughter is my oxygen and if push comes to shove, I will call my friend in the F.B.I. and have your ship stopped from sailing."

"You are mistaken, Mister Moore," remarks a now annoyed Captain who stands to attention feeling threatened, "go ahead, call your friend in the Bureau or at Langley or wherever else you may feel comfort in calling. I fear you will learn it will do no good," he says proudly raising his chin, clearly defying Ethan. "This ship carries a Bermuda flag and by law only the Bermuda Police has jurisdiction on board."

"This is an American port, damn you," mutters Sammy trying to make sense of what he is being subjected to.

"It appears that Miss Moore disappeared in International waters," comments Martin emotionlessly.

"What are you trying to say exactly?" asks Ethan fearing the worst.

"After consulting with S.E.C.O. Martin," replies a stern Captain, "we unfortunately suspect your daughter may have jumped off this ship and committed suicide.

"No!" shouts Ethan lashing forward to try and grab the Captain, but he gets detained by Martin and Sammy.

"Please calm down, Mister Moore," instructs Martin calmly, trying to hold him back.

"Chloe has a lot to look forward to, especially after starting a new life after her divorce," says Alexis knowingly. "So suicide is the last thing she'd do," she confirms making Ethan calm down and take a moment to breathe and step back from both Martin and Sammy.

"Maybe she drank too much and accidently fell overboard. It has happened before. Either way, the incident has already been reported to the Bermuda Police and they are waiting for our final report," says a confident Martin.

"This is a joke, right?" asks Ethan completely perplexed trying to make sense of everything he is hearing. "You mean to tell me that the Police located in another part of the world are just sitting tight, waiting on *your* report? A report which you clearly have concluded to be that my daughter, jumped?" he shouts and walks to the closed door. "She is aboard, maybe even held against her will and if you won't find her, then I will."

"We have thousands of new guests arriving for their cruise, Mister Moore," confirms Martin making Ethan stop and turn back at him.

"Good God man," mutters Ethan clearly enraged, "you call yourself a security officer?" he adds, pulling the door wide open. "First rule of an investigation is to seal off the area to avoid scene contamination. Evidently that doesn't apply here either, does it?"

"By sealing off an area, you are referring to the entire ship?" replies Martin calmly, "This can only be done by a forensic team, something that neither myself nor my team are, I am sorry to say."

"As a father myself, I understand your frustration, Mister Moore," replies the Captain sternly, "that is why, out of courtesy and nothing else, I will allow you to inspect my ship accompanied by two of my officers at all times."

"Thank you, Captain," replies a somewhat more relieved Ethan.

"But come 15.30 hours, you will need to leave and allow my men to continue with their investigation as we sail," remarks the Captain.

"I want full access to the ship's CCTV tapes," demands Ethan.

"The tapes will be handed over to the Bermuda Police along with our reports after our investigation," replies Martin emotionlessly.

"You can contact them directly of course and ask for a copy of the reports after they are filed," says the Captain.

"You say you are a father, Captain," asks Ethan taking one step closer, staring into his cold eyes.

"I have two daughters, yes."

"What would you do if they went missing and you were only given a few hours to try and make sense of their disappearance?" replies Ethan, seeing Captain Jones is at a loss for words. "You are wasting my time," he mutters and swiftly storms out of the lounge, leaving the Captain completely stunned.

Alexis and Sammy quickly rush out of the lounge.

"I will have my men escort him discreetly around, Captain," says Martin and walks out of the lounge leaving the Captain staring aimlessly at a wall, lost in his thoughts.

***

"This was our room," reveals Alexis as she, Ethan, Sammy and two security officers enter the stateroom and find a ship's steward in his twenties, cleaning the bathroom as he is making the stateroom ready for the next guests expected to arrive shortly. He finds Chloe's personal hair brush and make up, throwing them into a plastic bag.

"What do you think you are doing?" asks Alexis totally enraged, grabbing the bag from him.

"I have my orders," replies the unmoved steward. "New guests will be arriving shortly and I have to dispose of these belongings."

"Dispose?" asks a bewildered Ethan.

"I packed my bags earlier and left Chloe's here for her," she says walking to the wardrobe and opening the door, shocked to find Chloe's clothes and belongings are gone. "Where are they?"

"Everything has been moved to storage," replies the steward.

"I would like to have them please," states Ethan expressing frustration.

"I will make the arrangements," replies one of the security officers.

"Thank you," replies Ethan and looks back at Alexis, "where and when exactly did you last see Chloe?"

"At the bar last night," she replies confidently.

"She went off with the doctor," adds Sammy.

"What doctor?" asks a concerned Ethan.

***

"I got a call about two minutes after we arrived at the bar," replies a calm Morales at the infirmary reception desk. Ethan, Alexis, Sammy and the two security officers patiently observe while the nurse works on her computer at her desk.

"Who called you?" asks Ethan.

"My office got a call from stateroom 7405," replies a confident Morales who walks to the counter, picks up a clipboard with a false emergency report he had earlier fabricated in the event of an investigation. He extends it to Ethan who glances through it, "as you can see from the log, at twenty-six minutes past eleven in the evening I was paged for an emergency and so I politely bid Miss Moore good night, and left her at the bar to attend the call."

"That was the time we more or less saw her last," recalls Sammy confirming Morales's story.

"By the time I finished with the emergency in stateroom 7405 and returned back to the bar, Miss Moore had already left," replies Morales. "I already gave my statement to the security officer earlier today," he adds impulsively, touching the scar on his eyebrow, making Ethan suspicious.

"What did you do afterwards?" asks Ethan bluntly.

"Afterwards?" asks a now bewildered Morales.

"Yes, after you returned to the bar and saw Chloe wasn't there?"

"Well, I went to my room and went to sleep as it was a long

day and I was exhausted."

"Alone?"

"You know," replies a now nervous Morales, "I don't have to answer your questions and am doing so out of respect. But yes, I was alone."

"I see," replies Ethan thinking for a moment, then he glances at the connecting room leading to the theatre. "What's through there?"

"The O.R.," replies the nurse.

"I have far more important things to take care of than to give you a tour of my infirmary, Mister Moore," replies a frustrated Morales.

"What's in that room, doctor?" asks Ethan now pointing to another doorway.

"The examination room," replies Morales maintaining his posture, "where I treat patients when they arrive at the infirmary."

"I see," replies a frustrated Ethan who seems to have reached a dead end. "Thank you, doctor."

***

A small army of stewards are cleaning and preparing the Schooner bar as Ethan, Alexis, Sammy and the two security officers talk with the bartender from last night.

"You need to understand," says the bartender politely taking the picture of Chloe that Ethan hands him from his wallet, "the place was packed like it is every night. I must have served over a thousand drinks to a thousand guests. It's impossible to remember every face, I'm sorry."

Ethan scans the area and soon spots two CCTV cameras above the bar. "Who keeps the tapes from the CCTV?"

"We control all the ship's CCTV systems and storage of all footage on our hard drives," replies one of the security officers.

"I will need to view the tapes from those cameras from last night," demands a now hopeful Ethan.

"I am sorry, sir, but you are not authorised to do so. You have already been informed about this by my superior."

"Why is it that I get the feeling you are all trying to railroad me away from finding my daughter?" asks Ethan in frustration.

***

Walking along the Top Deck, Ethan, Alexis, Sammy and the two security officers walk together with hundreds of excited new passengers who are exploring the ship and shuffling in all directions.

"In all my years as a Detective, this is the first time I find a crime scene being blatantly and knowingly sabotaged," remarks Ethan in frustration. He stops to look out to sea, gripping the railing tight with his hands. "Suicide?" he mutters to himself trying not to believe it, focussing his eyes on the massive drop to the waters below.

"She wanted to open up her own business," explains Alexis as she stands beside Ethan and comforts him. "It just doesn't make any sense for her to do what they are saying."

"My God," says Sammy in horror, "she was a bit tipsy, what if she *did* fall overboard accidentally?"

"Depending on which deck she might have gone over, the higher the fall the less chances of surviving the impact with the water," replies one of the security officers.

"Plus if she did survive, hyperthermia would soon kick in," says the second security officer. "Either way, her chances of survival would have been slim to none, alone in those waters."

"I felt something last night and did nothing," barks out Alexis hitting the railing with her fists in anger.

"You wouldn't have known, Alexis. It's not your fault," replies a calm Ethan putting his arm around her shoulder.

"I could have called her," she remarks, "done something!"

"We are all trying to make sense out of all this but jumping to assumptions is not healthy for anyone," says Sammy trying to keep his cool with a clear and open mind.

"Yes," replies Ethan staring at the security officers. "It's as if they are trying to cover it all up."

"You mean like, sweep this whole affair under the carpet and hope it goes away?" replies Sammy.

"Something like that, yes."

"I am afraid time is up, Mister Moore," says one of the security officers glancing at his wristwatch, "I will now have to ask you all to please vacate this ship. We sail in less than thirty minutes."

"I am not leaving until I find my daughter, damn you!"

"The agreement was that you could stay until the ship sailed and that time has arrived, sir."

"I don't care. I'm staying."

"Then you will leave us with no other choice but to remove you by force."

"Give it your best try!" replies Ethan standing firm.

***

"Damn you all to hell!" shouts an enraged Ethan as he is being forcefully carried by four security officers down the gangway. "All of you should be ashamed of the way you are conducting your investigations!" he yells and notices how Martin watches from the centre of the gangway standing tall.

"Goodbye, Detective Moore," says Martin loudly, observing how they are removing Ethan from the ship, followed by Alexis and Sammy who are also escorted down the gangway by his men. "I promise we will continue with the investigation," he adds as Ethan composes himself, being prevented from entering the gangway by two terminal security officers who hold him back.

"Your investigation is a sham!" Ethan exclaims watching Martin's cold eyes.

"Please, don't make this harder than it already is," replies Martin as he walks back into the ship, leaving Ethan, Alexis and Sammy standing outside feeling helpless, hugging each other in tears as the gangway is retracted and the ship is about to sail.

"I don't understand," says a confused Alexis, noticing how they are removing the mooring lines from the ship, "why have they allowed the ship to sail? Chloe can still be somewhere on board."

"It's all a big money-making industry that has to meet deadlines and turnarounds, Alexis," replies Sammy knowingly.

"Alexis," asks Ethan calmly as he looks into her eyes, "was there anything strange about Chloe's behaviour these past few days?"

"In what way?"

"Did she meet anyone? Or say anything that sounded off?" he asks holding her firmly. "I need you to focus and think. However small of a detail that you may feel is irrelevant, I need to know."

"Well," she says gathering her thoughts and feeling embarrassed, "she did confide in me that," she pauses, finding it hard to say the words, "that, she had a one-night stand, a few nights ago."

"With whom?" he asks with a firmer tone clearly outraged.

"She didn't get his name. I'm sorry."

"Did she see him again?"

"Not that I am aware of."

"Think, Alexis. Anything else? An argument with someone. Um, a complaint she may have made. Anything!"

"What about the doctor?" says Sammy feeling concerned.

"His story matches with the ship's log," replies a frustrated Ethan.

"No, not last night," replies Alexis remembering the incident.

"What do you mean?"

"She first met him on the night we arrived on board," she replies feeling uncomfortable. "Chloe told me that he had made some sort of advances towards her."

"What sort of advances?"

"She said that he touched her face and asked if she had a cold."

"A cold?" mutters Ethan trying to make sense from this.

"It was strange," continues Alexis trying to remember everything Chloe told her. "She just felt uncomfortable around him."

"Did she report this?"

"I don't think so."

"Yet on her last night she had a drink with him. Why?"

"Maybe to make amends in some way as I did tell her that she may have overreacted and she did say that she was going to apologise."

"Why leave it till the last night though?"

The ship's mooring lines are now removed and the ship is slowly sailing out of the port where hundreds of passengers wave goodbye and the ship's air horn blasts away as a new cruise begins for the thousands of new passengers leaving Ethan, Alexis and Sammy impotent to uncover the truth about what happened to Chloe.

8
The Anguish

"As I explained to you this afternoon Mister Moore, the company is conducting an investigation in conjunction with the Bermuda Police and there is nothing else we can tell you at this time, except that no foul play has been discovered," explains a woman's voice as Ethan holds the telephone's receiver to his ear, clutching it firmly clearly not happy with that answer and staring at many family pictures hanging on the wall near him: *Ethan with his late wife. Ethan with Chloe. Chloe in a happy moment growing up.* I'm sorry but that is just not acceptable," he replies trying not to lose his temper, clutching the receiver so tight his knuckles are completely red.

He glances at a connecting glass door leading to the lit garden and pool outside, remembering how Chloe used to run to the pool when she was a young girl with her constant cheerful laughs. "No foul play?" he asks in bewilderment glancing at a clock nearby that reads *"23:05."* "What is wrong with you people? My daughter has gone missing on *your* ship, obviously something has happened." *"Statistics unfortunately prove that many people commit suicide on board by jumping into the ocean,"* replies the emotionless woman making him even angrier.

"Does your company have a default script that includes the word suicide, damn it?" he asks getting worked up and stares at a picture of *Chloe on a happy moment of her life,* hanging on the wall. "I know my daughter and that is something she would *never* do so best change your narrative because it's wrong, damn you!"

There is a slight pause and then the woman replies. *"On behalf of the company, Mister Moore, I sympathise with your loss and will keep you updated if any further developments should arise. Good night."* The line is then disconnected.

"No wait! You're talking as if she is already dead! Wait!

Hello!" shouts Ethan slamming the receiver down in frustration, then takes a deep breath to control his emotions. "Bastards," he mutters to himself feeling completely helpless and vulnerable trying to control his rage as he continues to stare at a picture of *Chloe in a happy moment smiling*. He lets out a blood curdling scream, unable to control his emotions any longer and breaks down in tears. He takes the picture from the wall and tenderly caresses Chloe's happy face with his hand. "Where are you, pumpkin?" he asks crying in desperation.

But then he thinks for a moment and glances around the spacious living room, remembering what he heard about Morales earlier today: He recalls Alexis saying. *"Chloe told me he had made some sort of advances towards her. He touched her face and asked if she had a cold. It was strange. She just felt uncomfortable around him."*

In deep thought, Ethan walks to the small bar and pours himself a whiskey reflecting on what Morales mentioned, *"you know, I don't have to answer your questions. But yes, I was alone."*

Walking to the sofa with his whiskey in his left hand and the picture on his right hand, totally lost in thought, he now recalls what the ship's Captain told him, *"We unfortunately suspect, your daughter, may have jumped off and committed suicide."*

Ethan slowly drops on the sofa and sips his whiskey while staring aimlessly, in a complete trance, now recalling what the chief security officer, Martin, told him. *"It is clear Miss Moore disappeared in International waters."*

Then recalls what Alexis also told him. *"She wanted to open up her own business. It just doesn't make any sense to do what they are saying."*

Sipping more whiskey he now recalls Sammy's words, *"It's all a big money-making industry that has to meet deadlines and turnarounds."*

Ethan shakes his head, deep in thought at what Alexis had shared next, *"She told me she had a one night stand a few nights ago."* He lets out another blood curdling scream and throws the glass in anger against a wall, smashing it into pieces and takes one last look at Chloe's picture in his hand before finally snapping out of his trance, focussing on the matter at hand.

"Okay," He mutters as he takes out his cell phone from his pocket and scans through his contact list, until he finds *"Alexis cell,"* and clicks on dial. He wipes his mouth and sniffs, listening to the ringing tone and waits for Alexis to answer.

"Hello?" says Alexis's sleepy voice over his cell.

"Alexis, it's Ethan, am sorry it's late but I need to know if you took any pictures during your cruise?" he asks with anticipation not moving his eyes from Chloe's picture, and her happy smile.

"No, I couldn't sleep, it's okay for you to call me," she replies with a soft tone, *"yes, I can send them to you if that will help,"* she adds innocently.

"Yes, please," he replies feeling hopeful but hearing her cries.

"I'm sorry," she says breaking down into uncontrollable tears, *"I wasn't with her last night."* She expresses feeling guilty, which makes him break out into tears. He clasps Chloe's picture against his heart, hugging it tightly.

"I won't stop until I get to the truth, one way or another. So help me, I'll kill whoever's responsible if they've hurt my baby," he vows with a cold expression on his face.

"Let me know how else I can help. Anything at all," she says shyly. "Send me the pictures for now and try to get some sleep. You are a good girl, Alexis, for always being with Chloe. Good night." He says emotionally as it's very painful for him right now to continue talking with her so he ends the call.

"Damn it!" he shouts, tossing his cell on the sofa beside him. He stands up and walks to the large dining table where he sits down in front of his laptop, sets Chloe's picture on the table beside him and types "Missing persons on cruise ships" into his web browser.

The laptop screen now shows a long list of links. Ethan clicks on the first one he sees which opens a *"YouTube"* video of an interview. The man's face is concealed as he shares his story to a famous reporter. A banner reads *"Cruise Industry whistleblower"*.

Ethan sits back and raises the volume as he carefully listens to the interviewee speaking on camera. *"Not only does a cruise ship have crime but it has more crime than in any metropolitan city on land. The place to get away with committing a crime is on board a cruise ship. The place to be a sexual predator and prey on innocent children is on a cruise ship. If you are a rapist, you are more likely to get away with committing the crime on a cruise ship in the high seas, obviously everything is happening on International waters where there are no policemen on the scene, where you cannot dial 911 or summon a police officer to come to the crime scene, so they are out there by themselves and most of the crimes are usually committed on the last night of the cruise. In the last decade alone there have been over 250 persons gone missing, not only passengers but crew members also."*

"That is an average of 20 to 25 persons disappearing every year."

"Which is an extremely low percentage from the over thirty million passengers sailing on average every year. Unfortunately for those who do go missing, most of those cases go unsolved and are brushed aside with a convenient phrase from the company that the person has taken his or her own life."

"You would image that a holiday under the sun, visiting exotic destinations and getting pampered aboard a luxury liner would be a place of happiness, not one where you'd be so depressed you would jump overboard to kill yourself. Besides, I can imagine better ways to take one's own life than to jump into the cold waters and wait to drown a horrible and painful death," explains the stunned reporter. *"Tell me more about the vetting process for a cruise ship employee."*

"I have been working in the H.R. Department for over five years and when the company tells us to employ people to cover for a ship that is either sailing or is about to sail, you better believe, the recruits have to be on board within hours sometimes, to meet those deadlines."

"Surely, that won't give the company enough time to complete the vetting process for the new recruits?" asks the Reporter on camera.

"In the haste, there is hardly any vetting process done in some cases."

"So let me put this into perspective then. Families on board who entrust

their children to members of the ship's crew, like stewards, monitors, lifeguards or even carers, for example, not knowing exactly who that stranger really is... run the risk of having their child abused in some way or form, because the company has failed to do a complete background check on who that crew member really is?"

"That is correct, yes. Not long ago, a waiter who was recruited from India, groped an 11-year-old girl in one of the ship's elevators and this was captured on the ship's CCTV, where you can clearly see the girl entering the elevator being followed by this individual who molested her and then ran away. What did the company do? They allowed that individual to leave the ship on the next port so he wouldn't be held accountable. Who ends up suffering? The girl and her indignant family who couldn't get justice for what happened to their daughter. On another case, a ship's steward recruited from Brazil raped an American lady on her first night aboard, in her own stateroom where she remained throughout the entire cruise, not receiving medical assistance for fear of that individual returning. We employ people from all countries and cultures."

"But the questions our viewers are probably asking is, do we truly know all of them?" asks the stunned Reporter. "The answer must clearly be, no."

"It is no secret that a cruise ship has more crime than in most cities and as long as passengers are made aware of this fact, the crime rates will continue to skyrocket until something can finally be done to prevent it."

"Can you elaborate more about crimes? What crimes?"

"Everything from rapes, groping, assaults, theft and drugs. In the past decade over two hundred and fifty people have mysteriously disappeared and more than half are still unexplained."

"More than half?" asks a shocked Reporter.

"That is correct, from passengers to crew members, who just vanish into thin air. Imagine, one of the crew members who was part of the children's entertainment staff aboard a Disney cruise disappeared one night without a trace and the company just said she must have jumped, for whatever reasons. The ship was registered in the Bahamas so a Royal Bahamas police officer was sent to the ship where he only had a few hours to conduct his *investigation before the ship turned around and sailed with thousands of new passengers, on the same ship that member of staff went missing."*

Ethan's eyes glow with hatred as he listens and watches anticipating the worst for Chloe, unaware that his cell phone is vibrating on the sofa as Alexis sends hundreds of pictures via a social messaging service.

"There is a worrying statistic that grabbed my attention," says the Reporter now reading from his notes. "On a cruise ship there are fifty percent more rapes occurring than on land. Sexual assaults seem to be on the increase as it appears to be a free-for-all for sexual predators, as they know they stand a better chance of getting away with their attacks on a cruise than on land."

"Just like I explained, yes. It is shocking to say the least."

"Why are they getting away with it?"

"Convenience of flying a different country's flag, as registering a ship in a foreign country means that it's that foreign country that is liable for any security breaches aboard when sailing in International waters. Also the fact that a ship has no police and it's impossible to call 911 when something happens. Who is going to come to your aide when you are in the open waters? You must bear in mind that a ship looks after its crew. It's a family and a tight knit community who protect their own. That's why no one talks on board and there are so many disturbing secrets."

"Why have you come forward and become a whistle-blower?"

"The world must learn the truth and as long as the current regulations continue in place, I fear the statistics will just continue to rise and we will continue to close the lid on it. There are major bucks in play and no one wants to rock the boat!" replies a candid interviewee. "If anyone watching this can learn from it and maybe even save them from harm or their own lives while on a cruise, then that's one life saved which is why I am doing this."

"Oh my God," mutters Ethan in horror leaning back on his chair in disbelief and slams the laptop closed as he cannot listen to this anymore. "Jesus Christ," he mutters and notices in the corner of his eye how his cell phone is flashing its red *"message"* light. He quickly runs to the sofa and reads a text message from Alexis.

"Hi Ethan, here are all the pictures I took from the cruise," it reads followed by hundreds of pictures. He sits down and carefully begins to swipe through them one at a time, carefully watching them on his small screen.

- Picture at the pier of *Chloe, Alexis with Ethan.*

- Many pictures on the ship's promenade deck of *Chloe and Alexis fooling around.*

Ethan holds his tears as he zooms in on one of the pictures where Chloe is laughing. He pauses for a moment, sniffs and then continues to swipe through more pictures.

- Many pictures of *Chloe and Alexis lounging on the Top Deck's lounge beds in their bikinis.*

Ethan swipes through many of the Top Deck bikini pictures until one in particular catches his attention and he swipes back to get a much closer look at it. It's a selfie of *Chloe and Alexis with cocktails laughing at the camera by the pool,* but something is bothering him. He zooms into the picture until he spots Morales standing in the distance observing the girls with a stern expression. "What are you doing there, Doc?" asks an intrigued Ethan.

He slowly continues to swipe through more pictures and soon finds another one that gets his attention. It's a selfie of *Chloe and Sammy asleep by the pool and Alexis laughing.* Ethan notices someone in the background and once again zooms in and is shocked to see Morales observing the girls with a stern expression on his face. "You again?" mutters Ethan finding this to be far from a coincidence.

He continues to stare into Morales's cold face, he remembers again what Alexis mentioned. "*Chloe told me he had made some sort of advances towards her. He touched her face and asked if she had a cold. It was strange. She just felt uncomfortable around him.*" It plays over and over again in his mind.

***

Inside the Detective's Room at the Miami's police station, over ten plain clothed detectives are working at their desks. Amongst them is Ethan reading a report on his police desktop computer. He has clearly been up all-night crying, as his eyes are bloodshot.

Detective Hank Shaw, in his early forties and overweight, walks into the office carrying a large box of doughnuts and slams it onto Ethan's desk.

"They didn't have any of the caramel ones left so I got you the strawberry ones instead," he says opening the box and taking out one of the seven doughnuts inside, offering it to Ethan. "You look like shit! Here, the sugar will wake you up."

Ethan is so captivated by the report on his computer monitor that he completely ignores the doughnut and starts reading out loud. "Did you know that representatives from Central America and the Dominican Republic established a minimum penalty for the crime of organ trafficking, where a person convicted of the crime will receive no less than five years in prison?"

"Jesus, Ethan, eat the doughnut, here I'll join you," replies Hank grabbing another doughnut from the box and taking a great big bite.

"Don't you see Hank?" replies an excited Ethan, who now takes his doughnut and bites it. "Those countries are rife with crime and criminals are encouraged to continue because there is no serious punishment. In the United States there are laws to protect the public against such crimes but when you board a cruise ship, and that ship enters into International waters, the laws change. You are no longer entitled to the same protection you may think you are. The cruise lines know this, the crew members know this, but the passengers are left in the dark. Sexual assault is the number one crime occurring on cruise ships and thirty three percent of those are committed against minors."

"Ethan. I pray they will find Chloe alive and well. I mean, how difficult can it be to find her?"

"The ship was sailing around the Caribbean."

"There, see?" replies Hank finishing his doughnut and now reaching for another one. "These are great."

Police Captain Hills, a stern African American seasoned cop in his late fifties, wearing an expensive suit, stands beside Ethan and grabs a doughnut from the box.

"Morning Captain," says Hank as he continues to eat.

"These are good," replies the Captain enjoying the doughnut. "You two, in my office, now."

Hills walks towards his office at the back, followed by Ethan and Hank who are licking their fingers.

Inside the small office, Hills sits down behind his paper-littered desk which has a big sign that reads *"Captain Hills."* He waits for Hank and Ethan to come inside.

"Close the door," he says. Ethan, who is the last to enter, shuts the door behind him. "Take a seat," Hills adds and waits for Hank and Ethan to sit down in the visitors' chairs.

"Ethan, how long have we known each other?" asks a concerned Hills, leaning back comfortably in his armchair. Hanging on the wall behind him there are many framed police commendation certificates, graciously on display.

"Nearly thirty years, Captain," replies an exhausted Ethan rubbing his eyes trying to stay awake.

"Thirty years, that's right," confirms Hills knowingly, "and in that time I have watched you and your family grow. Watched you marry Amber and sadly mourned her death, same as you," he adds finding it uncomfortable, "damn it, Ethan, I was at the hospital the night Chloe was born," he says emotionally. "Hell! We all went out and got drunk celebrating her birth and then every year after that we all went out and got drunk again as if it were part of a tradition."

Hank raises his hand timidly and clears his throat. "As

Ethan's partner, Captain, I also got drunk with you guys," interrupts Hank feeling left out of place.

"Damn it, Hank, don't interrupt me," barks Hills, "it's hard enough trying to express my feelings without having your sorry ass interrupting me every minute!"

"Sorry, Captain," mutters Hank sinking lower into his chair.

"Where was I?" asks a now distracted Hills.

"Getting drunk was a tradition, sir." replies Hank softly.

"So as I was saying," remarks Hills, "we have been through thick and thin in all those years, getting drunk yearly on Chloe's birthday and mourning the sad loss of your wife. I was honoured when you asked me to be Chloe's godfather and as such, we are a family and by God we are here to support one another, not only for the good times but also when push comes to shove!"

"I appreciate your candour, Captain." replies Ethan softly.

"When I learned last night about Chloe's disappearance it hit me hard, as I felt like I raised that girl as my own daughter and, damn it, I know exactly how you feel, Ethan. I want you to know that you have this department at your disposal in order to find her and bring her home."

"Thank you, Captain." replies a relieved Ethan.

"Officially," remarks Hills feeling uncomfortable, "it's out of our jurisdiction and therefore everything we do has to be kept under the radar."

"I am aware of that, sir."

"So tell me, what's the latest you have?"

"Captain, it's like opening a can of worms," explains an enthusiastic Ethan as he gets comfortable in his chair, "the crimes just continue and nothing appears to get done."

"You are one of my best, Ethan," says Hills and he glances at Hank, "you too, Hank."

"Thank you, sir," says a much happier Hank after that compliment.

"And I can only imagine what you must be going through," continues Hills, "but you need to stay focussed if you have a chance of finding the truth about what really happened on that ship." He then takes a moment to think. "What about that doctor you told me about last night, was it Morales?"

"Yes, Hugo Morales, Captain," replies Ethan emotionally, "I ran his name on our system."

"And Interpol's," interrupts Hank trying to chip in.

"Yes," continues Ethan with a grateful wink at Hank, "through Interpol also, and no match was found, nothing, it's as if the guy doesn't exist."

"Maybe Hugo Morales is not his real name," remarks Hills.

"Yes," replies an excited Ethan. Taking out his cell phone, he opens one of the pictures of Morales from Alexis's photos. "So I ran his face and again, nothing," he adds as Hills looks at the photo staring at Morales's cold face.

"He appears to be a ghost, sir," remarks Hank.

"If I have learned something in my time in the force," says Hills continuing to stare at Morales on the small screen, "is that no one is too clean. I don't like it. This man has so many red flags, we can use him as target practice five miles out!"

"What we do know he's from the Dominican Republic," adds Hank.

"What about the cruise company?" asks Hill returning the cell phone to Ethan.

"I have been calling all morning and I get the same narrative."

"Maybe you should see them in person," suggests Hills.

"I tried getting an appointment to meet their CEO based in Miami but all I get is a blanket of PA's blocking my every move."

Hills leans forward on his desk and stares straight into Ethan's eyes. "I cannot tell you what to do or how to do it," he says softly, "but when I was a rookie, I had a sergeant who taught me there were two ways to do things, the right way and the wrong way."

"I don't think I understand what it is you are trying to say," says a confused Ethan.

"Me neither, Captain," replies a bewildered Hank.

"If the right way doesn't work out, then in order to get results, you need to get them the wrong way. Follow my drift?" asks Hills watching how Ethan now understands and smiles impishly.

"I think I do," replies Ethan with a smirk on his face.

"Remember I can only cover your ass so far," explains Hills bluntly, "so don't screw it up."

**

Sitting alone in his SUV wearing a baseball cap and listening to the news on the car radio, Ethan stakes out a mansion at *"Miami Beach - Indian Creek Island,"* which is an elite neighbourhood for the super-rich and famous. As he patiently waits, tapping his finger on the steering wheel, lost in thought on this warm summer night, he notices how some neighbours walk their dogs under the light of the bright street lamps. He looks around at the impressive luxury mansions rising majestically along the entire street, each with large gates and CCTV cameras; some even with private security. He glances at his wrist watch and notices its *"22:45"*, then reaches over to the passenger seat where he has a prepared thermos full of coffee, a box of half-eaten sandwiches and night vision binoculars, as he is used to spending many nights on stakeouts as part of the job. He pours coffee into a mug and takes a drink, eats a sandwich as he continues to wait.

A security patrol car drives towards Ethan's SUV, stopping beside it. The driver, a uniformed security guard, shines a torch into the SUV at Ethan's face to see who is inside the suspicious vehicle.

"Do you need some help?" asks the security guard as Ethan tries to block the bright light from his eyes.

"Ethan Moore, Miami PD on a stakeout," replies Ethan showing him his Detective's badge, "now get that damn light off my face before you blow my cover."

Immediately the security guard turns off the light. "We got a report of a suspicious car being parked here for the past three hours. Hope it goes well, good night," replies the security guard and drives away.

"Damn rent-a-cops, nearly giving my position away like that," Ethan angrily mutters under his breath as he drinks more coffee. Suddenly, the bright headlights of a sporty Mercedes car shines closer, stopping by the closed gates of the mansion Ethan is staking out. "Here we go," he remarks as he swiftly picks up the night vision binoculars and looks carefully at the driver of the luxury car, noticing it's an elderly man alone, and smartly dressed in a suit. "Bingo," he adds softly and turns on the SUV ignition but leaves the headlights switched off as he continues to wait.

Ethan watches as the gates slowly open and the Mercedes drives through. He throws the binoculars into the passenger seat, shifts into drive and speeds in through the gates, following the Mercedes up a long driveway that leads to a magnificent mansion. The Mercedes eventually stops by a locked garage and the man promptly gets out of the car, shocked when an SUV with no lights speeds up and stops beside him.

"This is private property!" yells the man concerned for his welfare dialling *"911"* on his cell phone.

Ethan steps out of the SUV and walks intimidatingly to the man, taking the cell phone away from him, clicking to end the 911 call.

"Who are you, what do you want from me?" asks a now frightened and helpless man leaning against his car.

"John McArnold?" asks Ethan to confirm it's the correct man.

"Yes, I am he."

"You are a hard man to reach over the phone, so I thought it best to give you a visit," says Ethan walking closer to the man and pinning him against the car door.

"Please, don't hurt me," begs the man taking his wallet out, "here, there is over five hundred dollars in cash and my credit cards."

Ethan takes the wallet and throws it back at him. "I am not here for your money."

"Then what do you want?" John asks confused.

"Information about my daughter, Chloe Moore, who went missing on one of your cruise ships this week."

"I see," replies John softly, vaguely recalling reading a report about this incident, "what type of information?"

"How about we start with what really happened to her, damn you?"

"I don't know," replies a frightened man. "I was told she jumped!"

"You are the CEO of the company so you *should* know everything about what happens," shouts Ethan trying to remain calm. "I will ask you again, what happened to my daughter because, with God is my witness, she didn't commit suicide! Someone somewhere *must* know the truth!"

"Mister Moore, I am very sorry for the grief your daughter's disappearance is causing you, but you must understand, I am not that someone, as I know exactly as much as you do. This is an open case and my staff are conducting meticulous investigations to try and determine the cause of the disappearance. But all the evidence leads to the fact that she did jump. I am truly sorry but there is nothing else we can do but wait for the investigation to conclude."

"How can you investigate a crime scene that has been contaminated?" asks Ethan. Realizing everything is now lost he steps back, allowing the man to stand up straight. "I want copies of all the CCTV tapes from that ship," he demands.

Suddenly the front door of the mansion opens and two of the house staff servants, wearing suits, walk towards Ethan and John.

"Is everything all right, Mister McArnold?" asks a servant.

"Yes," replies John who swiftly walks to meet the two servants and stands behind them. "Mister Moore was just about to leave."

"I demand copies of the tapes," says Ethan firmly.

The man smirks and walks towards the open door escorted by his servants. As he reaches the door he turns giving Ethan one last stare. "I don't take likely to demands."

"God damn it!" yells Ethan as McArnold and the servants enter the mansion, closing the door behind them, leaving him standing all alone.

***

The doorbell is ringing, waking up a clothed Ethan who fell asleep last night on the living room sofa. He moans as he wakes up, glancing around to see what time it is, as the daylight shines into the house.

"Coming!" he yells as he stands up to make his way towards the door, knocking over a half empty bottle of whiskey resting on the floor by the sofa. "Damn it!" he yells, picking up the bottle and setting it upright on the dining table. He reaches the door and opens it, only to find a delivery company van parked in his driveway and a messenger standing at the door holding a clipboard. Chloe's two suitcases rest beside him.

"Mister Ethan Moore?" asks the friendly messenger.

"Yes," replies Ethan trying to block the sunlight from his sensitive eyes, feeling like he has been run over by a freight train. "What time is it?"

"It's just after nine."

"I overslept," replies Ethan rubbing his eyes.

"I have a delivery for you and will need you to sign please," says the messenger handing over the clipboard and a pen to Ethan. He swiftly signs and hands the clipboard back to the messenger. "Thank you, sir and have a good day," he replies and walks to his van leaving the suitcases at the door.

Ethan looks down at the bags, knowing they are Chloe's personal belongings and he takes a moment to gather his strength. Suddenly his cell phone rings from inside the house and he quickly rolls the two suitcases into the house, slamming the door shut, then he runs to the sofa where he picks up the cell phone and answers it. "Yea!" he says, yawning.

"We need to talk," replies Hills with an angry tone. "Meet me in thirty at O'Malley's for coffee," he adds then disconnects the line.

"On my way," mutters Ethan and throws the cell phone back on the sofa. He walks to the two suitcases and opens them both, revealing Chloe's clothes inside. He picks up a blouse and smells it, breathing in Chloe's all too familiar scent. He drops to his knees breaking down into tears, as the pain is just too much for him.

***

"Got a call from the chief this morning," says an angry Hills sipping a coffee inside O'Malley's Irish bar, where many patrons are enjoying their drinks and meals. This is a popular venue that Ethan and Hills have always used as their local establishment during their many years of working together, ever since they graduated from the Police Academy. It's a neutral ground, away from the hustle and bustle of the department's red tape and protocols.

"Did he call to wish you a good day?" asks an exhausted Ethan who is sitting opposite him in a corner booth drinking coffee and eating pancakes.

"Would you like more cream for them pancakes, Ethan?" asks a friendly Muriel in her fifties who pours black coffee into both Ethan and Hills's cups with her usual happy smile. She has been waitressing at the bar since she was eighteen and knows all the patrons like family.

"No thanks, Muriel, these are fine as they are." he replies and gives her a smile, watching how she strides to the next table to top up the coffees of her patrons.

Ethan looks back at Hills while he devours the pancakes.

"You should have been a comedian," replies Hills seriously pissed off, "you know damn well when the chief calls it's to chew my ass and I tell you, my ass has been chewed off big time because of your stupid stunt last night! Hell, not even probable cause to get a warrant!" barks Hills trying to control his temper and getting all worked up. "Jesus, Ethan, what in the hell were you thinking, going to the man's house and harassing him like that?"

"I didn't harass him, we just had a chat," he replies sipping more coffee. "So I tried the wrong way and it backfired, so what?"

"So what?" replies Hills sarcastically, leaning forward on the table nearly knocking over his coffee. "John McArnold's lawyer has filed a lawsuit, the biggest the city has ever seen, against the department for harassment. It names you in particular for breaking into his property and threatening him!"

"Just goes to show." Ethan responds coldly.

"Show what?"

"The power they have to bury their sins."

"Damn it Ethan, we are not in some half ass crusade here!"

"Damn right we're not!" yells Ethan angrily. "We are trying to find the truth about what happened to Chloe," he shouts, but tries to stay calm, noticing how some of the patrons curiously overhear.

Ethan takes a deep breath and takes a sip of coffee, then looks straight into Hills eyes. "Remember her, your god daughter?" he adds firmly. "And if that means staking out the CEO of the company and trying to talk to him to get answers, then that's what I did and so help me, I will do it all over again if I have to," he says pushing his half-eaten pancake plate aside in frustration. "He probably has a whole army of security with him by now. I had him and I let him go!" he adds, kicking the table in anger to release some steam. "He was never going to give me the CCTV tapes. What was I thinking?" he adds leaning back feeling a deep loss and regret for allowing McArnold to slip through his fingers.

Hills also leans back and watches how distraught his friend is as he tries to protect him. "Ethan, your judgement is impaired and it's causing you not to think straight."

"Chloe's belongings arrived at the house today," he says holding back his tears. "I could smell her scent on her clothes," he adds, breaking down into tears, making Hills hold back his own tears emotionally, as he watches his best friend fall apart in front of him. "She was the only family I had in the world and those bastards have taken that away from me and by God, they are going to pay!"

"Ethan, take a week, hell, take two weeks paid leave, I'll cover your ass and handle the chief, you won't have to worry about any flack," he says leaning forward holding Ethan's hand on the table.

"And as for family, man, you got us. Always remember that."

"Thank you."

"Do what you need to do, in order to try and find peace with this whole damn thing. Go home and rest, get yourself cleaned up, cos God knows, you can't find the truth, feeling sorry for yourself," he adds and they exchange an emotional look at each other, proving the long-established bond they share between them.

***

Ethan is heartbroken as he watches a home video on his TV of when Chloe had her twelfth birthday party at the pool out back. His late wife Amber, in her thirties and full of life, carries a large birthday cake with the name "*Chloe*" on it and twelve lit candle sticks. She walks across the living room towards the connecting garden door. The footage shakes as a young Ethan holds the camera while following Amber outside. "*Be careful honey, don't fall now,*" says a cheerful young Ethan walking closely behind her.

He captures how she turns around with a bright smile on her face. "*If I do, I know you will always be there to pick me up, my pumpkin,*" she replies tenderly.

Ethan continues to watch the home video breaking out into more tears as he vividly remembers that special day like it was yesterday, his eyes fixed like glue to the TV screen, wishing he had a time machine to travel back to those special years.

The camera now follows Amber moving toward a young and extremely pretty 12-year-old Chloe sitting patiently beside the pool with a young Alexis, and a handful of other children.

The camera then turns around capturing a younger Captain Hills, Detective Hank Shaw and four other detectives who now sing the "*Happy birthday*" song as Amber presents the cake to Chloe. "*There she is,*" says a young Ethan from behind the camera zooming into Chloe's innocent and happy face. "*My little Princess.*" He says watching how the young Chloe is clearly ecstatic as she blows out all the candles with her mother's help.

"*I love you, mommy and daddy,*" she says with a gentle and innocent voice.

"*And we love you too, honey,*" replies Amber while the camera shakes violently as Ethan is passing it over to someone beside him.

Now the camera points back at Chloe, where a young Ethan appears on screen giving her a tight hug, expressing his love for his daughter. *"I will always be here for you, baby. God, I love you,"* he says to Chloe, smothering her with kisses.

"And I love you always, daddy," replies a happy Chloe with a sweet expression on her face.

Ethan presses the *"pause"* button on the TV remote and the image freezes on Chloe's innocent face. He again bursts into more tears, as the torture of those memories are just too much to bear.

"God, I miss you!" he screams hugging himself and wailing on the sofa, clearly emotionally destroyed and in pain for not knowing where his daughter is, or if she is alive or dead. He takes a moment and thinks briefly looking at his cell phone. Unlocking the phone he clicks on the gallery, swiping through picture after picture until he finds the one where *"the girls are in the pool"*.

He zooms in on Morales lurking in the background. Ethan's expression clearly reflects anger and hatred as he studies Morale's cold face.

***

Ethan and Hank are firing their service firearms in the police firing range, wearing protective glasses and ear mufflers. Ethan is transfixed as he shoots repeatedly, re-loads and continues to fire at many pop-up target boards; some depicting the enemy and others innocent bystanders. His thoughts rage wildly as he hits all the targets with deadly accuracy until he runs out of bullets and stops.

Ethan glances at Hank who stopped firing moments earlier and is watching him with a concerned expression. "You got two friendly targets," says Hank putting his firearm back into his holster, "it's not like you, Ethan."

"They were collaborators," replies Ethan as he puts his firearm back into his holster and walks with Hank to inspect the target boards.

"How are you holding up?"

"I don't have any substantial evidence… nothing to connect the dots!"

"But you suspect this Morales guy, right?" Hank asks.

"All I have are two pictures of him in the background aboard a busy ship full of people."

"So it's coincidence that he's in two of a few hundred pictures?"

"Could be, I don't know, I'm not thinking straight, Hank," replies Ethan as he inspects one of the friendly bystander target boards he hit. "I just have a gut feeling he knows more than he's saying."

"Your gut feeling has never proved you wrong," replies Hank as he also inspects the friendly target board Ethan shot. "Definitely a collaborator," he remarks and they continue walking over to the next shot up target boards. "I know that feeling all too well," he adds and stops Ethan, looking into his painful eyes, "you once told me when I first joined, to follow my instincts and I am now reminding you of that."

"It's like hitting my face against a brick wall, Hank!" replies a frustrated Ethan. "All the leads I thought I had have dried up. Every door I try to open gets shut in my face. Everyone I talk with in that company are speaking from the same Hymn sheet!"

"It's a bummer, I know, but the hardest cases ever broken were always due to the smallest detail that someone first overlooked. You just have to find that detail."

"I was thinking, maybe going to the press," Ethan says.

"If it's true what you say about them, they probably own the press and the story will never see the light of day."

"Damn it, Hank, people are going missing aboard those ships and no one does a damn thing about it! The internet is full of sad stories like Chloe's. There is even a site called the International Cruise Victims Association whose president Kendall Carver lost his daughter on an Alaskan cruise and she was never seen or heard from again."

"What about the Bermuda Police?"

"I've been calling them for the past week and all I get is the standard bullshit of an ongoing investigation."

"Yep!" mutters Hank sympathetically. "I know that statement."

"The scene was contaminated by allowing thousands of passengers to sail on that ship that same afternoon. The investigation is a joke. I can't get any direct collaboration from the cruise company *or* from the investigating Police Department in Bermuda. Everyone is going on with their lives, as if nothing has happened and yet my daughter is nowhere to be found and I can't do a *damn* thing to uncover the truth!" he says, hanging his head in shame. "What kind of a cop am I, if I can't even find my own daughter?"

"The kind of cop who follows the rules," Hank blurts.

"Well maybe it's time I didn't, as clearly, doing everything by the book is obviously leading nowhere," Ethan lets out an emotional yell to calm down. Then gives Hank a petrifying stare. "I will beg, steal and kill for my daughter. She's all I have left."

Hank puts his hands on Ethan's shoulders and sighs. "You have told me how you feel and as your partner I am now going to advise you on what I would do if this happened to me. But know this, once you start, there will be no turning back," he says with a powerful tone. "Are you sure you are up for this?"

"Anything."

"Then we have no time to waste," he replies holding Ethan's shoulder and steering him towards to the exit. "I'll fill you in as you drive."

***

"These babies are top of the range," says a man in his sixties who is the owner of a local electronics store. He places a number of micro surveillance devices on the counter to show Ethan and Hank his latest acquisitions, while the store has and promotes all types of surveillance equipment on display.

"How about one of those lapel pin cameras?" asks Ethan as he takes one of the micro devices in his hand and admires it.

"It has to look inconspicuous," remarks Hank as he also admires the equipment.

"Oh, I got a beauty," replies a proud owner as he retrieves a micro lapel camera cleverly concealed as a US flag and extends it to them with a smirk on his face. "This baby operates within a ten-mile radius with crystal clear sound and full 8K image."

"Jesus," mutters Hank, seriously impressed.

"Show me how it works," Ethan urges.

***

Ethan walks into Hills's office and stands by the door. "Captain," he says standing straight, "you have a minute?"

"You know I always do, Ethan."

"I've been giving some thought about what you said and if the offer is still on the table, I will take those two weeks."

"I am glad you are finally coming to your senses," replies a much happier Hills. "If you need more time off just let me know. I want you back with batteries fully recharged, you hear?"

Ethan walks over and shakes Hills's hand in gratitude. "Thank you, Captain," he says sternly and walks away to exit the office.

"Hold it right there," barks Hills knowing Ethan too well, and knowing the handshake was a dead giveaway.

Ethan pauses and turns around, trying to give him an honest smile.

"What are you really up to?"

"It's best you don't know so if it goes south, you and the department will be protected and your ass won't get chewed up some more."

"I knew you were up to something," he shouts slamming his closed fists on his desk. "Damn it, how worried must I be?"

"From a scale of one to ten, I would say, a twenty."

"Can I at least get a hint, for old time's sake?"

"Let's just say, I am going fishing," replies Ethan with a wink, as he walks out of the office.

9
Fishing

Ethan and Hank are casually strolling along the pier at the Miami port close to the docked *"Poseidon of the Seas"* cruise ship, observing how a small army of workers load and unload many containers to and from the ship. At the same time hundreds of passengers are happily disembarking with their luggage after returning from their cruise.

"She is a big momma; I'll give them that," remarks Hank impressed at the gigantic size of the ship.

"That she is, Hank," says Ethan spotting Chief Security Officer Martin at the arrival's gangway, with a few of his security officers checking the boarding passes of the new arriving passengers who are now boarding the ship for the afternoon cruise.

"You can still back down if you want and no one will ever judge you for not doing this," affirms Hank.

"I will live with it for the rest of my life, if I don't do this, Hank," replies a confident Ethan.

"Then let's get your case from my car and get the show on the road," replies a supportive Hank with a smile, and they walk towards the busy parking lot.

***

Standing at one of the many check-in counters with an SLR camera strapped around his neck, Ethan tightens the *"all-inclusive bracelet"* onto his wrist. A young male check-in assistant smiles, handing him his printed boarding pass with his picture on it.

"You are in stateroom 7315, on deck eight," the assistant says with a friendly smile. "Your luggage will be delivered shortly to your room. When you're ready, please make your way to my colleague standing at gate six and he will direct you to the gangway. Enjoy your cruise and thank you for choosing to sail with us today."

"Thank you," replies Ethan with a confident smile, walking slowly away. He can't stop feeling how familiar this all seems, like Deja-vu. It wasn't that long ago that he was in the same building surrounded by the hundreds of similar passengers all eager to start their cruise.

***

Patiently waiting in line, a passenger, Ethan stands at the gangway lowering his head slightly, trying to avoid eye contact with Martin, who is supervising the arriving passengers with three other security officers manning an X-Ray machine and body scanner.

"Next," says one of the security officers at Ethan, motioning at him to walk through the body scanner. Ethan puts the camera onto the X-Ray machine's conveyor belt, then walks through the body scanner, avoiding eye contact with everyone. The X-Ray monitor is clear and so is the body scanner monitor, ensuring no one takes any illegal items on board.

"Your boarding pass please, sir," asks another security officer who takes the boarding pass from Ethan's hand and scans it on his computer, revealing Ethan's correct details on the screen with a green tick, thereby confirming he is a passenger on this cruise. "Thank you, Mister Moore and welcome aboard the Poseidon of the Seas," he adds with a friendly smile, returning the pass back to Ethan.

"Thank you," replies Ethan putting the boarding pass in his pocket and grabbing his camera from the conveyor belt. He walks past Martin, who is in deep conversation with one of his security officers on one side of the gangway not noticing many of the new arrivals entering the ship, including Ethan.

***

Ethan walks the narrow labyrinth of corridors passing many staterooms and excited passengers. He soon arrives at stateroom 7315 where he swipes the boarding pass over the keypad and the door automatically unlocks. He pushes it and walks inside the standard stateroom where he finds his suitcase has already been delivered. A beautiful decorative flower made from a white towel is on the bed, complimentary chocolates are by the pillow. "Huh," he mutters walking into the connecting bathroom finding everything is satisfactory. "Cool," he says to himself.

He locks the front door securely, picks up his suitcase and places it on the bed. "All right, let's begin," he adds and opens the suitcase revealing the clothes neatly packed within, gently introducing his hands inside where he pulls out a small laptop computer and a black bag which have been carefully packed at the bottom of his clothes. "There you are," he remarks softly moving over to the small desk where he sits down. Impulsively, he clears away the brochures from the desk, placing the laptop and the black bag on the desk.

Ethan takes a deep breath and proceeds to open the bag. Carefully he takes out the miscellaneous micro surveillance devices and the *"US Flag"* lapel pin, setting everything down in perfect order on one side of the desk. "Let's see you work," he mutters grabbing his cell phone and clicking on one of his many APPs, which is a picture of the *"US flag"*. This automatically activates the lapel's camera and he can see real live, crystal clear feed on his phone screen with full working moving audio bars.

"I love technology," he says with a proud smirk on his face.

***

Walking along the crowded and busy promenade deck, wearing the lapel pin on his polo shirt, a white baseball cap, navy blue shorts, sneakers and his professional SLR camera hanging by a strap around his neck, Ethan blends in as another of the thousands of tourists aboard this floating city. He walks along the many stores which he vividly remembers from the hundreds of pictures Alexis sent him which he has memorized. He cannot help noticing how many mothers allow their young children and toddlers to run freely amongst the crowds. He knows full well how easy it is for anyone to snatch them, recalling the hundreds of missing people to date.

He continues walking but soon his heart sinks as he realizes Chloe was walking in this very same promenade with Alexis and he imagines her standing on the same spot where he is now, as it's by the store where the girls bought their lovely pink dresses. "Oh God," he says softly to himself, "she was right here." He studies the dress on display, oblivious to the busy crowds all around him shuffling past in all directions. His heart is racing in overdrive and he extends his cell phone, viewing a picture on his screen of *Chloe and Alexis smiling by the window display pointing at the dress with bright smiles.*

Everything around him now moves in slow motion, he day dreams, smiling at *Chloe and Alexis laughing and giggling as they walk by the same spot where Ethan is now standing. Chloe smiles at her father as they continue to walk past him, hearing her young 12-year-old sweet voice telling him "I love you, daddy."*

"Excuse me, sir," asks a concerned young ship's steward who is standing beside Ethan noticing his lost expression. "Is everything all right? Do you need help?"

Ethan wakes up from his day dream and everything now returns back to real time. Taking a moment to catch his breath, glancing around hoping it wasn't a dream and that Chloe and Alexis did walk past just now, only to discover it was only his imagination.

"Are you feeling all right, sir?"

"Yes," replies Ethan clearing his throat and composing himself braving a smile. "I was just miles away in my thoughts. Thank you."

"In that case, enjoy your cruise, sir," replies the steward and he walks away leaving Ethan perplexed gathering his thoughts.

***

Hundreds of passengers are blissfully waving from one of the decks as the ship slowly sails away from its berth. Ethan watches by the railing, as Hank and over a dozen other people stand at the pier waving back at the distancing ship. The ship's air-horn blasts repeatedly. Ethan looks around holding back his tears.

***

At the Top Deck, Ethan walks around the spacious and busy pool area glancing at the picture of *"Chloe and Alexis taking a selfie with Morales lurking in the background"*, trying to pinpoint the exact location where that picture was taken. He cannot help noticing the hundreds of young woman in bikinis oblivious to any sort of danger as they sunbathe on their lounge beds, many of them completely alone.

"Christ," he mutters to himself softly, "it's a bloody free for all for predators!" he adds, suddenly noticing a familiar white post beside a door on a corner. Searching his photos he compares the white post to the post in one of the pictures and identifies that this is the white post where Morales was standing checking out Chloe and Alexis, meaning they must have been sunbathing just about where Ethan is now standing. He closes his eyes and can just imagine in his mind, *"Chloe and Alexis giggling and laughing as they take the picture while Morales lurks behind them, watching their every move."* A loud woman's scream wakes Ethan up from his thoughts and he turns around only to see how a woman is being carried into the pool by her boyfriend, screaming once more as the boyfriend throws her into the pool, splashing water in all directions. He sighs in relief and walks over to the white post, where he positions himself as Morales was when the picture was taken. He also notices this to be a good vantage point, having a clear and undisturbed view of the girls.

***

"Excuse me," says a now disoriented Ethan walking into the ship's infirmary towards a young nurse working at the reception, "I don't have my sea legs, I'm afraid and am feeling a bit nauseous."

"That's perfectly normal, sir," she says walking out to comfort him, ensuring he doesn't fall over. She helps him sit in one of the many visitor's chairs. "Stay here while I go and get you some pills that will make you feel better in no time," she adds walking back to the reception. Opening a drawer she takes out a small bottle of pills. "Take one of these and you will be as good as new in no time," she affirms with a warm smile, walking back to him.

"Thank you," he replies feeling drowsy, standing up when suddenly he loses his balance and drops hard to the floor. "Maybe it's something I ate, either way, I feel terrible," he mumbles and begins to breathe heavily.

"Stay with me now," says a calm nurse helping him up. She walks him into the connecting examination room, where she carefully helps him lie down on the table. "I will page the doctor. I want you to rest in the meantime and don't exert yourself," she says rolling an oxygen bottle on wheels to the examination table. She fits an oxygen mask over his nose and mouth, to help control his breathing.

"That's better," he says as his breathing returns to a more natural level which makes the nurse relax.

"There, see," she says comforting him as she walks to the door. "I will be right back." She exits the examination room and moves to her desk to page the doctor.

Ethan glances around to ensure he is now alone inside the room and he immediately removes the oxygen mask and stands up, walks to the partially opened door and looks out, observing how the nurse is trying to get a hold of the doctor by phone. "Like a charm," he says to himself softly as he closes the door and scans the room carefully until he soon identifies a good spot to place one of his micro cameras.

***

Morales is walking along the Top Deck casually glancing at a number of attractive women when his pager beeps and he looks at the number, realising its the infirmary. "Damn it, what now," he remarks to himself. He walks towards a locked ship's phone which he unlocks and opens, placing the receiver to his ear. He then dials a Centrex number and waits impatiently for the nurse to pick up.

"*Infirmary*," answers the young nurse with a soft tone.

"You paged me," replies an arrogant Morales.

"Yes, doctor, a patient arrived suffering from dizziness but it appears he may have something more serious, as he partially fainted and his breathing became erratic. He is waiting in the examination room."

"He might just be seasick," he says, clearly distracted by several teenage girls walking past him in bikinis towards the busy bar, "but keep him comfortable until I arrive." He hangs up the receiver into the phone box, smirking at the young girls.

***

Ethan has just finished hiding one of the micro surveillance devices on the top corner of the room in a perfect spot. He takes out his cell phone and looks at the receiving signal on his screen, which works perfectly. It shows the entire room with its wide-angle lens. He snaps his fingers and notices the audio bars moving, as the sound quality is also captured. "Okay," he mutters and casually opens the door.

Ethan walks out of the examination room waving at the nurse with a smile. "The oxygen did the trick," he adds walking faster towards the long corridor to exit.

"But the doctor is on his way," says the nurse with a loud voice, trying to stop Ethan from leaving.

"Sorry to have troubled you, have a good day."

"How strange was that?" she asks herself completely bewildered as he left the infirmary, leaving her all alone.

***

Walking down a long corridor decorated by colourful artwork and paintings, Ethan spots Morales coming toward him in the opposite direction. He gradually lowers the cap over his eyes and lowers his head, as he continues to walk forward without attracting attention to himself. Soon both men pass each other and continue walking. Ethan glances back observing how Morales keeps moving towards the infirmary.

***

On the Top Deck later that afternoon, Ethan stands by a railing overlooking the endless blue ocean stretching to the horizon. He feels the refreshing sea breeze blowing against his body, and the intense sun beaming down on this warm afternoon. His thoughts are running wild again, wondering if Chloe was also standing where he is right now, looking out to sea with her happy smile and undeniable laughter, which made her unique. He glances at the bar and decides it's time for a cold soothing drink to quench his dry thirst and starts walking towards the busy bar.

"*Dad!*" shouts Chloe's voice making him stop in his tracks and glance to where he believes the voice originated from. "Chloe?" he says hopeful she is still alive. But as he carefully scans the area in the direction he heard her voice, he soon notices Morales standing by a white post observing a young, 20-year-old woman, wearing a sexy red bikini, sunbathing alone on a lounge bed near the pool.

He now understands the voice was to warn him of a possible danger. "What are you up to?" he asks himself softly as he works his way around the spacious pool, using his police training to blend in around the hundreds of passengers, so as not to get noticed. Soon he manages to find the perfect spot to be inconspicuous as he positions himself on the other side of the deck, opposite Morales. He aims his camera at him, using the telephoto lens he zooms in closer so he can clearly see Morales observing the young woman. She is unaware that she is being observed. Ethan begins to take pictures:

- Camera Viewfinder: *Morales observing the young woman*. Click.

- Camera Viewfinder: *Morales touching the scar on his eyebrow*. Click.

"My instincts were right," Ethan says to himself as he discreetly continues to take pictures, "bastard!" he mutters, noticing another crew member, who happens to be Pavlov, standing beside Morales. He's holding a large Tupperware container with a blue lid. Ethan continues to take more pictures:

- Camera Viewfinder: *Morales talking with Pavlov*. Click.

"It's confirmed. Two," says Pavlov passing the Tupperware container over to Morales who casually takes it.

- Camera Viewfinder: *Morales receiving the container*. Click.

- Camera Viewfinder: *Pavlov walking away*. Click.

- Camera Viewfinder: *Morales observing the young woman*. Click.

- Camera Viewfinder: *The young woman smiling*. Click.

Ethan lowers the camera and stares at Morales confused. "What the hell are you up to?" he asks himself softly and then notices how the young woman stands up and walks towards the bar while Morales walks away, disappearing into the crowd.

"Damn it," he mutters but decides to follow his instincts and find out who this woman is, after all, she has the doctor's undivided attention so maybe he can use her to get to him.

He clears his throat and walks towards the bar, where he soon arrives, standing beside the young woman who is patiently waiting for the bartender to take her order.

"One piña colada, please," she says calmly with an angelic voice.

"Of course, madam," replies the friendly bartender.

"Make that two," says a cheerful Ethan getting her attention.

"Two piña coladas coming right up."

"Oh," she adds before the bartender begins preparing the cocktails, "can I have extra coconut milk on mine please?"

"Extra coconut milk coming right up," replies the bartender and he gets busy behind the bar preparing the two cocktails.

"So you are having piña colada, too," she says with a smile.

"It's my favourite cocktail," replies a warm Ethan.

"Get out of here!" she replies optimistically slapping Ethan's shoulder softly to express her delight. "It's mine, also."

"Well, that is a coincidence that deserves a toast," he replies with a bright grin, "once the cocktails arrive," which makes her giggle. "The name's Ethan," he adds, extending his hand politely.

"Joanne," she replies shaking his hand, as she finds him interesting.

Moments later the bartender arrives with two enticing cocktails and places the glasses in front of them at the bar. "Would you like anything else?" he asks courteously.

"No thank you," she replies picking up her drink and raising it to Ethan.

"How about you, sir?" asks the bartender noticing Ethan has the "all-inclusive bracelet," so no extra charge but he still needs to charge Joanne for her drink.

"That will be fine for now, thank you," replies Ethan as he also picks up his drink and clinks Joanne's glass. "To coincidence." He toasts and they sip their cocktails.

"What is your room number please?" asks the bartender at Joanne.

"6325," she replies with a smile.

"Thank you, I will charge the drink to your room," says the bartender and he walks to the nearby electronic register where Ethan discreetly observes how the bartender taps on a "*piña colada*" image and inputs in the numbers "*6325.*"

"I should have purchased one of those all inclusive drinks," she remarks, "maybe then I wouldn't get asked what room I am staying in by every bartender on this ship," she adds jokingly.

"Yes," he replies with a giggle, "these do help to stay discreet." He gets closer to her to get more comfortable. "So, are you travelling by yourself?"

"I am," she says, sipping her drink, "and you?"

"Actually," replies a now nervous Ethan as he has all the information he needed and doesn't want to drag the conversation much longer, "the wife and kids are by the pool over there," he adds pointing to the crowded pool and waving at strangers. Joanne suddenly loses her smile and steps back from him.

"I don't like getting involved with a married man, Ethan," she says candidly, "I hope you can understand," she adds and walks away with her drink, leaving him alone at the bar.

"Totally," he replies to himself and downs the cocktail in one shot, quenching his thirst.

***

Ethan walks cautiously along the labyrinth of corridors passing many closed stateroom doors until he eventually finds stateroom "*6325*" situated at the end of the corridor. He smiles as he passes a steward standing beside a cleaning trolley who is using a passkey to unlock a closed stateroom door, returning the passkey to the trolley's clip.

"Afternoon," says Ethan as he walks past.

"Good afternoon, sir," replies the steward grabbing clean towels from the trolley and walks into the room. Ethan takes the opportunity ensuring there is no one else in the area watching and impulsively, he grabs the passkey from the trolley's clip and quickly walks towards stateroom 6325. Without wasting any time, he swipes the passkey over the keypad. The door clicks open and he swiftly slips into the room, closing the door behind him.

Ethan knows Joanne can return at any moment so he doesn't have too much time. He drops the passkey into his pocket while scanning the room that is designed just like the rest of the staterooms. "All right," he mutters to himself as he soon identifies a good spot near the air conditioning vent. "That will do," he adds, taking out another micro surveillance device from his pocket, switching it on. He carefully conceals it by the vent, calculating where it should be pointing. Once he is happy he returns to the centre of the room, takes out his cell phone, clicks on the *"US flag"* APP and watches the screen. The live signal feed clearly covers the whole room, including the front door and the bed in detail, with its wide angle lens.

***

Back in the comfort of his own stateroom, Ethan carefully introduces the SD card he has removed from the SLR camera by inserting it into one of the laptop's card readers. He waits, staring at the desktop screen until a popup box appears asking to open the SD card. "Oh, yes," he utters to himself and clicks on the *"yes"* tab. All the pictures he has taken at the Top Deck appear as thumbnails on a new screen. "There you are," he adds clicking on the pictures one at a time to open them independently.

Ethan sees Morales observing Joanne in numerous pictures and then he studies the one of *Pavlov handing a container over to Morales*. Finding this rather unusual, he zooms into the empty Tupperware container, trying to make sense to why he would want that for. "What the hell are you up to?" he asks himself softly, then redirects his attention to Pavlov, zooming into his name tag that reads *Viktor Pavlov - Steward*. "Okay Mister Pavlov," he says reaching for his small notebook resting by the bed. He opens it to a page that says *"Morales?"* and he writes *"Viktor Pavlov?"* under it, continuing his private and unsanctioned investigation.

"Let's see what you are up to," he says as he clicks on a *"US Flag"* shortcut, double checking the cables of two external hard drives that are securely connected to the laptop. Soon the entire screen changes into a security surveillance multi-screen of two live feeds: The feed on the left from the infirmary's examination room camera, showing the room is empty and the feed on the right of Joanne's stateroom camera, showing the room is empty. Each screen has a running time-code with date and time, at the top of both feeds together with a continuous flashing red *"recording* "icon, as the cameras are constantly recording and downloading the footage into the laptop's external hard drives.

10
Below Deck

Away from the luxurious settings of the ship's fine dining and comfortable amenities for its passengers and beneath their lavish lifestyle there lies another city which has its own rules and hierarchical structure. Over one thousand crew members living below decks have to endure a more indispensable lifestyle, traditionally based on their nationality which designates in most cases the type of living arrangements they will have to endure throughout their standard nine months contractual employment aboard.

As in any hierarchy, the lowest position, in this case "the lowest jobs" which are normally "cleaners" are always placed at the very lowest deck of the ship, in shared cabins with communal bathrooms and showers which need to be shared by everyone living in that particular corridor.

In order for any member of the crew to access the decks above to commence their work day or go from one part of the ship to another without interacting with passengers, each cruise ship has a special massive corridor commonly named the *"I-95"* after the popular American highway, which is an impressive architectural design running along the entire length of the ship, although in other ships it's called the *"M-1"* after a motorway in the United Kingdom. This corridor is commonly found on Deck Zero in some ships but again this number can vary on different ships but it's always situated beneath the common passenger decks to ensure no passengers gain access to them.

The *"I-95"* is always busy with foot traffic by many crew members shuffling in all directions at any given time with dozens of trolleys and carts rolling past. This is where the crew can gain undisturbed access to different staircases and elevators along any part of the ship. This corridor was originally created to speed up productivity from the crew members and give the paying passenger more value for their money by getting a faster and more efficient service.

In this, the longest corridor on the ship, there is the *"Crew Mess,"* where crew members have their own space to enjoy drinks and snacks, *"The Crew Training Centre,"* which is an educational office where any crew member can learn and train in languages, banking, computers or other essential requirements to help them become better at their work, *"The Crew Medical Centre," "The Crew Lounge," "The Crew Galley,"* where they can enjoy their little time off by playing pool or just relaxing, *"The Staff Mess,"* and *"The Marshalling Area,"* which is a massive holding area where they typically store alcohol and whatever else required to be delivered to the staterooms, *"The Stores,"* and the *"Environmental centre,"* amongst many offices and other staircases leading further down to the lower decks of the ship.

Most passengers do not even realise this hidden deck exists, as passengers are normally too busy on the public areas of the ship being pampered without noticing, or wanting to notice, the different structures that exists below.

The passenger's main care is when they return to their stateroom after a day out enjoying themselves, they always typically find their stateroom has been cleaned, beds made with fresh new linens and their bathroom also cleaned and have clean towels waiting for them, without thinking for one moment that it was a poor under paid cleaner, working an average between 12 and 15 hours every day nonstop to keep their tight schedule, to earn a very basic and modest average one thousand dollars per month for their families back home, depending on the tips to boost that low wage and get a decent amount of money at the end of each cruise, thereby making all their hard work worth it.

Wearing a ship's steward's uniform, which he conveniently brought with him in his suitcase for this very purpose, Ethan walks along the hectic I-95 deck passing many of the active crew members who are so busy with their work. They don't even acknowledge him and on several occasions nearly having near misses, as Ethan is trying to get an orientation of where exactly he going and narrowly misses getting bumped by a number of the crew who shout the typical "*Open your eyes!*" or "*Look where you're going!*" As they continue along, but Ethan has other plans, he is searching for the crew's accommodation list which he knows has to be somewhere down here but doesn't know where. "You there!" Shouts the ship's second purser in his pristine white uniform who spots Ethan lounging carelessly around. Ethan stops to look at the purser walking towards him and glances around, making sure he was not shouting at someone near him.

"Me, sir?" asks a bewildered Ethan.

"Yes you," barks the purser angrily as he stands opposite Ethan, "where is your name tag and why aren't you at your station?"

"Well," replies Ethan playing dumb with a foreign accent, "you see, sir, I was transferred just before ship sail and I still try to find my way around, as for name tag, I left in cabin when I signed in but now, I don't remember where my cabin is, so I am lost, sir."

"God, another newbie!" remarks the purser knowingly, as this is a very common scenario. "Your cabin number is in your boarding card," he says keeping his cool, "show me your boarding card."

"I left that in my cabin by accident, sir."

"Where in God's name do they find these people?" asks a frustrated purser who has now seen it all. "See there?" he shouts pointing at an office way up ahead with a glass window in the distance. "Allocation unit, office ninety-two. There you will find the crew list which include their allocated cabins and daily work stations, so go there now, find your cabin, ask in the office for a copy of your boarding card to enter your cabin, get your name tag, smarten up your uniform and run to your station. And for the love of God, always carry your boarding card with you at all times, got it?"

"Yes, sir, I will do right now," replies Ethan and walks at a faster pace towards the office trying to get as much distance between him and the purser. "Jesus," he mutters to himself as he passes countless staircases going both upwards and downwards leading to other parts of the ship, "you need a bloody map just to find your way around," he adds in astonishment to himself, glancing back and noticing the purser has moved on.

He slows down and now walks at a normal pace, making his way to that office eventually arriving over a minute later and stands by the office door where a sign reads *"Allocation Unit"* and glances at a thick printed book hanging by a string. Through a tab system it shows an alphabetized list of details about crew members, and it's available to any of the crew who might need it. "Bingo," he says as he takes the printed book, glancing around noticing how everyone continue shuffling about without taking any notice of him.

Using his index finger he flips to the tab *"P"* and patiently scrolls the many pages until finding *"Viktor Pavlov - cabin 335."* He then turns the pages to the tab *"M"* and searches for Morales until finally finding *"Hugo Morales - cabin 684."* He grins and shuts the book saying, "Got you now."

Ethan faces the many staircases around noticing how they are all conveniently labelled with bulk cabin numbers such as *"Cabins 105 - 250"* making it easier to locate a cabin. "Okay, let's start with 335," he mutters to himself, and walks along the corridor of staircases until he spots a sign that reads *"Cabins 305-350"* and stops.

"Ok," he says quietly stepping down the staircase leading to the next deck below. He stops at the landing and stares down a long solitude corridor that stretches as far as the eye can see. "Talk about claustrophobia," he utters sarcastically and takes a deep breath.

Ethan keeps walking forward, reading the many cabin numbers as he proceeds further inwards, noticing a foul stench, barren white walls, no windows and a serious feeling of claustrophobia. He can only imagine what it must feel like to actually live down here in this lonely environment. "Bloody hell," he says to himself softly, glancing around completely alone.

He continues on until finally arriving at cabin number 335. Feeling the door for any vibrations in case there is someone inside, he knocks and waits for an answer. He takes the passkey he borrowed from his pocket, swipes it over the keypad and the door clicks open. He glances around the corridor to make sure no one is around, then walks into the cabin, closing the door behind him.

Ethan takes a moment to find the light switch, then he turns it on, revealing how small and cramped this cabin is. There are two bunk beds, one wardrobe, no windows or fresh ventilation and a connecting bathroom that is so small it's impossible to shower inside it. "Okay, Viktor, which one is your bunk?" he tells himself staring at the beds as he takes the micro surveillance devices from his pocket.

***

After successfully planting the device in Pavlov's cabin, Ethan walks down another long corridor passing many cabins. He takes the stairs to the floor above, and eventually stops outside cabin number 684 where he knocks and waits. Just like before, he glances around to ensure no one is watching and opens the door with the passkey. He quickly enters then closes the door behind him. Ethan scans Morales's cabin which is much more spacious than Pavlov's cabin on the deck below and quickly walks to a corner frame above the wall where he places another micro surveillance device carefully concealing it by the frame. He then takes out his cell phone, clicks on the *"US Flag"* APP and watches a perfect live feed on his screen of the entire room.

***

Walking along the I-95, Morales makes his way to his cabin to rest. His face clearly reflects anger but he does greet many of the crew members he passes with friendly greetings and waves, as they walk by.

***

Inside Morales's cabin, Ethan is busy searching through his wardrobe but finds nothing. He looks around and stares at the bunk beds, thinking to himself, "if I had to hide something maybe it would be under the bed." He impulsively looks under the bottom bunk bed but finds nothing.

***

Walking down a staircase to the lower deck, Morales moves along the lonely corridor and is about to reach his closed cabin door when his pager begins beeping. He stops, looking to see who it is. "Damn it!" he yells. It's the emergency code from the infirmary, but he hesitates staring at the pager.

***

From inside the cabin, Ethan overhears Morales just outside. With nowhere to hide, he frantically jumps into the top bunk and closes the curtains, leaving a slight opening. He watches how Morales walks into the cabin, quickly leans under the bottom bunk bed and takes out a small book, writing briefly on a page until the pager starts beeping again. "I hear you, damn it." he yells closing the book. He hides it back under the bed and quickly exits the cabin shutting the door.

Ethan can hear Morales's footsteps fading into the distance and lets out a sigh of relief as he climbs out of the top bunk. He leans under the bed and pulls out the book with anticipation, opening it. He scans through pages of dates, initials, quantities and sums of money. "What the hell?" he mutters to himself as he flicks through to the last page and finds…

INITIALS:	DATE:	QUANTITY:	VALUE:	SPLIT WITH:
S.F.	11th May 2018	2	$215.000	V.P.
S.K.	18th May 2018	1	$107.500	V.P.
N.V.	25th May 2018	3	$505.000	V.P.
C.M.	1st June 2018	2	$215,000	V.P.
N.L.	8th June 2018	4	$705,000	V.P.

"C.M.," he mumbles softly, "Chloe Moore?" he asks himself noting it was around the same date that she went missing, but it could just be another coincidence. "V.P.," he wonders, "could that be Viktor Pavlov?" He takes out his cell phone, clicks on the camera and begins to take pictures of all the pages in the book, so he can later investigate it further.

11
Grave Error

An attractive Bettina, 24 years of age and wearing a sexy bikini, is sunbathing all alone at the Top Deck pool area on a lounge bed. She's enjoying the warm sunny afternoon, unaware that Morales and Pavlov are standing at the upper deck observing her discreetly.

"That one is perfect," remarks Pavlov with a cold tone in his voice. "Bettina Hudson," he adds, "arrived alone and staying on deck six."

"She has good skin," says Morales pleased with her. "she looks after her body and health, so her organs will be as good as new," he adds impishly. "She will do nicely for your contacts in Jamaica," he adds and gives Pavlov a bitter stare. "Double the dosage."

"But that will most probably kill her."

"Then be sure to snatch her before she dies," replies a shrewd Morales, "it will save me the trouble of having to kill her later."

"Very well," says Pavlov and he walks away. Morales turns around and continues to observe Bettina below with an emotionless grin.

Ethan walks cautiously around the Top Deck trying to spot either Morales or Pavlov, as he has just changed back to his tourist clothes after spending a few hours on the decks below. Suddenly, out of the corner of his eye he spots Pavlov walking over to the bar. Taking evasive action so not to be seen, he stays behind the many white posts, aiming his camera at Pavlov.

Pavlov reaches the bar, giving a secretive nod at one of the two bartenders, who immediately acknowledges him and gets busy preparing an ice-cold cocktail. As he waits, he casually glances over at Bettina with lustful eyes. The bartender soon places an enticing cocktail on the bar by Pavlov's hands, then walks away to serve other waiting passengers.

"What's he doing?" asks Ethan to himself as he tries to watch through the zoomed camera but can only see Pavlov's back. In frustration he decides to move further around the deck to try and get a better angle. But in doing so, Ethan misses seeing how Pavlov gingerly takes a small wrapped paper from his pocket containing a mixed powder *"Methadone and Vicodin"* which has been finely ground and prepared for this occasion. Once he is confident no one is watching, he pours the large amounts of powder into the cocktail and using his finger, mixes it until the powder is dissolved.

Ethan finally finds a better position and aims his camera at Pavlov as he is now leaving the bar with the spiked cocktail. "Drinking on duty, Viktor?" asks himself softly and takes a few pictures:

- Camera Viewfinder: *Pavlov walking holding the cocktail.* Click.

Pavlov reaches Bettina, smiling and blocking the sun from her face. "Miss Hudson?" he asks in a friendly tone.

"Yes," she replies candidly raising her hand to her eyes trying to see his face, as he has the sun directly behind him.

"Compliments of the bar for winning this afternoon's bikini competition," he says excitedly while extending the cocktail to her.

"But I didn't enter any competition. There must be a mistake."

"You are Bettina Hudson, correct?"

"I am."

"Then there is no mistake, but if you don't want this ice-cold cocktail to quench your thirst, I will just return it back to the bar."

"No need, after all, it's already been made," she replies in excitement and gladly accepts the cocktail, sipping it. "Mmm, it's very nice."

- Camera Viewfinder: *Pavlov handing the drink to Bettina.* Click.

- Camera Viewfinder: *Bettina sipping the cocktail.* Click.

Ethan continues to watch through the camera's viewfinder, then notices Bettina laughing, downing the cocktail in one go. "Who gets special service?" he asks himself and takes one more picture of Bettina.

- Camera Viewfinder: *Bettina smiling after finishing her cocktail.* Click.

Suddenly, Steven, Bettina's boyfriend walks towards Bettina and surprises her. She lets out an exhilarating scream, hugging him and forcing Pavlov to step back with a horrified expression on his face.

"What are you doing here?" asks an elated Bettina.

"I thought about what you said and you were right, we only live once so I got to the port as fast as I could after you left and booked a cabin. I've been searching the entire ship to give you the surprise," replies an elated Steven who cuddles her and kisses her passionately.

"Excuse me," says Pavlov totally confused, walking quickly towards a nearby staircase.

Ethan can just make out Pavlov stepping up the staircase to the upper deck where he soon spots Morales staring at Bettina and Steven. "There you are," he mutters, taking their picture.

- Camera Viewfinder: *Morales watching from above.* Click.

- Camera Viewfinder: *Pavlov standing beside Morales.* Click.

- Camera Viewfinder: *Morales and Pavlov watching Bettina.* Click.

"What happened to the intelligence?" asks an angry Morales gripping the railing tight.

"The boyfriend came to surprise her."

"She will be dead by tonight and with the boyfriend now in the picture we can't bloody well use her!" he shouts under his breath trying not to lose his temper. They are both fully aware Bettina is no longer useful for their needs, as with the boyfriend around, there is no way they can discreetly get rid of her body thus ruining their meticulous and sinister plans.

Ethan continues to take pictures of Morales and Pavlov who appear to be arguing.

- Camera Viewfinder: *Morales clearly upset at Pavlov.* Click.

"What do we do now?" asks Pavlov, without emotion.

"We wait until I get the call that she has died, then you go into her cabin and plant some Methadone and Vicodin, so when the family performs her autopsy, they will put two and two together and hey presto, cause of death, by overdose," he replies deviously, clearly planning worst case scenarios ahead of time.

"What about the order?"

"It will have to be postponed as we will have to deal first with this bloody error so we don't attract any unnecessary attention," he replies calmly. "Another day won't matter."

Bettina and Steven walk away from her lounge bed holding hands, like the romantic couple they are, heading into the ship. Ethan decides to follow them, keeping his distance.

∗∗∗

Ethan walks tentatively along the luxurious corridors keeping Bettina and Steven well in his view, as they cuddle and kiss, walking towards her stateroom. Ethan notices the contrast between these corridors and the ones down below for the crew, finding it hard to comprehend why the company doesn't look after their staff better. After all, it is thanks to their hard work that the ship functions properly. keeping passengers happy and returning for more cruises.

Ethan soon notices the couple has reached stateroom 6285. Steven romantically pins Bettina against the door and erotically rubs his body over hers kissing her passionately. She quickly takes out her boarding card, swipes it on the keypad and they rush into her stateroom slamming the door shut. Ethan curiously walks towards the stateroom door where he listens to them obliviously beginning to make love inside.

***

Now in his stateroom, Ethan sits back in his chair patiently observing his laptop screen, which is split into four live surveillance feeds, each with their continuous running time codes:

- Top left screen: *Two nurses working in the examining room.*

- Top right screen: *Joanne's empty room.*

- Bottom left screen: *Pavlov's cabin where Pavlov sits on the top bunk typing on a laptop.*

- Bottom right screen: *Morales's cabin which is empty.*

Looking at his cell phone, Ethan clicks on the *"US Flag"* APP and the screen automatically changes to the same split surveillance feed he is watching on the laptop screen. He clicks on the bottom left screen and it changes into a full view of *Pavlov typing on his laptop.* "Gotcha!" he says in excitement, feeling content the system is working perfectly while hearing the crystal-clear sounds of Pavlov's keyboard keys punching away.

***

"Sure you don't want to come? I'm famished!" says an energised Steven getting out of bed with a wide smile on his face. He begins to put his clothes on after spending three hours making love to Bettina who is completely exhausted and just wants to sleep.

"You go on ahead, babe," she replies with a tired voice

feeling sleepy, "I will order room service, as I'm exhausted," she mutters softly making him feel more macho, believing she is feeling this tired because of his wild sexual love making.

He leans over her on the bed and gives her another passionate kiss. "You sleep and get more energy for tonight," he adds, grabbing her boarding card and promptly exiting the stateroom.

She hears the door close and closes her eyes. Moments later she gets a sharp agonising pain in her stomach. Her eyes flash open and she moans in agony, she touches her head, clearly feeling restless. The room begins to spin faster with every passing second, her body temperature rises beyond normal levels and her stomach convulses with unbearable cramps, forcing her to throw off the covers from her naked body that continues to heat up like a furnace as she doesn't understand what is happening to her. She does not realise that the harmful narcotic powder Pavlov gave her earlier is now effecting her fragile system. Unless treated immediately, she will be dead within the hour.

Although Morales and Pavlov still have the power to save her young life they prefer instead to just sit back and let her die, clearly demonstrating their malicious actions as they literally play God, choosing who lives and who dies aboard their ship. They know only too well that if they raise the alarm to save her, her statement would undoubtedly implicate Pavlov for giving her the spiked drink. This would mean receiving unnecessary attention, something they certainly do not want.

"Help!" Bettina whimpers softly, breaking out in cold sweats, unable to move or shout. "Someone!" she cries but then her body begins to shake with violent, uncontrollable convulsions on the bed. She screams inaudibly in agony lasting for a good two minutes until soon enough she sighs her last breath and dies with her eyes wide open, staring at the ceiling. Bettina's lifeless body remains motionless with her arms and legs spread out on the bed and drool oozing from her mouth. Her lips are blue, her face completely pale and her pupils fully-dilated.

***

Ethan walks out of the Grand Restaurant wearing a smart suit after having a lovely dinner. It's a beautiful evening as he walks along the luxurious inner deck, decorated to the highest standards of luxury with priceless paintings, crystal chandeliers, bronze statues of ancient Greek Gods such as *"Poseidon," "Apollo," "Zeus," and "Eros."* He makes his way along the crowded deck towards the foyer, passing many passengers shuffling in all directions wearing their elegant evening attire. Everyone is ready for a great night aboard, prepared to enjoy their evening trying their luck at the Casino, watching one of the live shows at the Grand Theatre or just taking a romantic stroll along the Top Deck enjoying the cool ocean breeze. Flowing with unlimited alcohol and rich foods to their heart's desire, helping to make wonderful memories of this unforgettable cruise.

Ethan soon arrives at the foyer and glances around, hearing a live band playing majestically as a talented performer sings the cover of a popular music track. Continuing down the grand staircase where people are enjoying drinks at the foyer's bar, Ethan observes the amazing sunset filtering through the many windows along the foyer.

***

"Sorry I took a while but there was this massive line at the windjammer and I couldn't find my way back," says Steven as he walks into the stateroom and leans on the bed to kiss Bettina. But he soon becomes terribly worried as something is seriously wrong. She is not responsive to his touch and her eyes are staring aimlessly at the ceiling with drool all over her mouth. "Bettina!" shouts a concerned and now frightened Steven as he tries to wake her up, only to find she is not breathing.

"Oh, God!" he shouts clearly not knowing what to do and he freaks out, panicking he picks up the cabin's phone and dials *"9"* which is the ship's guest service desk. *"Hello? How may I help you?"* asks a friendly woman's voice on the other end of the phone.

"My girlfriend," he replies frantically, "she is not breathing!" he shouts breaking up in tears. "I think she's dead!" he adds wailing like a baby, totally unprepared and in complete shock.

"All right, sir, please calm down and tell me in what stateroom is she in?" She asks with a firm tone.

"I don't know," he replies unsure of the room's number and quickly looks at the boarding card still in his hand, "yes, 6285, please send someone!" he pleads hysterically, glancing at the body wondering if he had anything to do with her death as he is totally confused.

"The medical team will be with you momentarily, sir." she says with a tranquil voice trying to calm him down.

"Please hurry!" he asks, thinking about her family, knowing it will be devastating for them to receive this sad news. "What am I going to tell her mother?" he asks himself staring at her opened eyes, still clutching the phone's receiver in his hand.

***

As Ethan strolls along the Top Deck he cannot help gaze at the spectacular sunset and red skies that stretch deep into the horizon. He holds tight to the railings, thinking about Chloe also admiring these amazing views, knowing full well she would have thoroughly enjoyed them. "Where are you, pumpkin?" he asks himself, emotional but holding back his tears.

***

The young nurse and Morales barge into stateroom 6285 holding two emergency response bags and pushing a gurney. Steven immediately intercepts them at the door. "Thank God you arrived!" he shouts nervously, clearly distraught, motioning with his arms to the bed. "I found her like this," he adds and the nurse immediately performs CPR on Bettina's body.

"Did she take any medication?" asks Morales as he helps the nurse with the CPR by doing the compressions. The nurse takes a ventilator from one of the response bags and places the mask over Bettina's mouth, squeezing the pump, thereby sending air into her lungs.

"Not that I know of," replies a confused Steven. He's completely unaware that Pavlov is walking discreetly into the stateroom, cautiously making his way into the connecting bathroom where he meticulously plants several *"Methadone and Vicodin"* pills, making it look like Bettina was an addict and must have overdosed.

"She is unresponsive!" shouts the nurse as she continues to squeeze air into her lungs while Morales applies continuous compressions to her body's chest.

"Better call it." he replies and stops the compressions, realising she is gone.

The nurse stops the ventilator and looks at her watch. "Twenty-one, thirty-five hundred hours," she confirms with a heavy heart knowing Bettina couldn't be saved.

"No!" yells Steven breaking into tears, sobbing and wailing. "Steward," says Morales to Pavlov, "help us take the body to the infirmary."

Pavlov immediately wraps the body with the bed sheets and helps Morales transfer it from the bed and onto the gurney while the nurse comforts Steven.

"We did everything we could, sir," she tells him softly while Morales stares at the body thinking what a waste of perfectly good organs. If only the boyfriend hadn't arrived, we would already be removing her kidney and liver. But it's impossible to do it now as the family will most likely want an autopsy done and her organs must be intact to avoid any red flags and alarms going off.

***

Pushing the gurney into the examination room in the infirmary, Morales and Pavlov observe the nurse comforting Steven as they walk behind. "Help me lift the body, Pavlov," says Morales. Pavlov helps him transfer the wrapped body onto the examination table. "Nurse, please help him fill in the necessary paperwork," says Morales. The nurse nods her head sympathetically and walks Steven still tearful outside to her reception desk where the arduous paperwork will now need to be filled out in detail.

***

Continuing to watch the amazing sunset, Ethan is completely lost in his thoughts about Chloe, so much that he doesn't hear a continuous notification ping coming from his cell phone. Moments later the phone vibrates. He snaps out of his trance and grabs his phone, staring at the screen. The *"US Flag"* APP sensor is flashing, detected movement in one of the surveillance cameras.

He clicks on it, showing the live feed of the infirmary where he can see a dead body on the examination table. Morales and Pavlov are removing sheets from around it, and soon they're admiring the naked body. "What the hell?" he mutters softly as he zooms into the face of the body. He's shocked to see it's the same girl from earlier that afternoon, recalling how Pavlov gave her a cocktail by the pool. "Christ almighty," he adds in disgust. "What have they done?" He runs towards one of the doors, trying to safely manoeuvre around passengers walking in all directions.

***

Ethan rushes into his stateroom, shuts the door and sits down at the desk, opening the laptop. He types a password which automatically activates the surveillance screen, then clicks on the live feed from the infirmary, noting it is automatically recording. Turning up the volume, he listens to Morales's and Pavlov's conversation.

***

"This has cost us dearly, damn it," says Morales, perturbed, staring at Bettina's naked body while Pavlov stands calmly beside him, glancing at Steven outside.

"If only he would have arrived two minutes earlier," recollects Pavlov without showing any remorse, glancing back at the body, "she would still be alive."

"After the boyfriend leaves, put the body in the ship's morgue," instructs Morales coldly. "We will resume our operation tomorrow," he adds confidently, and touches the scar on his eyebrow.

***

Ethan writes *"Dead girl from pool after Viktor Pavlov gave her a drink" "Coincidence or foul play?"* and *"Resume operation"* in his notebook, circling it with a big question mark. Tapping the question mark with the tip of his pen, he continues to watch and hear their every move on the screen knowing something bigger than he ever imagined is happening aboard this ship, and the death of this innocent girl is just the tip of the iceberg.

"I will inform the Captain about the death so we can make the necessary arrangements with the Jamaican authorities for the body to be released from the ship, and maybe give the family time to fly out," says Morales, walking with Pavlov towards the door. "Be sure to transfer the body tonight," he adds, "I don't want it stinking up my infirmary," he says.

They exit the examination room but the audio can still be heard clearly. "I will have the body out of here in fifteen minutes," confirms Pavlov.

Ethan remains watching the screen, lamenting how sad to just leave the body of that beautiful girl alone inside that room, knowing those two had something to do with her death. But he doesn't have any tangible evidence at this time and knows he must keep digging to try and prevent more deaths and tragedies from occurring.

12
Vigilante

Relieving his anxiety and stress, Ethan takes a moment to himself sitting at a corner table in the Schooner bar, where he enjoys a nice glass of bourbon. He watches the nearly one hundred other passengers listening to a great entertainer playing the piano and singing a popular cover song. Many of the passengers sing-a-long, keeping the atmosphere cheerful. Everyone is clearly having a nice time.

Ethan glances around, casually noticing that the bartender serving many drinks to waiting passengers is the same bartender he interviewed when he first came on board the ship after Chloe's disappearance.

Suddenly, a girl's loud scream can be heard followed by her laughter coming from a corner table on the other end of the bar, getting Ethan's attention. He notices she's a young girl, around 14 to 16 years of age, attractive figure with green eyes, long blonde hair and a sexy dress. She's cramped into a booth with four adult men in their thirties enjoying shots of alcohol, all of them are laughing and shouting, clearly having fun.

This makes Ethan think to himself, *"this doesn't look right."* *"Could it be that they are trying to buy her drinks to then take advantage of her?"* He feels completely paranoid, as he doesn't know what to expect from this cruise lifestyle that appears to be a paradise for sexual predators, hiding behind the legality of being in International waters.

"Here they are!" shouts a fifth man who swiftly stumbles towards the corner table carrying a tray filled with about twenty shots. He sets the tray on the table where the girl takes one of the shots and downs it in one go, slamming the empty glass onto the table beside a collection of twenty other empty glasses. Then the five men grab a shot each and down them in one go, slamming their empty glasses on the table. They all break out in joyful cheers.

Ethan continues to observe this table as his instincts are telling him something is not right. He watches how the girl takes two more shots and downs them one after the other, slamming the empty glasses onto the table, letting out another excited scream. This makes the men cheer.

Ethan manages to catch a glimpse of how drunk the girl now appears to behave. Then within seconds the five men nod at each other, as if giving themselves a secret message, and they all simultaneously stand up without attracting any unnecessary attention to themselves. They help the drunk girl up and escort her out of the bar. Immediately, Ethan downs his drink and follows them, as he feels they are up to something bad.

***

"Where are you taking me?" asks the drunk girl, slurring her words and trying to stand up straight as she is being ushered along the labyrinth of corridors by the five men. They know exactly what they are doing, anticipating a great night with her, unaware that Ethan is following them from a distance.

Ethan activates his *"US Flag"* lapel pin in the event of gathering evidence if this is going to end up as he fears, into a gang rape. Suddenly one of the five men runs forward to a closed stateroom door number 6237, and swipes his boarding card to open it, allowing the other four men to quickly push the girl into the room. They slam the door shut behind.

Immediately, the girl is thrown onto the bed and two of the men violently tear off her sexy dress and panties, revealing her perfect, naked figure. The other three men all begin to take off their clothes without losing anytime. "What's happening?" she says slurring as she doesn't understand where she is or what is happening to her, trying to focus but being so drunk she just lays on the bed. Seconds later one of the naked men climbs on top of her body and sticks his slivering tongue into her mouth, forcing her legs apart and holding his erect penis with his hand as he guides it into her vagina where he proceeds to penetrate and rape her while two other men firmly hold her arms and legs tight, ensuring she cannot move. Laughing and cheering they all watch the rape and eagerly awaiting their turn to be inside her. The desperate girl continues to shout, "no!" But they are not interested, as there is no turning back now.

Using the passkey, Ethan storms into the room horrified to see his instincts were right. He can only imagine this is what may have happened to Chloe, making him angrier. "Stop it right now!" he yells in a firm tone, brutally grabbing the man forcing himself on the girl. He throws him to the floor but the other four men simultaneously attack Ethan. Within seconds he is on the floor being kicked everywhere and all he can do is to cover his face from the brutal attack. Then he tries a bluff, "The police are on their way and will be here any second!" he shouts. The five men immediately stop the beating, stare at each other and hesitate.

"Hey, man, if he knows where we are then so must the cops," yells an anxious man who quickly grabs his clothes lying on the floor and runs out of the room.

"The hell with this," yells another man who also grabs his clothes from the floor and runs out of the room, being followed by the other three men, fearing a lengthy jail sentence if they get arrested.

Ethan stands up with a bruised head and bloody nose feeling his body aching. He quickly covers the girl with a blanket and cradles her, comforting her as she cries feeling ashamed. "Shush now," he tells her with a soft voice, "it's over, those bastards won't hurt you anymore," he reassures her.

He picks up the phone and presses the number *"9"*. *"How may I help you?"* asks a friendly woman's voice on the other end of the line.

"I wish to report a rape in stateroom 6237," Ethan confirms.

***

Pavlov is slowly pushing the gurney with Bettina's covered body along the I-95, as he is making his way towards the ship's small morgue which has freezers for four bodies. Every crew member he passes, just continues walking away, as no one is curious to know what has happened. It is clear he is pushing a dead body but no one wants to get involved, especially with Pavlov.

***

Inside stateroom 6237, the girl's concerned mother, in her forties, is hugging her distraught daughter on the bed. Both are in tears while a nurse places bandages on the girl's heavily bruised arms and legs.

In a corner of the room, holding a bag of ice to his head to try and stop the swelling, Ethan is giving a statement to Chief Security Officer Martin. "And that is when you decided to follow them to determine what their intentions were," asks Martin attentively as he takes the statement in his notebook.

"It was by pure luck that I noticed them at the bar," replies a candid Ethan. "If I hadn't then, I am afraid the outcome," he adds, glancing at the shocked girl in tears, "would have been much different."

"We best get her to the infirmary now to run some tests," says the nurse to the mother.

"Do you have rape kits on board?" asks a concerned Ethan, noticing how the nurse discreetly nods her head confirming they do.

"We need to go to the medical centre now, sweetie," tells the mother softly to her daughter. The girl clings on tighter to her, totally traumatised and afraid of stepping outside, fearing she will be attacked again. "I am not letting you out of my sight ever again," she adds emotionally, "we will do this together."

She kisses her daughter on the forehead wrapping her in a

blanket. Wiping away her tears, she helps her stand up. With the nurse's help they walk the girl towards the front door. Ethan and Martin watch them leave, then the mother stops, turns around and looks at Ethan, giving him a compassionate smile. She wipes grateful tears from her sore eyes, feeling thankful he stopped the brutal sexual attack from escalating. "Thank you for stopping the attack and saving my baby, sir."

"I just did what I hope any other person would have done if it happened to my daughter, madam."

"It's my husband's birthday today and she was insistent she wanted to go to the teen club to make new friends. My husband even encouraged her to do so, as we expected her to be safe in that club," she adds and breaks down into more cries. "I never would have imagined she would have been taken by those men, given large amounts of alcohol to make her drunk, so they could then rape my baby while her father and I were out enjoying a show to celebrate his birthday. I will never forgive myself for that. She is only fourteen."

"The world must open their eyes and realise a cruise ship is not as safe as it is portrayed on fancy advertisements and TV commercials." Ethan answered.

"Will those men be captured?" she asks vehemently.

Ethan gives a confident look. "Justice will be made and those monsters will be held accountable for their actions, you have my word."

"Good," she replies emotionally and with the assistance of the nurse they slowly walk the girl out of the room.

"Those men are still out there," says Ethan.

"They won't get far, as after all, we are standing in their stateroom, so it's just a matter of time my men and I apprehend them and throw them in the ship's brig where they will remain for the duration of the voyage," Martin replies.

"Crime prevails on board your ship but nothing gets done

about it, as after all, we are in International waters, right?" Ethan asks.

"What is it you want, Mister Moore?"

"I pray to god my daughter didn't go through an ordeal like that young girl went through tonight," he replies indignantly. "I want a public announcement to be made to all the passengers on this ship, warning them that sexual assaults happen, that people die and people do go missing aboard these ships without a trace. Everyone is entitled to know the truth and reality that they are not in the safe environment they believe they are in. That is what I want for now."

Martin grunts in amazement and walks towards the front door knowing full well that the request for the public announcement will never happen. "You are clearly upset," he says, stops and looks back at Ethan, "I thank you for helping that girl, Mister Moore, but we don't need a vigilante on this ship."

"Maybe if you had a vigilante or a team of marshals on board, my daughter would have been home with me right now!" replies Ethan trying to control his emotions. "But because your rent-a-cops didn't do their job correctly, as they cannot be everywhere, my daughter is still missing and I fear presumed dead by now."

"I will remind you, Mister Moore, that you are just another passenger aboard this ship and I must insist that you do not take any form of action to try and impair our open investigation into your daughter's disappearance or to go anywhere that is off limits to passengers," he replies firmly and takes a step closer to Ethan. "I must also remind you that you do not have any form of search warrant or special privileges, nor do you have any legal jurisdiction aboard, so if you step out of line and create a panic on this ship, I will see to it personally that you are removed at the next port of call, wherever that may be," he threatens rigorously. "Do I make myself clear?"

"Crystal clear," replies an enraged Ethan keeping his cool, knowing Martin is totally correct and he basically doesn't have a leg to stand on if he does screw up.

"Good night then," replies Martin. Not wanting to go into a debate he exits the stateroom swiftly leaving Ethan clutching his fists in anger, glancing at the bed and feeling his aching body.

***

A new day and the sunrise on the horizon is a spectacular view as the ship's hull graciously ploughs through the calm open blue waters. Many of the passengers are just waking up or heading to the Windjammer restaurant for their morning buffet breakfast.

Ethan enjoys a large breakfast glancing around at the hundreds of passengers who fill their plates with all sorts of food. He touches his swollen head and moans slightly as his body is still aching from last night's beating. He spots the mother of the girl from last night sitting at a table near his. He observes how she, her husband and the girl are trying to eat some food but they are clearly distraught. Ethan glances over to the window to continue watching the spectacular sunrise on the horizon.

"Excuse me," says the girl's father who is now standing beside Ethan. "My wife told me what you did for our daughter last night."

"Please, it was nothing," replies Ethan.

"She is my only daughter and means the world to me," he says and extends his hand. "Thank you."

Ethan shakes his hand remaining silent and the man then returns back to his table where the mother emotionally cries and whispers, "Thank you," to Ethan with her lips, then focusing her attention on her traumatised daughter.

Ethan is moved by the gesture but he doesn't seek recognition for what he did, he grabs his SLR camera resting on the chair beside him and walks away feeling sad, when suddenly his attention is drawn to Morales standing on the other side of the ample room, staring at something.

Ethan quickly moves around, using the passengers shuffling in all directions as cover. He discreetly positions himself behind a coffee dispenser where he can just make out Morales closely watching, Joanne from a distance. She's sitting alone enjoying her breakfast. "Doesn't the man ever stop?" Ethan asks himself under his breath and quickly aims his camera at Morales and takes a picture:

- Camera Viewfinder: *Morales watching Joanne.* Click.

- Camera Viewfinder: *Joanne eating her breakfast.* Click.

Morales then walks away and mingles with some of the crowd where he soon disappears, leaving Ethan wondering if Morales is actually stalking his victims before he does something to them. If that is the case, it means Joanne is clearly in danger. But he cannot tell anyone, especially the ship's security, as then they will throw him off of the ship and he will never complete his private investigation, and possibly never find out what really happened to Chloe.

***

Inside his stateroom, Ethan sits at the desk watching the laptop screen, fast forwarding all four split screens which are continuously recording on the hard drives. He is playing last night's feed to see if he missed anything. The four screens show:

- Top left screen: *Pavlov taking Bettina's body away on the gurney and after much fast forward, the nurse walking into the examining room with the mother and the raped girl where a lengthy examination and treatment is meticulously conducted by two nurses under the close supervision of the mother who constantly stands beside her daughter holding her hand.*

- Top right screen: *Joanne sleeping alone all night on her bed, occasionally moving sleeping positions as the hours pass.*

- Bottom left screen: *Pavlov's cabin where his roommate is drinking heavily and eventually falls asleep and hours later Pavlov walks in, changes and goes to sleep on his bunk bed.*

- Bottom right screen: *Morales eventually entering his cabin and after taking a shower and goes to bed completely naked where he gradually falls asleep.*

Ethan closes the laptop and looks at the door.

***

Walking along the busy and popular Top Deck, Ethan slowly follows Morales, who in turn is discreetly following Joanne. She constantly glances out to the open sea, sliding her hand over the railing as she walks along, feeling lonely.

Ethan takes a picture, adjusting the zoom accordingly:

- Camera Viewfinder: *Morales following Joanne.* Click.

Joanne stops, gazing out at the open ocean. She closes her eyes to feel the cool sea breeze on her face, taking a deep breath of the fresh air, which makes her feel more alive.

"The ocean is as beautiful as your eyes," says Morales standing beside her, making her quickly turn around and blush, as she finds him to be very attractive.

"Thank you for that sweet compliment, Mister?"

"Hugo Morales," he says holding her hand and kissing it tenderly, portraying himself as a true gentleman, "I am the ship's doctor."

Ethan hides behind a nearby white post and takes pictures of Morales kissing her hand while she continues to blush.

- Camera Viewfinder: *Morales kissing Joanne's hand.* Click.

"At your service, señorita." Morales adds with his flamboyant accent.

"My," she utters holding her breath as she is completely enthralled by his charm, "a Spanish gentleman," she adds shyly, "and that accent, mmmmm, how I love it. My name is Joanne."

"What a pretty name you have, señorita Joanne," he says knowing he has her charmed. He takes a step closer. "Do you mind if I," he adds holding his palm near her face, "feel your temperature?"

Joanne feels his hand and moves closer to him. "Am I hot enough for you, doctor?" she says in a seductive tone, pressing his palm firmly against her face. This makes him grin mischievously knowing she is going to be an extremely easy snatch.

- Camera Viewfinder: *Morales touching Joanne's face.* Click.

Ethan lowers his camera observing Morales and Joanne talking, which makes him recall what Alexis told him, "*Chloe told me he had made some sort of advances towards her. He touched her face and asked if she had a cold. It was strange. She just felt uncomfortable around him.*"

Ethan goes into a trance and can see in his mind Chloe standing by a railing talking with Morales until he puts his hand on her face, making her uncomfortable, forcing her to step away.

Ethan snaps out from his trance and continues to watch Morales conversing with Joanne by the railing.

"I am as fit as can be," she says with her sensuous voice moving closer to him, making him feel nervous as he doesn't like her being so dominant, "but you are welcome to examine me in my room in more depth if you don't believe me," she adds and bites her lower lip making him nod his head, taking a step back.

"Not today," he tells her with a stern tone, and he walks away leaving her completely perplexed standing alone.

"I'm sorry if I came on too strong, as I thought you wanted me?" she says with a confused voice.

Morales stops and smiles at her. "Oh I do," he tells her confidently, "and I will have you, make no mistake about it, just not today," he adds, walking away leaving Joanne clearing her throat and feeling embarrassed. She glances around hoping no one was watching.

"What the hell is he playing at?" asks Ethan, his eyes following Morales.

***

Wearing protective glasses and ear muffles on the Starboard Deck, Ethan aims a double barrel shotgun out to the open sea and shouts "Pull!" Immediately, a steward, waiting by the clay pigeon machine, yanks hard on a string releasing two clay discs catapulting them high into the air out to sea.

Ethan follows them with his reflex action, swinging the barrel of the gun at the flying discs, keeping them in his sights. He squeezes the trigger, making a loud bang and the first disc is hit, breaking into pieces. He quickly aims at the second disc, squeezes the trigger, and accurately hits it, shattering it with ease.

A number of enthusiastic passengers clap as Ethan opens the breach of the weapon, automatically ejecting the two empty shells from the barrel. They land on the deck near a dozen other empty shells, as he has been here for some time now.

"Well done, sir," says the excited steward, "that is thirteen out of fourteen."

"Load them up again please," Ethan replies while loading two new shells into the barrel unaware that Morales is walking towards him from behind. Soon he's standing behind him, clapping his hands twice.

"Investigating pigeon clays, Mister Moore?"

Ethan recognises Morale's cold voice and grips the now loaded weapon tight in his hands, closing the breach and cocking it, making it ready to be discharged. He stares at the horizon grinding his teeth, trying to control his rage at the monster standing behind him.

"Maybe you are flexing your Miami PD authority on the fish at sea, Ethan," remarks Morales sarcastically, trying to provoke him. He notices how Ethan slowly turns around and gives him a penetrating glare, staring straight into his cold and emotionless eyes.

"I find shooting very relaxing," Ethan says staring at Morale's impassive demeanour.

"What are you doing on board? I already told you, I left your daughter at the bar and when I returned, she had gone." Morales says, changing the subject.

"I remember what you told me, Hugo."

"So?"

"My boss convinced me to take time off, so I thought, why not take a cruise to get my mind off things," he replies callously, "and what do you know, here I am."

"And here you are," replies Morales sardonically, observing how Ethan grips the loaded weapon tapping his index finger repeatedly over the trigger.

"Mister Moore, sir," says the waiting steward, "the clays are ready."

"Pull!" He shouts hearing the sound of the clays being released. He impulsively swings around, aims and shoots down both clays accurately within seconds with two loud bangs, releasing his outrage and anger.

"Well done, sir, that makes fifteen out of sixteen," says an impressed steward as the passengers continue to clap in excitement. Ethan opens the breach of the weapon, staring emotionlessly at Morales, automatically ejecting the two empty shells from the barrel where they land on the deck near the other empty shells. He slowly takes two new shells and puckishly reloads them into the shotgun, then he closes the breech of the weapon.

"Two!" shouts Ethan.

The steward immediately begins to reload two more clays into the machine, as Ethan tentatively aims the business end of the barrel at Morales and cocks the weapon ready for firing. "Isn't that right, doctor?" he adds trying to control his temper. He rests his finger over the trigger and fights with all his might not to squeeze as he needs to know what really happened to Chloe.

"Two, was it not?"

Morales doesn't budge, nor is he intimidated by the loaded weapon and carefully puts his finger on the barrel, pushing the gun to one side. "Come now, detective," he utters in a low but frosty voice, "you of all people should know to never point a loaded weapon at anyone, unless your intention is to shoot." He notices how Ethan begins to sweat and is clearly distraught. "Many accidents happen at sea," he adds menacingly, leaning his face closer to Ethan's face, obviously taunting him, "and we don't want another one now, do we?" he adds with a grin. Morales walks away making Ethan more outraged as he lets out a sigh of anxiety.

"Pull!" shouts Ethan completely enraged. He hears the clays being released, flying into the air, and he lets out a blood curdling scream as he turns around and fires both shots clearly missing the clays, as he is not focussed on them anymore. "God damn it!" he utters, staring at the open ocean knowing his cover has been blown. But he can't understand how, as he has been taking all the right steps to remain inconspicuous.

***

Morales and Pavlov walk along "Deck A" passing many passengers along the way. They soon stop to admire the ocean and lean forward against the railing. "I get the impression he is on to us," exclaims an upset Morales completely disturbed. "It is no coincidence he is on this ship," he says thrashing the railing with his fists in anger, "he can jeopardize our operation and we have too much riding on this to allow it to be ruined by his nosing around."

"How do you want to handle this?" asks Pavlov keeping his voice down so no one overhears.

"I want him gone," replies a snarled Morales, giving Pavlov a sinister stare. "But first I want to make sure he is travelling alone."

"I will make the usual enquiries."

"If he is with someone, then make it look like an accident."

"And if he is alone?"

"Then eliminate him and dispose of the body discreetly."

Pavlov nods his head in agreement, staring out to the ocean in deep thought "I think I know just the spot," he replies with a conniving grin on his face.

13
The Trap

In his stateroom, Ethan scans through the day's recorded surveillance feed on his laptop from all four cameras but finds nothing of importance. He glances at his wristwatch and sees it is *"23:06"* when suddenly, a very faint knock is heard at the door grabbing his attention. Before he can answer someone slips a folded piece of paper under the door.

Ethan spontaneously slams the laptop screen closed and swiftly runs to the door, opening it, but no one is outside. It's as if the paper magically materialized. He grunts and walks back into the stateroom closing the door. He picks up the piece of paper, unfolds it and reads a handwritten note: *"I know what happened to your daughter and where she is. Come alone tonight at midnight. Deck 00, cabin 142."* His eyes are hopeful as he crushes the paper in his hand. This could be the break he has been so desperately yearning for. He sits down on the bed feeling a weight has been lifted off his shoulders.

In less than an hour he may finally discover what really happened to Chloe and maybe, God willing, he can bring her home safely. He opens the crushed paper, grabs his cell phone and takes a picture of the note.

***

Walking along the endless I-95 corridor, passing a small army of crew members shuffling in all directions, Ethan checks his watch which reads *"23:42."* He looks at the piece of paper in his hand to confirm the deck and cabin number where he needs to be in less than twenty minutes time. Taking a left turn he notices a flight of stairs with a sign that reads *"Deck 00."* He casually walks down those stairs, glancing around to make sure no one is following him.

As Ethan continues further downwards onto the bottom deck, the lights grow dimmer, which can easily make anyone feel claustrophobic. But he is not afraid and he continues until reaching the landing, staring down a lengthy narrow solitude corridor which has many closed cabin doors on both sides. He takes a deep breath and walks slowly along, reading the cabin numbers until he eventually arrives outside of cabin 142, looking at his wristwatch which now reads *"23:59"*.

Ethan gulps, glancing around both directions of the corridor and finds there is no one in sight, as he is completely alone. "Don't freak out now, Ethan," he tells himself under his nervous breath. Looking at the closed cabin door, he knocks twice and waits. A few seconds later the door lock clicks and he cautiously pushes it open, looking inside the seemingly small and badly lit room. "Hello," he says but there is no answer, making him even more nervous. "I got your message," he adds, taking a few steps into the room.

Then he hears soft cries coming from the back, and can just make out a naked blonde teenage girl crouching in the corner, "Are you all right?" he says loudly, expressing concern, as he rushes to her aide. But suddenly he is knocked on the head with a metal rod rendering him unconscious. His body collapses to the floor beside the girl. Unfortunately, in his haste, he didn't remember the first rule of entering a possible hostile room, which is to check behind you.

An hour later, Ethan moans in pain as he gradually awakens with a massive headache, only to discover his wrists have been tied up with tie wraps to a water pipe near the cabin's ceiling. He attempts to break free but is unable to, though he soon discovers his legs are not tied up. When suddenly he hears the chilling sound of a chainsaw starting up and revving, which gets his undivided attention.

He looks around, trying to focus his eyes in the dimly lit room. Soon he sees a crew member slowly walking towards him, stepping over a plastic sheet that is covering the entire floor. Ethan realizes this is not going to end well. "What do you want from me?" he shouts, as he closely watches the tip of the chainsaw getting dangerously close to him. Terrified, his eyes open wider with horror as he is clearly trapped with no apparent way out.

Another two crew members walk into the room and stand guard by the door, watching how their mate is now a few feet away from a petrified Ethan. "It was a trap, wasn't it?" shouts Ethan from the top of his voice trying to be heard over the loud revving noise. "You lured me down here to kill me, didn't you?" he adds realising its hopeless. No matter how much he tries to break free, he is unable to do so as he now watches how the tip of the chainsaw is raised over his face getting nearer to his eye.

The crew member revs the chainsaw clearly taunting him, making him more enraged. "If you are going to kill me, damn you, at least tell me where my daughter is? Let me die knowing what you bastards did to her?" Suddenly the chainsaw is lowered and the revving stops but the engine is left idling.

"Take her away," says Pavlov walking into the room. "No need for her to watch what we are going to do to him," he adds, and the two guards standing by the door quickly grab the crying girl forcing her out of the cabin. "Make it quick," he tells the crew member holding the chainsaw, and he exits leaving Ethan and the crew member alone.

"Whatever they are paying you, I can double it," says a desperate Ethan trying to plead for his life.

"It's not about money, don't you get it yet?" mutters the crew member, revving the chainsaw loudly and raising it up menacingly into the air, ready to begin hacking up Ethan's body into small pieces. But just as the chainsaw plunges down to Ethan's head, he holds on tight to the water pipe, lifts up his body and brutally kicks the crew member in the face, locking his thighs firmly around his neck and squeezing as tight as possible to try and strangle him.

The crew member yells, brandishing the chainsaw all over the place trying to cut Ethan anywhere possible. But Ethan finds the right moment and kicks him hard, catapulting him backwards, as the chainsaw falls on his body and hacks off his left leg, splattering blood in all directions. The crew member's blood curdling screams continue, making Ethan squeamish as he watches the wounded man desperately try to stand up. But he's losing too much blood and is unable to do so. "Let me help you!" exclaims Ethan. But the crew member is in so much pain he doesn't listen to reason and instead takes out a handgun from his pocket. He aims it at Ethan to shoot him instead, trying to focus but the pain is making it difficult to concentrate.

Ethan uses his police training, pulling hard and fast on his wrists, repeating the technique several times until the ties snap off and he is free. He drops to the floor where he impulsively kicks the gun away from the crew member's hands. Then Ethan takes off his belt and makes a tourniquet around the man's thigh, an inch above the amputated leg. "I know it hurts," he says to the anguished crew member, "but I am going to get help," and he grabs the gun from the floor. "Where are they holding the girl that was here?" he asks.

"I don't know," replies the crew member in agony trying to focus after losing so much blood. "Please, help me."

"I will send help, just hang in there," replies Ethan and he quickly exits the room, only to encounter another crew member just exiting the cabin next door. They both engage in a violent hand to hand fight, punching, kicking, pushing and shoving until finally Ethan overpowers him and kicks him so hard the crew member loses consciousness.

Ethan hears footsteps approaching as someone is now walking down the staircase in the distance. He can just make out the silhouette of a steward who hesitates as he spots Ethan standing over the unconscious body of the crew member in the middle of the corridor. Impulsively he runs back up the staircase.

"Wait!" shouts Ethan as he runs towards the staircase chasing after the steward. Ascending the stairs he comes out at the infamous I-95 where he stops. Glancing left and right he tries to spot the escaped steward, holding the hand gun tightly.

A small army of crew shuffle in all directions watching Ethan pant and sweat with the gun in his hand. Noticing their wondering eyes, he puts the gun into his pocket as he doesn't know where the steward has gone and doesn't want to alarm the passing crew.

Just when he thought all was lost, from the corner of his eye, he can just make out the steward hiding in one of the nearby stores watching him. "You there!" he shouts taking the gun from his pocket and running towards him.

The steward dashes down the corridor being chased by Ethan who tries to aim the gun at his legs to slow him down. Be he doesn't fire as there are too many crew shuffling in all directions and he doesn't want to wound any innocent bystanders or kill someone accidentally. So he presses on, running faster and faster until he bumps into several Filipino waiters carrying large trays stacked of plates. The dishes crash to the floor breaking everything.

"Look what you've done!" shouts the angry waiters. But Ethan continues to run after the steward, who himself has collided with several crew members, also crashing to the floor. This gives Ethan valuable time to catch up and throw himself onto the steward where they both engage in a violent hand to hand fight.

"Who sent you to kill me?" shouts an enraged Ethan, pounding his fists harder into the man's now bruised and bloodstained face. Passing crew immediately step in, forcing them apart, restraining them both while other crew stop to curiously watch. "Let go of me!" demands Ethan as he tries to break away finding it impossible to do so.

"He is crazy!" shouts the steward as he too tries desperately to break free. "He has a gun!" he adds and the crew release him. He runs away wiping the blood from his nose, leaving Ethan to let out a blood curdling scream as he continues to be restrained.

***

"I warned you, Mister Moore," says Martin slamming the hand gun on his desk staring at a handcuffed Ethan sitting on a chair inside his office.

"I already told you, they have a young girl below deck, blonde, green eyes, imprisoned somewhere in the ship," he says holding his temper. "The guy in cabin one four two, who attacked me with the chainsaw, did you get him to the medical centre? He can tell you who ordered him to kill me."

"My men went to the cabin on Deck zero zero, number one four two, where you were allegedly held captive, and they found no trace of anyone there or of any foul play, Mister Moore," he explains calmly. "No blood and no crew member with an amputated limb."

Ethan manages to take out the piece of paper he received and slams it on the desk beside the gun. "It was a trap, they left this for me. I went down, they knocked me unconscious and when I woke up, I was tied to a pipe where they were going to hack me up before I managed to escape."

Martin takes the crushed paper with interest and reads it, "be it as it may, there is just no evidence to support your statement."

"Then how can you explain the gun?" asks Ethan firmly. "It's surely not mine and I certainly didn't bring it aboard past your tight security detail."

"You were caught in an area that is off limits to the passengers, chasing after one of the stewards with a lethal weapon."

"Yet the question is, where did I obtain said weapon."

There's a knock at the door and Martin opens it slightly, giving Ethan enough view-of-sight to observe Pavlov standing on the other side. "Don't do anything stupid, Mister Moore, you are in enough trouble as it is already," says Martin and he walks out to speak with Pavlov leaving Ethan alone in the room.

Ethan looks at the handcuffs on his bruised wrists and leans back in the chair, trying to stay focussed and make some sense of all this.

He casually glances around the office, noticing a number of commendations hanging on the wall and several photographs, one in particular catches his attention. *"Martin, Morales and Pavlov in full uniform laughing on the Top Deck of the ship surrounded by attractive women in bikinis."* It is evident that Martin may be part of whatever Morales's operation is.

Suddenly the door opens and Martin comes back into the office, walks over to Ethan and slowly unlocks the handcuffs with a key then removes them from Ethan's wrists.

"It is late," says Martin without emotion standing with a menacing posture. "Go to your stateroom and rest, Mister Moore. We will be in Ocho Rios by sunrise."

Ethan takes a moment to digest what is happening and it now makes perfect sense that whatever Morales and Pavlov are up to, they need help and who better to help them than the chief of the ship's security. Ethan now realises this is beyond what he ever imagined. A whole organisation using all the resources the ship has to offer while hiding behind centuries old and antiquated maritime laws that have not been adequately updated for today's modern cruise ships. It is now also clear that Morales knew he was aboard the ship, after Martin got his statement when he saved that girl from the gang rapists. So he must have told Morales, who in turn quickly tracked him down. All the puzzles are slowly coming together.

"Did you hear what I just said?" Martin asks.

Ethan snaps out of his trance and gives a warm smile. "Yes, thank you," he adds and looks around for the piece of paper.

"Looking for this?" he mutters knowingly as he raises the paper in his hand. "I will keep this, together with the gun, for my report."

"Of course," replies Ethan as he stands up and walks past him. "Thank you," he adds, calmly exiting the office.

***

Ethan carefully removes the laptop and hard drives from the desk by placing them on the floor, then pushes the now empty desk against the front door of his stateroom. This gives him a few extra valuable seconds, if anyone tries to open the door during the night. It will hit the desk and make a sound which will wake him up, giving him time to protect himself from an attack. Completely exhausted, Ethan then drops to the bed and falls asleep.

14
The Betrayal

Recently docked at the beautiful Jamaican port of Ocho Rios in the very early hours of the morning, while many passengers are still sleeping or just waking up, Bettina's mother patiently waits at the lonely pier beside a taxi. She wears a black outfit and cries into a white handkerchief, as the body of her daughter is carefully removed from the ship on a gurney by two local undertakers. They respectfully place the body into the back of a local hearse.

Martin walks down the gangway followed by Bettina's boyfriend and they both approach the grieving mother to comfort her. "On behalf of the Captain and everyone aboard," says the shrewd Martin giving her a hug, "please accept our sincere condolences for your loss."

"They told me that she overdosed," she says finding it hard to believe. "My baby never took drugs."

"They are taking the body to the local morgue," he says as the hearse slowly drives away. "We sometimes don't really see what our children actually get up to," he adds with a sombre tone, "until it is sadly too late."

"It was you, wasn't it?" she says giving the boyfriend a cold look.

"I swear on my mother's grave that I didn't give her anything."

The mother is too exhausted after travelling many hours to get to Ocho Rios before the ship arrived, and doesn't want to argue with anyone. "I have to make the arrangements to bring her home with me," she says completely devastated, walking towards the waiting taxi, totally perplexed and indignant about what has happened. The boyfriend walks beside her and they both get into the taxi which soon drives off to catch up with the hearse.

Standing alone on the pier, Martin glances up at the ship's deck where Morales and Pavlov are watching from above, knowing the error they committed has finally been eradicated.

***

Ethan is already awake and has just finished a soothing shower. He feels sore, and his clearly bruised body is hurting everywhere after last night's struggles and fights. He takes clean clothes from the wardrobe, navy blue shorts and a Hawaiian shirt with sneakers. He pushes the desk back to its original position then carefully returns the laptop and hard drives to the desk, switching it on. He quickly scans through last night's surveillance footage in fast forward on the screen:

- Top left screen: *Morales working at the examination room and getting surprised by Pavlov and two stewards who bring the wounded crew member with the amputated left leg and immediately Morales orders them to take him to the OR where it's clear Morales will spend the next few hours operating on him.*

- Top right screen: *Joanne sleeping alone all night on her bed, occasionally moving sleeping positions as the hours pass.*

- Bottom left screen: *Pavlov returning late to his cabin where he eventually sleeps.*

- Bottom right screen: *Morales eventually entering his cabin at 04:26 and dropping to bed completely exhausted.*

"Just some more evidence and I will bring your whole operation down," he says out loud, flipping the laptop closed knowing the surveillance feed continues to be recorded on the hard drives. He walks to the door, opens it and finds his cabin steward waiting outside in the corridor.

"Good morning, Mister Moore," says the steward with a friendly smile, "would you like me to have your stateroom cleaned today?"

Ethan takes a fifty dollar bill from his wallet and hands it to him. "Not today either and make sure no one does."

The steward pockets the tip with a smile. "I understand your privacy and respect it, sir," he says and walks away, leaving Ethan at ease knowing no one will enter his stateroom today either. He has been giving the steward a fifty dollar tip every morning since he began the cruise to make sure they keep away, as he doesn't want anyone messing around with the laptop or the hard drives.

***

Joanne is amongst the hundreds of passengers disembarking on this sunny morning to explore the stunning Ocho Rios town, and the atmosphere is lively. Ethan discreetly follows Joanne keeping a safe distance as she walks out of the terminal building and finds a market where she curiously begins to browse at souvenirs.

Ethan blends in with the crowd of tourists as he follows her without attracting any attention to himself. He notices when she waves at a young 20-year-old attractive woman passenger, who is also browsing. They start talking and laughing and continue walking together, so obviously with her new friend, Joanne will at least be safe from Morales or Pavlov.

***

Ethan walks along the Top Deck and can sense someone watching him. He turns around but there's no one. *"My God,"* he thinks to himself, *"I'm getting paranoid!"*

***

In his stateroom later that afternoon, Ethan plays the recordings from the morning surveillance footage:

- Top left screen: *Morales is comparing many photographs which he is taking out from one of the drawers and then gets startled as one of the nurses enters the examination room and clearly disturbs him, making him swiftly throw the pictures back into the drawer as if he were trying to hide something.*

Ethan rewinds the footage and pauses the image on the main screen, to where Morales is holding one of the photographs in his hand. "What are you hiding?" he mutters softly, zooming into the photograph. But he can barely make out a woman's face as the zoomed image is too pixelated and he cannot clearly see who she is. He decides to press play and watch the recorded live feed in real time:

"I told you to always knock!" barks Morales at the nurse.

"I am sorry, doctor," but a mother has just arrived with her 10-year-old daughter who is suffering from severe sunburn."

"Very well, bring the girl in and help the mother fill out the forms."

The nurse exits and promptly returns walking a timid girl in a bikini into the examination room, then exits, leaving her alone with him. "What is your name?" he asks, helping her to sit down on the examination table.

"Amanda," she replies with an innocent tone as he takes a bottle of lotion from the counter and begins pouring lotion all over his hands.

"Stay still Amanda, this will make you feel better," he says standing behind her and rubbing his hands all over her face and chest, making him excited. "It's okay. I won't hurt you," he adds feeling how she cries as the pain is just too unbearable for her. When erratically, he pins the girl down to the table and begins to sexually fondle her. Making him aroused he kisses her on the neck, reaching his hand down for his clearly erect penis.

Ethan's eyes open wider with rage as he watches in horror. "That bastard!" he mutters under his breath clutching his fists, knowing that what he is watching has already happened and there was nothing he could have done to prevent it.

***

Standing by a railing of the ship, Ethan is looking out at spectacular Turtle Bay while talking on his cell phone. He glances below at the many passengers returning from a wonderful day in the Jamaican town.

"I tell you, Hank, the bastard is one twisted fuck!"

"How old did you say the girl was?" asks a stunned Hank on the other end of the cell phone.

"The nurse said she was ten."

"Jesus."

"I have enough evidence against him to take him out."

"Don't do it yet, Ethan, you still don't know where Chloe is. If you get Morales now, he may not talk and you may lose the only chance you have of ever finding her."

"I know, damn it. It's just leaving that predator roaming free on this ship is putting more girls in harm's way."

"You have strong evidence against a paedophile but you only have circumstantial evidence for human trafficking, and that is the evidence you need to shut him and his team down for good," continues Hank.

"I am sending you some pictures now," Ethan says pressing *"send"* on a number of saved photos. "You should have them any moment now." The pictures included screen grabs of the attack on the 10-year-old girl by Morales, parts of Morales's coded book and Pavlov giving Bettina what appeared to be a spiked drink resulting in her death. "If anything should happen to me I want you to get them to our friend in the Bureau so they can build a case against them."

"You just watch your six and don't do any more stupid heroics, you're not a kid anymore, you hear?"

Ethan moans as his sore body still aches. "Yeah, I hear."

***

In the evening, as the ship sails into the horizon under a beautiful and stunning orange sunset, Ethan enjoys his dinner at the busy and crowded Grand Restaurant. He is seated a few tables behind Joanne's table, where he can watch her and her attractive woman friend blissfully enjoying their dinners, making toasts with champagne, and kissing each other passionately on the lips.

***

Back in his cabin, Ethan glances at a digital clock beside his laptop which reads *"02:36."* His eyes are glued to the split screen as he patiently waits for Morales to go to bed so he can swing into action:

- Top left screen: *The dark examination room as lights are switched off and no one is inside.*

- Top right screen: *Joanne and the attractive young woman passionately making love on the bed.*

- Bottom left screen: *Pavlov sleeping on the top bunk.*

- Bottom right screen: *Morales cuddling his naked body on the floor erratically banging the back of his head repeatedly on the wall, clearly deranged.*

Ethan knows this is as good a time as any and stands up.

***

Ethan breaks into the examination room and closes the door behind him. He turns on a small flashlight, shining it around the dark room as he makes his way to the drawer he saw earlier on the laptop's screen where Morales hid those photographs. He reaches the drawer and finds it's locked. "Shit," he utters.

Glancing around he spots a pair of scissors on a cabinet and using one blade he fiddles with the lock until finally the drawer clicks open. "Still got it," he remarks as he slowly pulls out the drawer and finds a number of medical instruments and notes inside. "I swear it was this one," he mutters feeling slightly confused. But just as he is about to close the drawer, he notices the tip of a white envelope concealed at the very back. "Hello," he utters curiously, taking a picture as evidence to verify where the envelope was hidden inside the drawer.

Ethan picks up the envelope and opens it, finding a small stack of photographs inside which he flips through in horror:

- Photograph: *A young unconscious woman lying on the examination table with livers removed from her body.*

- Photograph: *Another young unconscious woman lying on the examination table with her heart removed from her body.*

- Photograph: *Another young unconscious woman lying on the examination table with both her eyes and her kidney removed from her body.*

"Jesus!" he shouts trying to control his tone. Gagging and swallowing several times, he takes a number of deep breaths to calm down and compose himself. "You got this, Ethan," he tells himself frantically flipping through all of the photographs, one as gory as the next, but none of them are of Chloe. "Thank God you're not one of them, pumpkin!" he says to himself and carefully lays all the photographs on the examination table where he calmly takes individual pictures of each of them.

***

Sitting at the laptop, Ethan types a long email to his friend at the FBI, glancing at the digital clock that now reads *'04:58'*.

- Last paragraph of the email being typed on the screen: *"So I am attaching the shots of the pictures I took and the video file of him abusing the little girl and I need you to please ensure a full investigation gets underway, thank you. Ethan."*

Ethan double-checks all the attachments carefully and then clicks the *"send"* button. The email takes a while due to low WIFI until finally the email is sent, making him more relaxed knowing that between Hank and his friend in the FBI they now have enough solid evidence to incarcerate Morales.

***

Chloe is running along the labyrinth of dark corridors on the ship completely petrified as she is being chased by a faceless man brandishing a shiny knife who is menacingly catching up. Her agonising screams echo through the hallways, and she soon reaches a closed cabin door. Banging on it anxiously she shouts for help, then glances at the man, now only a few steps away, as he raises the knife into the air and plunges it mercilessly into her on the shoulder. "Help me!" she yells apprehensively knowing she is all alone and no one can help her.

Suddenly, the sound of the ship's fog horn blasts and Ethan wakes up covered in a cold sweat and bloodshot eyes. "Chloe!" he yells glancing around his stateroom with an accelerated heartbeat until soon realising it was all just a nightmare.

The sound of the ship's fog horn being blasts continuously, as the ship anchors at the Cayman Island harbour on this lovely warm morning.

***

After having a quick breakfast, Ethan stands on "Deck A" watching a small fleet of tender boats transporting hundreds of passengers to the port so they can enjoy their day. He takes a few pictures of the port with his SLR camera hanging around his neck. Casually glancing to his right, he erratically ducks behind a white post, when he spots Morales and Pavlov walking nearby and passing him.

"Shit, that was close," he says to himself catching his breath and watching how they make their way towards the Grand foyer. He immediately follows, keeping his distance.

Inside the crowded Grand foyer Pavlov soon spots Heather, a sexy 19-year-old blonde model who has been working aboard the ship for just under five months as a dancer. She walks towards him with a great big smile on her face showing off her elegant summer dress.

"That's her," Pavlov secretly tells Morales who promptly notices and grins maliciously as they continue to walk towards her.

"She will do just fine," replies Morales with an impish tone.

"Heather," says a now happy Pavlov, raising his hands as she arrives and giving her a friendly kiss on each cheek. "You look stunning as always."

"You are too kind, Viktor," she replies blushing with a striking British accent.

"Allow me to present to you the ship's doctor."

"Hugo Morales," she immediately interrupts extending her hand, "may I just say it is an honour to finally meet you, doctor."

"The honour," he replies seductively as he takes her hand and kisses it tenderly, "is all mine, Heather."

Ethan aims his SLR camera and takes a picture:

- Camera Viewfinder: *Morales kissing Heather's hand as she smiles.* Click.

Heather turns and points at a door that leads to a nearby gangway, "so, shall we?" she adds excitedly and they all walk along the crowded foyer. "Viktor tells me you are taking me to see some great sights," she says enthusiastically.

"This will be your unforgettable cruise, Heather," replies a sinister Morales.

"I haven't been off this ship in a long time so imagine my surprise when I was given a day pass and allowed to disembark, thanks to you, of course, Viktor," she says holding Pavlov's arm in gratitude.

"It helps to know which strings to pull," replies a confident Pavlov as they navigate their way through the crowds.

Morales casually glances back, knowing Ethan is following them as this is all part of a conniving plot to trap him using the girl as bait. He smiles, spotting Ethan trying to hide behind some passengers. "Are your men ready?" he tactfully asks Pavlov, motioning to him that Ethan is following behind. Pavlov just nods his head to confirm that they are.

***

At the gangway, Martin supervises two of his security officers scanning the boarding cards of every passenger entering the gangway and boarding the tender boat, so they can enjoy their day in the beautiful town. The scanner's computer monitor clearly shows a picture of the passenger being scanned with a red tick, meaning they have disembarked.

Morales, Pavlov and Heather reach the gangway, then wait behind a small line of passengers who are being scanned by the security officers. Morales gives Martin a secretive nod, and Martin casually takes a scanner and walks towards Morales, Pavlov and Heather.

"Boarding cards please," asks Martin, noticing how his men are busy with the rest of the passengers, including Joanne and her lover.

Morales, Pavlov and Heather take out their boarding cards and extend them to Martin. He first scans Morales's card then Pavlov's and lastly Heather's. "Thank you, enjoy your day," he says gesturing for them to board the waiting tender.

Heather boards first completely elated, followed by Pavlov. But before Morales boards he motions to Martin with his eyes that Ethan is nearby.

Martin nods and casually walks to the computer where he types on the keyboard and Heather's scanned details promptly appear in red. He discreetly glances around to ensure no one is watching and presses a key, which deletes her from the system as if she never disembarked, instantaneously removing her picture from the screen. The tender is now full and sails slowly towards the land port.

Ethan is behind a number of passengers as they slowly walk down into the gangway. He notices a new tender arriving and that he must catch that one in order to be able to follow Morales.

As the two security officers continue to scan the passengers' boarding cards, Martin swiftly intercepts Ethan with an emotionless stare. "Boarding card please," asks a conniving Martin, waiting as he takes out his boarding card and extends it.

"Seeing the sights, Mister Moore?"

"They say the Cayman's are a pearl, so it would be a shame to miss its beauty," replies Ethan as Martin scans his card and steps aside to allow him to board the tender.

"Enjoy your day, sir."

"Thank you," replies Ethan feeling rather uncomfortable, walking past Martin as he boards the half-full tender boat.

Martin casually walks back to the computer where he types on the keyboard, and Ethan's scanned details promptly appear in red. He discreetly glances around to ensure no one is watching and quickly deletes him from the system, as if he never disembarked and his picture is instantaneously removed from the screen. "Good bye, Mister Moore," he utters to himself softly and continues to supervise his men.

Inside the second tender boat, Ethan waits patiently as it's now full and no more passengers are allowed to board. The tender soon departs slowly towards the land port. He takes out the *"US Flag"* lapel pin and proudly wears it on his shirt, keeping a close eye on the first tender boat which is about to arrive at the port.

The first tender slowly docks and two ship's stewards help all the passengers disembark, wishing them a good day in the town, watching how everyone quickly disperses in all directions. Morales, Pavlov and Heather are the last to disembark, purposely standing at the pier.

"Finally got my feet on solid ground," says a blissful Heather taking in a deep breath, glad to have some well-deserved free time away from the monotony of the ship.

Morales grabs her arm and gives her a fake smile. "Let me show you around," he says and pulls her along towards a nearby side street, while Pavlov walks towards a local bar in the opposite direction.

"Isn't Viktor coming with us?" she asks with concern,

apprehensive about being ushered rather forcibly away.

"He has a pending matter to resolve first," he replies glancing back at the second tender boat that is about to dock, anticipating Ethan will be arriving soon. "But I promise you are going to have all the fun in the world," he adds making her feel more relaxed. They walk into a side street and disappear out of sight just as the second tender docks and Ethan soon disembarks.

Ethan stands at the busy pier glancing in all directions, not able to locate Morales, Pavlov or Heather anywhere. "Shit!" he mutters under his breath, watching passengers browse through the markets along the pier.

Ethan soon manages to get a glimpse of Pavlov drinking a beer outside a local bar up ahead. "There you are," he says to himself, with a sigh of relief. He discreetly mingles with the crowd, making his way towards the bar.

Pavlov spots Ethan, as he has been waiting for him, and impulsively puts his beer on a table and walks deeper into the town, thereby leading Ethan to follow him. And Ethan does follow, rather effectively, and a foot chase now begins weaving through the crowded streets, as they play a game of cat and mouse.

Ethan, however, is concerned he cannot locate Morales or Heather and can only assume they will be meeting with Pavlov at any moment. Listening to his instincts he continues following Pavlov, blending, with the busy crowds.

***

Morales and Heather are now walking along a quieter part of town where only a few of the ship's passengers can be seen, as this is a more neglected area. The buildings seem to be rather abandoned and dirty, but she is excited to be exploring and doesn't take too much notice of the drastic contrast. She continues walking beside Morales, all the time being watched by a number of locals from every corner.

"So, doctor, are you married?"

He chuckles at the question, "not me."

"Maybe you just haven't found the right partner yet."

"Oh, I've found the right partner," he says, and grabs Heather's arm firmly as they approach a blue door, making her feel rather uncomfortable.

"You're hurting me," she says trying to break away from his tight grip but she's unable to, just as he knocks on the door twice.

"Shut up and keep quiet."

"I have a crush on you, you know," she admits openly, "have had since I first saw you watching me dance a while back."

"That's too bad."

"What do you mean?"

The door swings open and two rough looking men, both in their twenties and wearing casual clothes, stand in the doorway with smirks on their faces.

"Don't tell me you're doing house calls," she asks jokingly trying to hide her escalating fear and concerns. Her eyes scope the area trying to find the courage to run as she has a nasty feeling about this. She looks back at the two men from head to toe, flashes her gaze at Morales, feeling her arm aching from his tightening grip. "I want to return back to the ship now, please."

Without any warning, the two men brutally grab her as Morales lets go of her arm. They force her into the house, slamming the front door shut.

Heather's muffled cries for help are reduced to a whimper, as one of the men covers her mouth with his sweaty hand pushing her into a specially prepared bedroom with boarded up windows. He savagely forces her onto the bed where the two men swiftly tie her arms and legs with ropes, spreading her legs apart while Morales just watches by the bedroom door as she struggles to try and escape.

"I trusted you!" she yells crying in desperation, when one of the men violently punches her face so hard she stops struggling, nearly losing consciousness, making it easier for them to finish tying her up. Morales now walks forward, as blood drips from her nose, and he takes a prepared syringe with a cap on the needle from his pocket, removes the cap, inserts the sharp needle into a vein in her arm and mercilessly injects the dark liquid, making her go completely unconscious.

"That was your mistake," he replies with a stern expression, returning back to the door where he leans against the wall and watches how the first man impatiently tears off her clothes, revealing her toned and sensuous naked body. At the same time, the second man takes off his clothes, revealing his now naked body. Maliciously, he climbs on top of her and begins to rape her, spreading her legs further apart as he pounds his erect penis deeper into her vagina.

"Be gentle!" yells Mia, a Madam in her late forties who stands beside Morales watching the rape. "Don't damage her like you did the last girl you idiot!" She turns to Morales and smiles handing him a brown bag, "this one is young and attractive. She will fetch a nice sum. You have done well."

Morales takes the bag from her hand and checks the stacks of hundred dollar bills inside, making him happier. "As I always do."

"My Saudi contact wants virgins," she adds now watching how the first man ejaculates over Heather's chest, then he climbs off of her. Immediately the impatient second man begins to rape her again, making Mia feel a bit horny and she rubs her fingers sensuously down Morale's arms. "The younger the better. I need two for next week."

Morales puts his hand on Mia's face and kisses her intimately on the lips as they hear the grunts of pleasure from the second man pounding faster and faster as he is about to reach an orgasm. "I will get three," he tells her softly. "Two for the Saudi's and the third for the Sheik."

He walks out of the bedroom but stops and looks back at Mia. "Just tell your goons not to penetrate them when I deliver them, or else they'll lose their virginity. After all, we do have a reputation to uphold," he confirms just as the second man ejaculates over Heather's chest.

Mia walks over to Heather, observing her lavish body and erotically runs her fingers from her vagina all the way up her semen-stained chest to her lips, where she caresses them. "Will this one be missed, Doctor?"

"She doesn't have much family and has been alone on the ship for five months, so she can disappear like the rest of them without a trace," Morales replies confidently walking towards the closed front door with his money, leaving Mia with a bright smile on her face.

***

Pavlov continues to lead Ethan away from the busy streets and into a quieter but neglected part of the town where just a few locals walk the partially empty streets. He occasionally glances back ensuring Ethan is predictably following behind.

He grins maliciously as he turns a corner, then runs down a narrow dead-end alleyway where he stops by a closed door, opens it, walks inside, and closes it softly so as not to make a noise.

Ethan soon reaches the alleyway that he saw Pavlov turn into just moments earlier. He hesitates as he cannot see him, glancing around in bewilderment. "What the hell?" he mutters in frustration to himself, as he cautiously walks into the alleyway, studying his surroundings.

He doesn't understand where Pavlov has vanished to, but soon hears footsteps approaching from behind and looks back at the entrance of the alleyway. He watches in horror at two men standing tall, each holding a large shiny machete in their hands. It is in this moment that he realises he has fallen into a trap. "This isn't good," he mutters to himself. He quickly glances forward at the dead-end wall, then back at the only exit behind him which is guarded by two armed men.

Clenching his fists, understandably concerned, Ethan nervously looks around trying to find another way out. But the alleyway has a brick wall at the end and the only way out is through those men. He notices two doors and tries frantically to open them, but they are both locked. He now stares at the emotionless men walking slowly towards him, brandishing their intimidating machetes with a clear intent to kill.

"I am a police detective and I mean you no harm," he shouts, desperately looking for a way out.

"I eat pigs for dessert!" replies the first man with a Russian accent.

"You have no jurisdiction here, detective!" shouts the second man also with a Russian accent, as they continue moving closer.

Ethan begins walking backwards clearly petrified by the size of those sharp machetes. "I've got money!" he tells them, while frantically searching for a way to escape or find something to use for protection, but there's nothing.

"Your money is no good to us," replies the first man as Ethan now reaches the brick wall at the end of the alleyway, still desperately scanning the area to find a way out.

Just as the two men walk past the door, Pavlov comes forward, standing behind them, watching how they approach a trapped Ethan.

"Why are you doing this?" shouts Ethan panting in sweat, knowing he is clearly outnumbered. "I am an American Citizen, damn you!"

"You ask too many questions!" shouts Pavlov, sternly.

"If I am going to die I want the truth, Viktor," he yells, "where is my daughter?"

"Swimming with fish, Mister Moore!"

Ethan is overcome overwhelmed with sorrow and rage and he drops to his knees, letting out continuous agonising cries, as he now knows the dreaded truth about his beloved Chloe. It is what he had feared all along, removing the small glimmer of hope he had of ever finding her alive.

The two men stop within feet of Ethan. Pavlov takes one step forward where he gives out a command in Russian. "Ubey yego i sdelay eto bystro." (Subtitled: *Kill him and do it quickly.*) They both immediately raise their machetes into the air and are about to strike by hacking off Ethan's head.

"How did she die?" asks a devastated Ethan crying emotionally as he removes the camera strap from his neck, carefully setting the camera down in a corner by the wall.

"I suppose you are entitled to know before you die," replies Pavlov watching his men wait impatiently, "from Deck D, just like the rest of them."

The first man shouts, lashing forward to strike Ethan with his machete. Suddenly Ethan uses his Martial Arts skills and defends himself as best as he can, blocking the man's arm which prevents the machete from striking him. Simultaneously, the second man shouts and lashes forward, as the two men fight Ethan who continues desperately to block all their strikes while delivering kicks and punches. He focuses on his training motivated by revenge, and he's determined to remain alive.

This clearly upsets Pavlov as he watches the gruesome hand to hand combat sequence. Ethan is sliced repeatedly with the sharp blades on his arms and legs but continues to fight on with all his strength, fed by his rage and adrenaline.

"Khvatit uzhe igrat'. Ubey yego!" yells a now nervous Pavlov. (Subtitle: *Enough playing around already. Kill him!*)

Rendering many blows, Ethan manages to overpower the second man and take away his menacing machete, erratically flipping it, then stabbing and killing the man without remorse. He then brandishes the bloodstained machete toward the first man, engaging in a machete fight which results in both of them receiving cuts on their bodies.

By this time Pavlov has had enough as he takes out a switchblade from his pocket and walks closer to the horrific fight with the intention of stabbing Ethan. But it's nearly impossible as the machetes continue to be brandished sporadically in all directions.

"Tell me this!" shouts Ethan in tears. "Did she suffer before you killed her?" he adds, turning around to block the man's machete. This gives Pavlov the opportunity he needed to stand behind Ethan and ram the entire length of his switchblade into Ethan's arm. Ethan lets out a blood curdling scream as he swings around and brutally hacks off the man's head in a desperate outburst of rage. He watches the decapitated body drop to the ground in a pool of blood. He tries to hold his balance, clearly exhausted and losing blood from his many wounds.

But Pavlov brandishes his bloodstained blade at Ethan and they continue the fight. "Yes she did," replies a taunting Pavlov to make Ethan lose focus.

"I am going to make you suffer before I kill you, you bastard!" replies Ethan as he continues the harrowing fight. "Haven't you had enough killing?"

"When you have served in Afghanistan for mother Russia, then you have seen enough killing," Pavlov yells.

"Why did you kill my daughter?"

Pavlov storms at Ethan and is about to stab him in the chest, but Ethan moves away at the last moment, elbows him and pins Pavlov against the wall. "You won't murder an unarmed man, detective," he says with a mischievous grin on his face, dropping his switchblade to the ground and raising his arms into the air to be arrested.

"Who paid $215.000 dollars for her?" shouts Ethan, clutching tighter to the machete's handle trying to stay focus as he is clearly having difficulty keeping his balance.

"The sex trade is big business, Mister Moore," replies an impish Pavlov, "but an even greater one is the organs trade!" he adds, erratically rolling on the ground, using his military training. He kicks the machete away from Ethan's hand, and it lands on the ground far away. Both men now engage in a brutal fist fight with no rules as they bite, punch, elbow, kick, scratch and pin each other down several times, until finally Ethan seizes the upper hand and mercilessly punches Pavlov's blood covered face repeatedly forcing him to drop to his knees.

Ethan picks up the nearby switchblade and stands behind Pavlov, like an executioner, grabbing firmly onto his hair with his left hand and pressing the blade's tip tightly against Pavlov's throat with his right, pulling his head back as far as it can go.

"I will ask you one last time. What happened to my daughter?"

Pavlov spits and laughs briefly. "In my country there is saying," he says keeping his cool, "problems will always stay until you tell the truth. Me, I am your problem because I will never talk."

"In my country we have a saying also," replies Ethan completely enraged, "there is more than one way to skin a cat, you fuck!" He mercilessly presses the blade's tip into Pavlov's throat. "That's for Chloe," he says coldly staring into his upside-down dark eyes.

"Suka blyat!" (Subtitle: *Fuck you!*) Shouts Pavlov with a smirk on his battered face, clearly defying Ethan, which makes Ethan more upset as he lets out a blood curdling scream and savagely slits Pavlov's throat like a pig.

Completely surprised at this unexpected move, Pavlov gasps for air, feeling his own warm blood splatter all over his chest, until he soon dies.

Ethan drops the lifeless body to the ground, watching a pool of blood quickly accumulate under it. Then he drops to his knees completely exhausted, breaking down into tears with a wailing cry.

"God forgive me for what I have done."

***

Covered in blood with his clothes slashed and bloodstained in many places, Ethan limps as best as he can feeling he will be falling unconscious at any moment. He can barely sustain himself and tries to fight it. Feeling the strap holding the SLR camera around his bruised neck he stumbles along the streets cuddling his arms around his chest. He notices many locals and passengers staring at him in horror as he slowly makes his arduous way towards a pharmacy sign. The pharmacy door is open and he barges inside then leans forward on a counter where a local female doctor in her fifties rushes to his aide from a back room. She holds his head, watching how Ethan is clearly delirious and about to lose consciousness.

Nearly two hours later, Ethan opens his eyes and finds himself lying on a bed, inside the back room of the pharmacy. The female doctor has removed his torn clothes and has been stitching up all of his cuts, requiring over five hundred stitches all over his bruised and battered body. "You are lucky to be alive," she tells him, without never losing focus on the stitching, though she is clearly tired but determined to save him.

"Where am I?" asks a drowsy Ethan.

"Safe in my pharmacy," she replies and motions to his clothes, intact wallet and camera, which she has carefully set aside for him.

"The ship," he asks and tries to stand up.

"Stay still," she says in a dominant tone, "the ship is still at the harbour. Expected to sail in under three hours from now," she replies, making him more relaxed, as he realizes he can still get to Morales.

"What happened to you?"

"I got mugged," he replies with a sigh not wanting to tell her the truth. "They tried to take my wallet but I fought them away," he adds, feeling the needle prick his skin as she continues with her work. "Thank you for helping me," he adds making her smile, as she barely ever gets a *"thank you"* from her patients, finding this gesture a welcoming one from a stranger.

"You are most welcome," she replies as she continues stitching.

***

Resting on a lounge bed at the Top Deck beside the pool, Joanne sips a cocktail and smiles as she watches Morales walking towards her. He eventually stands over her blocking the sun from her face. "Well, hello there, stranger," she tells him with a sensuous voice.

"Tonight is the last night of the cruise," he says.

"Yes and I was wondering when I was going to see you again."

"It is time we had that drink."

"Oh, it's time, is it?" she asks sarcastically.

"I will call on you tonight," he replies putting his palm against her face. "And I promise, it will be an unforgettable night."

Joanne blushes and takes a moment to reply. "Well, with an offer like that, how can a girl refuse?"

"Schooner bar, eleven o'clock?"

"I will be there, doctor," she replies holding his palm firmly against her face as he winks at her, then walks away.

***

Staggering along the labyrinth of corridors wearing new clothes he purchased from the local market in town, Ethan reaches his stateroom and swipes the boarding card to open his door. He barges into the room and slams the door shut behind him. "Okay," he mutters softly, then removes the SLR camera from his neck strap. He sets the camera on the floor and crawls under the covers exhausted.

15
The last night

The ship sails graciously towards the horizon on this spectacular evening; the last night aboard. The passengers are enjoying it to the full at the busy Schooner Bar, where an entertainer sings a popular music cover while playing the piano, making sure everyone is having a memorable time. Over one hundred passengers are seated around every table and standing by the bar while they enjoy their cocktails and drinks.

At the bar, the bartender gives Morales two freshly prepared cocktails then walks away. Morales casually glances at a corner table where Joanne is happily swaying her head to the rhythm of the music, wearing a sensuous and attractive summer dress.

He then glances up at the CCTV cameras, knowing he's in a blind spot but nevertheless, he leans over the drinks, carefully taking out a small envelope, and cleverly empties a while powder substance into one of the cocktails without attracting any attention to himself.

Morales discreetly mixes the powder in the cocktail with his finger until it's dissolved, glancing around to ensure no one is watching him. Once satisfied, he puts on a smile and walks to the corner table, where he sits down beside Joanne. He gives her the spiked cocktail and clinks her glass with his. "To a special night," he toasts and she clinks her glass back to make a second toast.

"To us," she replies with a warm smile and sips her cocktail. "Wow! What is this?" she asks, finding its sweetness addictive, and she downs the entire cocktail in one satisfying go.

"It's just something I concocted," he replies impishly, also downing his drink in one go making her giggle and laugh. He furtively looks at his wristwatch then smiles at her.

"You have to give me the recipe, but in the meantime, be a star and get me another," she says, making a puppy-dog face and giggling.

"Coming right up," he replies as he stands up holding both empty glasses, and walks towards the bar with an impassive stare.

***

Soaked in sweat, tossing and turning, moving his head vigorously from side to side on the bed, Ethan is having a nightmare. He suddenly lets out a blood curdling scream and, waking himself up, sitting petrified on his bed. He gazes around trying to calm down, and notices it's still dark. He looks at the digital clock by the desk that reads: *"00.57"*.

"Sweet Jesus," Ethan mutters to himself, moaning in pain as his entire body is bruised and aching. He eventually manages to get out of bed and walk into the connecting bathroom. He flicks on the light switch, squinting as the bright light hurts his eyes for a few seconds.

Ethan removes his clothes so he can see his own reflection in the large mirror, to examine his horrific wounds that have been treated and stitched up professionally. "Now I know how Frankenstein felt," he mutters painfully under his breath, leaning forward to the cold-water faucet where he opens the tap. Putting his hands under the running water he splashes cold water onto his unshaven but bruised face, thereby waking up in a flash. He then pops a few pills the female doctor gave him earlier for the pain. "Christ," he remarks as he again splashes his face and takes another look at his sorry reflection on the mirror. "You look like shit," he confirms to himself, turns off the water and walks out of the bathroom.

Flicking on the room light, he observes the SLR camera on the floor and walks towards it, opens the memory card compartment and extracts the SD memory card from inside. He then flips open his laptop on the desk and watches the split screen that is still automatically recording onto the hard drives.

Clicking a button on the keyboard, he now sees the desktop and can hover the *"cursor key"* over the *"US Flag"* APP. He hesitates, gathering the courage to click on it, which he does, and the screen changes to the video recording from the Lapel Pin's camera.

Ethan watches a timeline of the recorded footage from that afternoon in the town: fast forwarding to where he's walking along the ship, boarding the tender, then jumping to the vicious attack in the alleyway, watching the entire event unfold through the camera's wide angle lens. He then jumps to the very end of the fight, just before killing Pavlov.

- Laptop screen in full HD image and clear sound: *shaky POV image, Pavlov's head from the back, as Ethan is about to slit his throat. "This is for Chloe," he says followed by Pavlov's "Suka blyat!" and then Ethan's blood curdling scream as he slits Pavlov's throat and drops his lifeless body to the ground.*

Ethan finds it unbearable to watch and pauses the shaky image, closing the APP with a click while wiping his clammy, sweaty forehead with his shaking hands. He takes several deep breaths in and out to relax. "It was self defence," he mutters to himself trying to calm down, then clicks on the surveillance screen to watch the split screens:

- Top left screen: *The dark examination room as lights are switched off and no one is inside.*

- Top right screen: *Joanne's stateroom also dark and empty.*

- Bottom left screen: *Pavlov's empty bunk at the top and a steward sleeping on the bottom bunk.*

- Bottom right screen: *Morales cabin which is also dark and empty.*

"Tonight is the last night," he says knowingly, viewing the time on the digital clock that now reads: *"01:21."* He stands up without noticing the top left screen: *Morales has switched on the lights of the examination room and is helping a drowsy Joanne into the room, carefully placing her down on the table.*

Ethan has his back to the screen as he opens the wardrobe and decides what clothes to wear.

- Top left screen: *Morales fondles Joanne's unconscious body and rubs his hands all over her breasts.*

Ethan takes out a pair of trousers and a shirt, then sits on the bed. His side is to the screen so he cannot see what is happening in real time at the infirmary. He painfully puts on the trousers, moaning in slight agony, then looks for his shoes on the floor and spots them. "There you are," he says reaching down and grabbing them both. He slowly puts them on, one at a time as he moans in pain with every movement.

- Top left screen: *Morales ripping off Joanne's dress and panties, and climbing on top of her now naked body where he begins to force himself into her, grunting as he penetrates her repeatedly while savagely raping her, knowing she cannot fight back.*

Ethan takes a deep breath to try and regain his strength when he realizes he's hearing distant grunts of pleasure. He turns slowly to the laptop, horrified to be seeing a violent rape automatically recording in real-time, and realising it's Joanne. "God! No!" he shouts, grabs his cell phone and storms frantically out of the room closing the door.

He makes his way slowly, feeling nauseous, along the labyrinth of corridors. Trying to focus on where he is going while holding his cell phone, he clicks on the *"US Flag"* APP, now watching, *A completely naked Morales injecting a syringe into Joanne's arm.* "God, give me strength," he says fearfully as he continues to run as fast as he can.

∗∗∗

Opening a cabinet, Morales picks up a shiny scalpel, admiring its razor-sharp edge while staring at his own reflection on the blade as if he were in a trance. Moments later he snaps out of it and stares back at Joanne's naked body on the examination table. His ejaculated semen is still splattered all over her chest.

Morales is unable to ejaculate inside any woman, due to his sexual frustration and childhood trauma: It was a trauma spanning back decades to when his uncle first abused him at only eight years old. He forced him to perform oral sex, forced him to swallow his semen and then, he cut the boy's eyebrow with the tip of a kitchen knife, as a warning and a threat of what would happen if he ever told anyone about their secret. So frightened Morales endured the sexual abuse until he was sixteen, which was when he gathered enough courage, overwhelmed by years of accumulated hatred, to finally confront and overcome his uncle. While he was being savagely penetrated, screaming in agony, he managed to grab a kitchen knife he had earlier planted under the bed and proceeded to brutally and fatally stab him over one hundred times in a violent rage. Then standing over the body he sliced off his uncle's penis and chewed it up into minced meat with his teeth, thereby ensuring his uncle would never abuse him again, even though he was already dead. This action caused Morales to become mentally unstable and see sexual abuse as a normal way of life. It opened him up to letting his darkest demons run wild, which is why he has to sit over his victims at the moment of climax to show his dominance and power over them.

Morales walks to a counter and sets the scalpel down. He carefully takes a filled flask and pours the liquid solution into the Tupperware container until its filled half way, then he picks up the scalpel. Standing over Joanne he carefully rests the tip of the blade against her lower abdomen, wiping sweat from his forehead before making precise multiple incisions. He opens her abdomen, splashing the table, floor and his own naked body with her blood.

***

Reaching a junction of corridors, Ethan attempts to focus but his head is spinning around. He drops to his knees trying to stop the dizziness. "Come on Ethan, focus!" he shouts and slaps his face several times in desperation.

***

Morales carefully removes the first kidney, placing it into the Tupperware container with great care. He then returns to the examination table where he begins to cut out the second kidney.

***

Ethan stumbles, staggering forward along a corridor. He knows he is lost but is determined to find the infirmary to save Joanne.

***

Morales is now finishing the delicate operation, successfully removing the second kidney from Joanne's mutilated body. He carefully places it into the Tupperware container beside the first kidney while ensuring they are both fully submerged in the liquid solution. He then seals the container with the blue lid and stows it inside the freezer.

He then glances down at his body which is spattered with her blood and looks at Joanne's bloody and mutilated body. Raising his bloodstained hands to his face he touches the scar on his eyebrow, remembering, as he always does, the hatred for his uncle for making that wound when he was eight years old, when it all began and his innocent life changed, forever.

***

Suddenly, the infirmary doors are forcibly kicked open and an exhausted Ethan storms into the long corridor passing the reception area. He kicks open the closed examination room door, watching in horror as he is too late, it is empty. Morales and Joanne are gone and all that remains is a bloodstained examination room and table.

"God, no!" he mutters leaning against the door so he doesn't fall over. Then he remembers what Pavlov told him before he was killed. *"From Deck D, just like the rest of them."* Ethan stands muttering, "Deck D," then he runs slowly out of the infirmary.

***

Acting as if she passed out, Morales walks Joanne, fully dressed and held closely in his arms, along "Deck D." He takes her to the corner railings where he cautiously studies the area, making sure there are no witnesses watching. Loud music vibrates from the lower deck as a party is in full swing and passengers are having a blast, singing, shouting and enjoying themselves. Once satisfied, Morales mercilessly picks Joanne up and lifts her over the railing. He hears her soft moans of pain as she is beginning to wake up. And he watches the menacing dark cold ocean below, as there is no turning back.

"For God's sake, Morales, don't do it!" exclaims Ethan with difficulty as he pants and leans against a door, aiming his cell phone at Morales recording a video of the act. "Let her go. It's over!"

Holding her weight in his arms, Morales turns to Ethan with a mischievous grin. "It's not over, Mister Moore," he replies, knowingly, "and this will never end, as there is too much money involved and the demand is far greater than you can possibly imagine."

Joanne's agonising moans grow louder until Morales turns around, facing the railing and maliciously throws her overboard without a second thought or care. Ethan lets out a blood curdling scream as he runs forward, holding onto the railing. They both watch Joanne plummet towards the dark, cold waters below where she eventually splashes in, legs first.

"Stop the ship!" shouts Ethan, but his voice is muffled by the loud vibrating music playing below deck. "Woman overboard! Stop the ship!" he shouts again.

"Don't bother, detective," says a mischievous Morales, "she will be dead any second now, if she's not dead already."

"You bastard!" he yells, throwing himself at Morales and they engage in a hand-to-hand combat fight. Both men are trained in Martial Arts, but Morales is the strongest.

"If it's any consolation, your daughter was one of the best fucks I have ever had," taunts Morales.

"I am going to kill you just like I killed your Russian friend, you sick bastard!"

Morales notices how weak Ethan is, observing the many wounds he has, so he maliciously punches the wounds hard, making him bleed. Ethan yells in sheer agony as they both continue the violent and brutal fight.

"Don't flatter yourself, Mister Moore. I have many other friends to take Viktor's place," he reveals. But he misjudges Ethan's surprise kick which renders him unconscious as he blacks out.

***

Morales gradually opens his eyes and finds he is inside his own examination room staring up at the ceiling, which means he is on the table. Feeling his wrists are bound he tries desperately to break free but finds he is strapped down by his legs and arms, completely immobilised.

Ethan takes the Tupperware container from the freezer, setting it carefully on the counter. He watches the recording on his phone of Morales extracting the kidneys from Joanne and how he stored them into the container. Now he understands what Morales has been involved in, the organ trafficking trade as well as the human trafficking sex trade.

"Let me go," mutters Morales trying to escape.

"You ran a black-market organ trafficking operation using innocent girls you first raped and then killed, dumping their bodies overboard," explains an overwhelmed Ethan, putting his face near Morale's face, "to cover your tracks, and you did it just for money!"

"It's the perfect crime, Mister Moore. No witnesses. No bodies. They just go missing," confesses Morales, "and with time, forgotten."

Ethan holds an empty syringe which he found in a cabinet, in his left hand. He stands over Morales holding a full medical bottle in his right hand.

"You injected her with this, didn't you?"

"I injected all of them with that, yes. Even your slut daughter."

Ethan glances at the label on the bottle, which reads *"Tetrodotoxin."* He inserts the needle into the bottle pulling back on the plunger, filling up the syringe until it is completely full to the rim.

"What are you going to do?" asks a now concerned Morales.

"I am going to give you a taste of your own medicine, doctor," he replies, setting the bottle on the counter. Then without any warning he forcibly stabs the needle into Morales's arm, jamming the plunger down hard and forcing the liquid into his vein. Morales fidgets, trying to break free but is unable to.

Ethan throws the empty syringe on the counter and shows his phone to Morales. They watch the recorded footage of Morales removing Joanne's kidneys. "She was your last victim, you worthless shit!"

"You have to understand. It was just business. You were the only father who came looking for your daughter."

"You chose the wrong girl," he replies once again, leaning his face closer to Morales's face, hearing his breathing slow down as the Tetrodotoxin takes its deadly effect. "How many innocent women did you butcher?"

"Hundreds," replies a now delirious Morales. "I have lost track. I, I," he adds trying to stay focussed, "keep a record, it's all in my... in... my diary."

"Was my daughter dead when you threw her overboard?"

"The drug," replies Morales tediously, "doesn't, kill you. It just paralyses you. You can... still... feel... just cannot... move."

"You mean all those women drowned?" asks a shocked Ethan.

"If they, survived the fall, yes, they cannot swim, because… because," tries to explain a clearly drugged Morales, who is having trouble, "of the drug… so they… will drown… soon enough."

"How much money have you made at the cost of all those innocent girls?"

"Millions, I will, give you however much… you want, in exchange, for my… for my… release."

"No amount of money can ever bring back my daughter," replies an indignant Ethan who picks up the bloodstained scalpel from the counter and shows it to Morales.

"Yoooooou… are… not… not… a doctor."

"And you, you bastard, are no saint!" he replies stabbing the scalpel into Morales's arm then twisting it, watching his eyes express pain but he is unable to move. "That was for your first victim," he adds. Then Ethan erratically stabs the scalpel repeatedly in a wild, frenzied rage, over and over into Morales's arms, hands, legs and shoulders. "A hundred victims, deserve a hundred stabs, Hugo!" he shouts getting blood spattered all over his face and clothes.

"Pleeeeeeeeeesssssssssssssssssssss," moans Morales in complete agony, but motionless while Ethan continues the horrendous stabbing reducing Morales's body to pulp.

"That's what Chloe must have begged you for, but you never showed her any mercy, now, did you?" shouts Ethan completely enraged and in tears. Then, he suddenly stops to take a break, watching Morales bleed all over from his horrendous wounds. Ethan looks at the kidneys in the container, then stares back at Morales. "Oh no!" he yells and slaps Morales across the face. "You won't get out of it so easy."

***

Ethan pushes Morales in a wheelchair towards "Deck D." He slams the chair hard against the same railing where Joanne was thrown overboard. Then he leans into Morales's ear noticing how he stares aimlessly at the darkness in front of them.

"Is this where you threw my daughter overboard?" he asks, but gets no reply as Morales can no longer talk. But Ethan knows deep down in his heart this is the spot. "Then you can ask her for forgiveness because tonight I am not a police detective but a grieving father, not only to my daughter but also to all those other victims you killed and dumped overboard like trash!" he says coldly.

Impulsively, Ethan grabs Morales, lifting him onto the railing, when suddenly Martin kicks Ethan in the back. He lands on his face on the deck, while Morales crashes hard beside him.

"You should have stayed in the Cayman Islands, Mister Moore," he says, brutally lifting Ethan up and holding him over the railing.

"If there is one thing I hate, it's to see a corrupt officer," replies Ethan, and with all his might and strength he kicks Martin hard in the chest, forcing him to drop Ethan on the deck. "Even if it's a lousy rent-a-cop!" he adds, walking towards Martin, forcibly punching his face in repeatedly.

"You arranged for the sex trafficking victims to go ashore and then covered their tracks, didn't you?" he yells, continuing to pound Martin's now bloodstained face, over and over again without mercy.

"Fuck you," utters Martin trying to stand up.

"No, fuck you!" shouts Ethan as he stands back and kicks Martin so hard that he falls backwards onto the railing. Ethan immediately charges towards him, lifts him up and throws him overboard. Martin screams as he plummets to the cold ocean below, splashing head first into the water, resulting in his immediate death.

"Bastard!" shouts Ethan as he walks over to Morales. He lifts him to his feet, staring into his now petrified eyes, then pushes him overboard. He watches him plummet into the dark and cold waters below, splashing in feet first, finally riding the world of an unscrupulous monster. Ethan breaks down into tears as he continues to stare at the dark waters below, knowing justice has finally been served.

Morales survived the landing into the ocean but has two broken legs, just like Chloe and many of his other victims suffered, giving a poetic justice to his cruelty. As his body bobs on the surface he watches the ship sail further away into the horizon. He softly moans in sheer horrendous agony, fully aware he will be drowning any second now as he is unable to swim or remain afloat.

Suddenly, an unexplained force rises from beneath the waves, grabs his legs, pulls him down making sure he drowns a painful death. This force can be best described as a collective energy from all the innocent victims who suffered the same fate. They have been waiting for this moment to obtain their revenge, as they drowned alone in these perilous waters leaving no trace behind, seeking their own justice from the monster responsible for their untimely deaths. Morales continues swallowing water as he is being forced further downwards, where he eventually drowns and disappears, forever.

***

The ship is berthed at its dock beside the pier by the terminal building in the busy Miami port. Hundreds of passengers are disembarking from the ship as hundreds of new passengers continue to arrive. The ship is doing its weekly turnaround and is set to sail later that afternoon.

At the back of the ship, an ambulance is waiting with its rear doors wide open, so as not to attract the attention of the passengers embarking on the gangway in the centre of the ship. Two paramedics carefully walk a bruised Ethan, on a stretcher, out a rear gangway of the ship flanked by four FBI agents. Hank follows carrying Ethan's laptop, two hard drives and SLR camera, and then Captain Hills, who is holding the Tupperware container with Joanne's kidneys inside, the envelope with the mutilated photographs together with Morales's black notebook. They all make their way towards the ambulance and the paramedics carefully push the stretcher into the back of the vehicle.

Hills and Hank stand outside the ambulance waiting, as one of the paramedics fixes a drip into Ethan's arm. Three agents also wait near the ambulance while Ethan's FBI friend John, the fourth agent, climbs into the back, to remain by Ethan's side.

"The e-mail you sent me was horrific, Ethan," says John totally stunned. "You helped save many lives by dismantling this operation."

"Thank you for coming to my rescue, John."

"That's what friends do," he replies and tenderly holds Ethan's hand comforting his old friend. "Now rest and I will get your full statement at the hospital later on after they patch you up," he adds. Then John climbs out of the ambulance and stands beside Hills. "I will take the evidence now, Captain, for our investigation."

"Certainly, John," replies the eager Hills, nodding his head to Hank who immediately hands the laptop, hard drives and SLR camera over to John.

"It's all there," confirms Ethan." All the evidence, video footage of the doctor caught in the act, pictures of some other victims, motives and confessions."

"We watched the footage on your computer, Ethan," says a distraught Hank. "It's monstrous what they did."

"Sick doesn't even come close," says an equally distraught Hills.

"Hopefully with this breakthrough it will help us to better understand how crimes are committed aboard these floating cities, so we can finally curb the crime and save lives."

"You honestly believe this is just the tip of the iceberg, don't you?" asks Hills.

"That somewhere out there in other cruise ships similar crimes are being committed?" suggests John, knowingly. "Yes I do," he confirms and gives a confident combined nod at everyone. "If you'll now excuse me gentlemen." He joins his three waiting FBI agents and they walk towards the cruise terminal building.

"There is something that I just don't understand," says a bewildered Hills.

"What's that?" asks Ethan.

"In your statement, you said Morales escaped and jumped overboard to keep from getting caught, knowing full well he would probably drown."

"He must have committed suicide in the prospect of facing jail time," replies an emotionless Ethan.

"Yet on the video feed from the surveillance camera we saw, you had him strapped to the table," replies Hills totally baffled. "There is no way in hell he could have escaped from you."

Hank clears his throat and interrupts, "The video feed was interrupted immediately after he confessed to the crimes, Captain, so for all intents and purposes, we got our man!"

"Yes but how did he get to the deck to jump in the first place, that's what I don't understand. Why was the feed terminated?" asks Hills perceiving Ethan threw him overboard.

"Must have been interference from the ship's radar systems, I guess," interrupts Ethan, glancing over at Hank looking for some more help.

"Radar, my ass!" remarks Hills sarcastically, knowing there is more to the statement Ethan made. "Cut the crap, Ethan. You know damn well if you had anything to do with his death the department can't afford the publicity of having a rogue cop on the streets."

"We also have him groping that girl a few days ago on tape, sir," says Hank trying to deflect Hills from questioning Ethan.

"Ethan," says Hills, leaning further into the back of the ambulance, "be straight with me, from a friend, to a friend, you know I will protect you, for Chloe's sake," he adds emotionally, "just tell me the truth. How did the doctor end up going overboard?"

Ethan slowly smiles while staring at both Hills and Hank noticing the two paramedics waiting in the background having a smoke. "Poetic justice, Captain." He remarks with a dominant tone. "That bastard won't harm anyone else, anymore, and that is what really matters."

"You saw him hit the water?"

"And I watched him drown," he replies with a stern expression.

"They say revenge is a dish best served cold," says Hank, "I don't suppose it gets any colder than the ocean."

"All right then," replies Hills nodding his head in support of his friend. "If I had been in your shoes and I had him like you did, I would have thrown him overboard in a heartbeat," he adds with a smile on his face. "But again, that's me," he remarks, clearing his throat. "I will go along with your statement as God knows these radars sometimes get a glitch in them."

"Thank you, Captain," replies Ethan with a sigh of relief.

"You did good, Ethan. Maybe next time you will use your vacation time to actually go and enjoy yourself," he adds, giving him a wink. Then he glances at the waiting paramedics, "all right, take him to the hospital."

One of the paramedics climbs into the back of the ambulance while the second one closes the rear doors, jumps behind the wheel and drives slowly away, leaving Hills and Hank standing alone at the pier staring at the Tupperware container.

"On the book we recovered from Morale's cabin, I counted

two hundred and sixty-eight initials, Captain."

"Better make that two hundred and sixty nine, Hank," replies Hills noticing Joanne's kidneys inside the container.

"My God, what a monster! Those poor girls never stood a chance, did they?" he replies, as they both walk towards the cruise terminal building, passing many workers who are busy loading and unloading pallets of stores and other provisions onto the ship. They also walk past the same man who has been waiting for hours by his parked SUV for Pavlov to bring him the requested kidneys, unaware of what has transpired.

The kidneys are on their way to the hospital where hopefully they can be used to save someone else's life, so at least Joanne's death will not be in vain.

Hills walks into the terminal building, but Hank stops to take one final look at the impressive ship where hundreds of passengers are boarding completely ecstatic, as they are about to start their cruise.

16
A New Beginning

Boarding *"The Ghost of the High Seas"* cruise ship, berthed opposite her sister ship the *"Poseidon of the Seas,"* at the other end of the Miami port, are hundreds of passengers about to begin their six-day cruise.

They are unaware that watching from "Deck A" above, is a uniformed officer who is meticulously observing every passenger entering the ship. He has an emotionless expression on his face, until he soon spots a stunning young woman, in her early twenties wearing an attractive short dress, who has a beautiful figure. She walks alone onto the ship with an excited look on her face, as she is ready to have fun and enjoy her week-long cruise.

The officer enters the ship through a nearby door and walks into the impressive Grand foyer, a similar layout to the Grand foyer on the Poseidon cruise ship. He leans down from a higher deck and carefully watches for the stunning young woman to grace the foyer with her presence. He holds on tight to the railing, patiently waiting but also observing how every passenger who comes into the foyer is completely flabbergasted at the beautiful surroundings and luxurious decorative items the ship offers. Then, the young woman comes into view, and she too is overwhelmed by the amazing foyer.

The mysterious officer watching from above opens his eyes even wider. When suddenly, a young security officer, Ivaylo in his thirties, wearing a smart white uniform stands beside him.

"Find out if she is alone and what stateroom she is in," he tells Ivaylo softly with an Eastern European accent.

Ivaylo doesn't reply and just walks away leaving the man clutching the railing tighter with a malicious gaze on his face. His cold eyes watch closely as Ivaylo soon intercepts the young girl with a bright and friendly smile on his face.

"Welcome aboard," says Ivaylo, also with an Eastern European accent. He notices how the young woman is impressed with his good looks and charm.

"Thank you," she says with a Bulgarian accent.

"My name is Ivaylo and I am one of the security officers on board the ship," he says, and politely extends his hand watching how she blushes, and happily shakes.

"I am Nadezhda," she says shyly, "it means hope."

"How nice," he replies, "where are you from, Nadezhda?"

"I'm from Bulgaria but you can call me, Nadia."

"Well Nadia, it will be my pleasure to escort you to your stateroom and I will be happy to answer any questions you may have along the way. Tell me, are you travelling alone?"

"Yes I am," she answers, innocently, not knowing how harmful her few words can be. "My parents paid for this cruise as a graduation present, so I am all alone and I am going to have the best time of my life. I am going to party, get my body tanned and who knows? Maybe a little romance, no?" she adds, giving too much information to this stranger whom she has just met but trusts his position and uniform, so the least on her mind is danger.

"Tell me, what is your cabin number?"

"Uhm," she replies as she doesn't remember, but soon takes out her boarding card. "Here it is, 6204," she says with a brighter smile.

"Then we must go in the elevator to deck number seven," he says, casually placing her hand on his arm, walking her slowly towards one of the four elevators in the foyer. "This will be a cruise you will never forget," he adds knowingly.

"Oh, thank you! I can't wait!" she replies with anticipation for a memorable and joyous vacation. She does not notice Ivaylo giving a malicious smirk to the officer watching from above, as they know they have just found one of their many victims on this cruise.

Epilogue

The International Cruise Victims Association is helping change legislation to make cruising safer for all passengers and crew. Many of the events portrayed in this novel have been based on the real true events that many victims have endured. Below are a few of the countless of true life statements from victims and family members that have been obtained with the kind permission of "The International Cruise Victims Association" where the below statements have been extracted from and generously authorised for publication in this novel by its president with the hope that everyone is made aware of the reality of how unsafe it can be to be on a cruise ship in International waters without taking into consideration your surroundings and letting your guard down.

This novel is in memory of my friend and former president of the late Mr Kendall Carver and the over 250 persons who have gone missing on the High Seas through the years and the hundreds of other victims who have been subjected to sexual or other forms of abusive crimes and even deaths aboard cruise ships around the world. More tragic stories can be read in the International Cruise Victims Associations official website where you can also help.

https://internationalcruisevictims.org/victim-stories/

Statement from Jim Walker

(WALKER & O'NEILL P.A.) MARITIME LAWYERS,
SUITE 430, 7301 S.W. 57TH COURT,
MIAMI, FLORIDA, U.S.A.
Tel: 305 995 5300

Cruise lines have a unique business model. Rather than incorporating their business and registering their cruise ships in the United States, they incorporate in distant countries like Liberia (Royal Caribbean), Panama (Carnival Corporation) or Bermuda (Norwegian Cruise Line and Princess Cruises) and register their ships in countries outside of the United States in order to avoid all U.S. income taxes, U.S. wage and labour laws (minimum wage and overtime regulations) and occupational health and safety laws.

Unlike the airline industry that is closely regulated by the Federal Aviation Administration (FAA), there is no U.S. federal agency regulating the operations of cruise lines. The FAA has the authority to shut an entire fleet of planes down for safety reasons, but there is no such governance of cruise ships by U.S. authorities. A ship is subject only to the law of the country under whose flag it sails. The regulations in those countries are much more lax than in the United States.

Cruise ships are supposed to follow guidelines set by the International Maritime Organization (IMO). But the United Nations (UN), does not have any authority to enforce its own guidelines. It cannot impose fines or criminal sanctions against cruise lines that ignore its recommendations. This obligation of enforcement is the responsibility of the flag states, like the Bahamas, Panama, or Bermuda, which have little to no interest in overseeing U.S. based cruise ships on the high seas. These countries have few laws governing cruise ships to enforce, which is the main reason why cruise lines register their ships in such jurisdictions in the first place.

As a result, a cruise ship flying a flag of convenience, from places like Panama or the Bahamas, is virtually a lawless environment. There are relatively few employees on cruise ships from the U.S., the United Kingdom or Canada, except perhaps a few dozen staff members such as singers, dancers, or musicians, who compromise less than 5 percent of the cruise ship's crew roster. The cooks, cleaners, waiters, bartenders, and cabin attendants on cruise ships are primarily from India, Indonesia, or the Philippines.

Crew members on these ships often work 12 hours a day, 7 days a week, for as many as eight to ten months, and for as little as less than $2.00 per hour. There are no rights or mechanism for crew members to join labour unions. Cruise lines quickly terminate the employment of crew members who complain about their work hours or conditions. Cruise lines have inserted one-sided arbitration clauses in their employment contracts, which prohibit crew members from filing lawsuits in the U.S. and require the application of the law of the country where the cruise ship is registered which provide few rights to overworked or injured seafarers.

Cruise passengers leaving ports in the U.S. like Miami, New Orleans, Galveston, Los Angeles and Seattle, typically do not realize that they are subject to the laws of the flags of convenience where the ship is registered. Most cruise lines hire crew members from hiring agencies which do not perform background checks on their prospective employees. Non-U.S. crew members are not subject to screening on sexual predator data bases which do not exist in countries like India or Islands in the Caribbean. The majority of rapes and other sexual crimes which are committed on cruise ships are committed by crew members.

Although the U.S. Federal Bureau of Investigations (FBI) has jurisdiction over cruise ships flying with flags of convenience, when a U.S. passenger is a victim of a violent crime, the FBI has a poor record of investigating violent crimes and rapes on cruise ships. The vast majority of rapists on cruise ships are not arrested or prosecuted but are flown back to their countries free to seek employment on a different cruise ship operated by another one of the cruise lines which do not share crimes committed by an employee against a cruise guest.

The International Cruise Victims (ICV) organization was founded in December of 2005 when families of victims killed or raped on cruise ships banded together to seek legislation to deal with situations of lost or raped individuals on the high seas. They met while they attended a hearing before the U.S. Congress on the issue of cruise ship crime. Kendall Carver, who became the President of the ICV, was the father of 40-year-old Merrian Carver, who went overboard from a Celebrity cruise ship under mysterious circumstances. Even though the cruise line knew that this woman was missing from the cruise ship, the cruise line did not notify the FBI or other law authorities. After hiring a private investigator to board the ship and investigate the crime, Mr. Carver learned that his daughter's cabin steward had allegedly noticed that Ms. Carver was missing from her cabin early during the week-long cruise and had notified his supervisor who instructed the crew member to "not worry about it and keep working." Her personal items were unceremoniously disposed of by the cruise line at the end of her cruise.

George and Maureen Smith, the parents of George Smith III, were notified that their son went overboard from a Royal Caribbean cruise ship during his honeymoon cruise under disturbing circumstances. The cruise line knew that another cruise passenger was videotaped remarking that he had thrown George overboard, but the cruise line concealed the tape from the family and blamed George for over-drinking.

Laurie Dishman, a 35-year-old woman from Sacramento, California, was raped by a ship security guard during a birthday cruise which she took with a life-long friend. When she reported the crime, the ship's security department forced her to prepare repeated statements before it would permit her to seek medical treatment. When she finally was allowed to see the ship physician, he ordered her to return to her cabin and collect the sheets from the bed where the crime occurred and any other items she felt were relevant.

These families, all who were treated shabbily by the cruise lines, thereafter, attended six (6) congressional hearings over the course of the next five years to lobby lawmakers to enact legislation to improve the safety of cruise ships.

In 2010, Congress passed the Cruise Vessel Security and Safety Act which, for the first time, requires the cruise lines to report to the U.S. Coast Guard (and later, the Department of Transportation) and disclose certain crimes to the public such as: suspicious deaths, missing U.S. nationals, assaults with serious bodily injury, thefts over $10,000, and sexual assaults. The ICV was also successful in lobbying Congress to pass legislation which requires cruise ships to be equipped with rape kits and anti-retroviral medications for rape victims, as well as automatic non-overboard systems which will instantly alert the bridge whenever someone goes over the rails of a cruise ship into the water so that the ship can initiate rescue efforts.

Mr. Carver's goals were to create transparency in crime and missing passenger reporting and install man overboard systems on cruise ships. The cruise lines fought back vigorously. The cruise industry treated Mr. Carver like a villain and essentially painted a bulls-eye on his back. The cruise lines spent tens of millions of dollars lobbying Congress to oppose Mr. Carver's proposed legislation. But ultimately Mr. Carver prevailed.

Over the past dozen years, I've seen numerous cruise executives and cruise line defense lawyers come and go – as well as PR crisis managers and lobbyists in the cruise industry trade organization. Many have left the industry. But the ICV is still standing, and cruising is safer today because of Kendall Carver.

***

Statement from Kendall Carver

https://internationalcruisevictims.org/stories/merrian-carver/

Merrian Carver, a 40-year-old woman, disappeared from a Royal Caribbean cruise to Alaska in August of 2004. Her Steward reported her missing for 5 days to his supervisor and was told to *"just do your job and forget it."* At the end of the cruise, Cruise line officials simply boxed up her belongings and even disposed of most of her items.

Royal Caribbean Cruise Line made no attempt to contact either the FBI or her family when she turned up missing and had not used her room. Cambridge Police took several weeks to even trace her to the cruise ship delaying the search for almost one month.

Once the Cruise line was contacted, it took them 3 days to confirm she had been on the cruise, 26 days after she had disappeared. They then confirmed that she was on the ship and after the second night did not use her room. However, they also indicated that this was not uncommon since she could have stayed with someone else and could have gotten off in Vancouver and they would be not record kept to confirm her departure from the boat. Since we could not really determine what happened we hired Private Investigators plus a Boston Law firm to start a major investigation. By then the trail was cold.

Our goal was to speak to someone on the ship that had seen Merrian. Attempts by the Private Investigator met with only frustrations indicating that there was no reports issued by the Steward and nothing unusual happened during the Cruise that Merrian was on. Finally, on November 4, 2004, an investigator was sent onto the ship. He was then advised that he could not speak to anyone of the ship and they would not provide the name of the Steward that had taken care of Merrian's room. They also indicated that the videos were erased every two or three weeks and there was no review of the videos concerning our missing daughter.

Since no progress was being made, subpoenas were first issued on December 2, 2004 for information concerning our daughter. The law firms then tried to arrange for an interview with the Steward and after meeting with no success, it was necessary to obtain a Court Order at the end of December to require that the Steward and the head of the hotel be disposed.

These depositions took place on January 16th and 17th of the year 2005. At that point, we realized that our daughter had been reported missing daily for the last 5 days of the cruise and nothing was done to search for her. Also we learned that the cruise line had disposed most of her items.

Again, another subpoena was issued on January 24, 2005 for additional material. By February 9th only one item had been sent to use as a result of these two subpoenas. That was a poor-quality picture of Merrian getting on the boat.

Finally, we made the decision to go directly to the Board of Directors and CEO pleading for their assistance. Each member of the Board received the depositions showing the cover-up. No one from the Board responded to this plea but finally the Head of Rick Management called to indicated that we would receive the requested material in our subpoenas plus any other material in their possession concerning Merrian.

We did obtain documents written by Cruise Line employees setting up the cover-up of any information concerning our daughter's case.

We also determined from their own documents that they had reviewed the video's concerning our daughter on the 26th day of her disappearance. Also, videos were on a 30-day cycle. This means that there should have been a video of Merrian. The material we had been given over the months was inaccurate about that fact the videos are kept on 2 to 3 weeks and there was no review by them of these videos.

After additional months went by, we still did not have all requested information so started the process to take legal action against the Royal Caribbean Cruise Line.

***

Statement from Jamie Barnett

https://internationalcruisevictims.org/stories/ashley-barnett/

On October 14, 2005, my daughter, Ashley Barnett, her boyfriend, and two other couples, boarded Carnival Cruise Line's Paradise in Long Beach, California for a 3-day cruise to celebrate her 25th birthday. Less than twenty-four hours later, Ashley was dead.

According to her boyfriend, he and Ashley went to the casino and a concert, and then returned to their cabin. At approximately 2:30AM, there was an alleged disagreement. The boyfriend returned to the casino, while Ashley retired for the evening. Her boyfriend said that he returned to the cabin at approximately 4AM and joined Ashley, who was asleep. Early-afternoon he awoke and went upstairs to join friends, leaving Ashley, who he says was asleep, to rest. He returned to the cabin at approximately 2PM and was unable to awaken Ashley. He ran into the hallway screaming that his girlfriend wasn't breathing. Another passenger heard his cries and responded, telling him to call 911.

A nurse arrived and began CPR. An emergency broadcast was made to summon the ship's doctor. The doctor arrived but efforts to resuscitate Ashley were unsuccessful. According to the ship's records, she was pronounced dead at 2:45PM.

At approximately 6:00 PM, I learned of this nightmare from the ship's nurse, who informed me of my daughter's death. She had no answers as to what had happened to her. I demanded to speak with her boyfriend, but I was told that he was currently in questioning.

Later, I was informed that he had been cleared from the questioning, but declined to speak with me. Because the boat was docked in Ensenada, the Mexican authorities boarded the ship to determine if a homicide had been committed. The FBI was also notified. Later that night, with her boyfriend and the rest of the group on board, the Paradise set sail. Though the ship was scheduled to return to the Long Beach port within 36 hours, Ashley was left behind, alone in a Mexican morgue.

The following day, her boyfriend contacted me. He claimed not to know what had happened to my daughter, but continued to say that some of his medications were missing – Methadone and Vicodin.

When the ship returned to Long Beach, the FBI began its own investigation. As per their request, I was waiting at the harbour. I believed the FBI would find answers as to what happened to my daughter. I stood in the rain for four hours. Finally, the agents interviewed me; however, they revealed very little.

Five days after her death, my daughter's body reached the United States.. The process of getting her home was both tedious and torturous. I hired a private pathologist to conduct a forensic autopsy. His study indicated that her organs were healthy and her body was in pristine condition, with some evidence of alcohol consumption. There were no signs of trauma. Weeks later we learned the cause of death. Ashley died of the toxic effects of methadone.

Ashley would not have taken methadone. Ashley was adamantly anti-drug, and she would never have knowingly taken methadone. To prove this, we requested a test of Ashley's hair follicles. The results were clear. No drugs, including methadone, were found in her beautiful, long hair. The test was unequivocally "negative" for habitual drug use.

How did this drug end up in her beautiful, healthy body? Her boyfriend claims that he would never have given her this drug. A year and a half has passed since Ashley's death, and our question remains, "Who did?" Despite four trips to meet with the authorities in Ensenada, Mexico, we have no answers. To date, the FBI investigation remains "open", but to our knowledge, no continuing action is underway.

I wake up every morning, wishing I could hold my daughter just one more time. And I pray that no other mother ever has to live this nightmare.

***

Statement for Dianne Brimble

https://internationalcruisevictims.org/stories/dianne-brimble/

For two years, Dianne had saved to take a cruise around the South Pacific. Although she was the mother of three, she was only able to save enough to take her youngest daughter, Tahlia, with her on the trip of a lifetime...

On September 23rd, 2002, the P&O Pacific Sky departed Sydney, Australia. Dianne and Tahlia boarded the ship, along with Dianne's sister, Alma Wood, and Alma's daughter, Kari Ann. All four had planned to share a cabin for the 10-day/9-night cruise.

As they embarked on their cruise, Dianne and her accompanying family members enjoyed a "sail-away" party, which gave them a chance to relax, have a couple of cocktails, and watch the sun go down. Following the party, they decided to have dinner and talk about their plans for the following day. After dinner, Alma, Kari Ann, and Tahlia decided to head back to the cabin and call it an early night. Dianne accompanied them back to the cabin to kiss Tahlia "goodnight", and later left for the nightclub.

The following morning, Alma realized that Dianne had not returned to their cabin. At breakfast-time, Alma had her paged but was later called to the ship's Medical Centre, where she was told that Dianne had passed away. Her naked body had been found on the floor of a cabin, occupied by four unknown men.

As the cruise continued on to Noumea, Dianne's daughter, sister, and niece, were forced to endure an additional two days on the ship, before they could disembark and fly back home to Australia. At the same time, remaining family members in Australia had been provided with no other details, other than the fact that Dianne had died.

237

It wasn't until detectives boarded the ship in Noumea and continued on the cruise that her family members become suspicious about the circumstances surrounding Dianne's demise.

After a number of weeks, the family finally learned that Dianne had consumed a large amount of GHB or GBH (Great Bodily Harm – A date-rape drug also known as Liquid Fantasy), which contributed to her death. This "so-called" fact, combined with a litany of delays and excuses, made it extremely difficult for the family to comprehend exactly what had taken place.

A Coroner's inquest only began in Sydney, Australia, in March 2006. The investigation into Dianne's cause of death is still underway, which has currently uncovered a number of dreadful circumstances surrounding her death. There is no doubt that something happened to Dianne over which she had no control. The cruise operator has a number of questions that still need to be answered. Hopefully, those answers will be presented when the inquest resumes on June 13th, 2006.

The family's reasons for posting this story are to…

Highlight the circumstances, surrounding Dianne's assault and death. Stop this same tragedy from happening to other cruise passengers. Contribute to changing current cruise line security procedures. Ensure that any individuals responsible, who may have had an involvement or the ability to have prevented Dianne's death, be held.

***

Statement for Rebecca Coriam

https://internationalcruisevictims.org/stories/rebecca-coriam/

In June 2010, a 23-year-old British citizen named Rebecca Coriam was interviewed in London for a shipboard position with Disney Cruise. She was hired over hundreds of other applicants, and received four months of training at Disney facilities in Florida. She then worked for four months on cruises to and from the Bahamas, after which she returned to Britain for two months.

Her next assignment was working with other young people on board the Disney Wonder, based in Los Angeles. She was on board the ship when it left port for a Mexican cruise on March 21, 2011. She sent a message via Facebook to her parents in Britain that she would call them the next day. Their next report was from a Disney official saying that Rebecca had missed her work shift and could not be located. Since then, despite some evidence suggesting that she may still be alive, there have been no confirmed sightings of Rebecca Coriam.

The mysterious case has attracted international attention and allegations that Disney was not totally forthcoming with information. "The investigation into Rebecca's disappearance was appalling," said Stephen Mosley, MP for the City of Chester, home of the Coriam family.

The last confirmed sighting of Rebecca was on March at 5:45 a.m., about three hours before she was scheduled to begin work. A shipboard security camera recorded her presence in a crew area, talking on an internal telephone. She reportedly appeared to be upset. A young man walked up to her and asked if everything was all right.

She clearly replied, "Yeah, fine," after which she hung up.

After she failed to show up for work, crew searched the ship but found no sign of Rebecca. U.S. and Mexican navy vessels searched international waters where the Wonder had been sailing, also with no result.

Three days after her disappearance, a detective from the Bahamas, where the Wonder is registered, flew to the ship to investigate. He reportedly spent several days on board, but nothing is known what, if anything, came of the investigation.

Rebecca's parents, Mike and Annmaria Coriam, flew from England to Los Angeles, where they met the Wonder upon its return to port. They have said that the Bahamanian detective told them that he had investigated for only one day, not several, and that he interviewed only a few crew members and no passengers. They also said that they were brought on board the Wonder only after the passengers had disembarked.

They said the captain told them he believed that Rebecca had been washed overboard from the crew pool area, a story they found implausible because of the high protective walls around it. (The crew pool is on Deck 5 of the ship.) They later met with Disney executives and with the woman with whom Rebecca had been talking on the phone. Later they were brought to her cabin and given her belongings.

In early May 2011, a few weeks after Rebecca's parents returned home, her bank sent them an e-mail saying that someone had tried to gain access to one of her accounts on April 19. "The fact that her credit card's been used could only mean someone has stolen it or she's still alive," Mike Coriam told a British newspaper. The card was not among her possessions.

In September, an uncle of Rebecca's said the password to her Facebook account had been changed. He did not know by whom.

One day before the anniversary of her disappearance, her father received an e-mail from a woman who said she was "85 percent sure" she had seen Rebecca with a dark-haired man in Venice, Italy, the previous August. The family's website had roused her memory, the woman said. "It was very upsetting for everyone to think she could be out there somewhere after all this time," her uncle said. However, he noted, Rebecca's passport was among the items her parents retrieved from the ship.

That October, a British journalist sailed on the Wonder and discreetly asked questions. Several crew members who had been on the ship at the time of Rebecca's disappearance spoke to him on condition of anonymity. They suggested that more was known about her fate than Disney or the Bahamian police had publicly admitted.

The journalist concluded that Rebecca, an avid jogger, had probably slipped and fallen while jogging along a Deck 4 track. However, none of the security cameras in that area showed any sign of her. A crew member told him that Rebecca had gone overboard from the crew pool on Deck 5, and that this was common knowledge on board. "Disney knows exactly what happened," one worker said. "Everything here is taped." Noting the high walls surrounding the pool, and an abundance of security cameras, the journalist was sceptical.

The possessions reclaimed by Rebecca's parents included a slipper, or pair of slippers, which reportedly were found near the crew pool. However, a crew member said they were not the size or style that Rebecca would wear.

The Coriams agreed that they were too small for her, and said no forensics had ever been done on them.

Describing Rebecca as always cheerful and upbeat, her parents dismiss the idea of suicide, as do her friends among the crew. "[W]e know she would never harm herself," said her father. "We just know. That's why we have been totally mystified from day one." The Coriams said Disney officials had told them that Rebecca was drunk and furious on the footage, banging her head into the walls, but the video gave no evidence to support these claims. They also said the woman on the other end of the phone conversation told them Rebecca had been upset initially, but quickly cooled down. At the end of the talk, she said, Rebecca announced that she was going to her cabin.

"We've never believed she simply disappeared overboard and

drowned," said Mike Coriam almost two months later. "Maybe she fell in the water and was picked up by a fishing boat. Maybe she lost her memory and is in a little village in Mexico. Maybe she was attacked. Maybe she was on board after all and got off."

Whatever the truth, the British journalist has said that the Coriams have received no further updates from Disney on the progress of the investigation, and that the Bahamian detective has never returned any of his phone calls. The Coriams have been joined in their criticism of the investigation by British government officials, Rebecca's friends among the crew, and advocates for victims of other incidents on cruise ships and their families. The latter, especially, note that 170 passengers and crew have disappeared from cruise ships since 2000, many without being seriously investigated or widely reported.

***

Statement for John and Chantal Hopkins

Two Children Sexually Assaulted by a "Carnival Cruise Line" Employee

https://internationalcruisevictims.org/stories/john-and-chantal-hopkins/

In July 2004, on the last night aboard a Carnival Cruise ship, our cabin steward called the cabin occupied by our 13-year-old daughter and her 12-year-old friend. The two 18-year-old girls, who were also sharing the same cabin, had gone dancing. It was the last evening for them to enjoy the cruise, their high school graduation gift. My husband and I were sleeping in the adjacent cabin, but had always left both balcony doors open.

At approximately 12:30 AM, our cabin steward called and asked the younger girls if they would like drinks delivered to their cabin. They replied, "Yes, a COKE". However, when he arrived, he delivered beer, rather than the sodas they had requested. Upon gaining entry to the room, he proceeded to sexually assault both children by French-kissing both of them... and continued by pulling down the skirt of the younger child, my daughter's 12-year-old friend...

Immediately following the assault, both girls ran to our cabin, literally shaking and hysterical, and alerted us to what had just transpired. We were so shocked and so upset that we immediately proceeded to the Purser's Desk (with the girls) to report the assault. While reporting the assault, my husband was actually told by the desk attendant to keep his voice down!

Three security personnel accompanied us back to the girls' cabin, where we each of us gave our written statements. The unopened beer cans still remained in the room for their own observation.

After taking our statements, the security crewmembers left the cabin, but not before pitching a marketing statement for us to consider booking our next cruise with Carnival. How insensitive and inappropriate was that? We were so stunned with their response. We could not actually believe what we were hearing... Within one-hour of two children being sexually assaulted and nearly raped by a Carnival employee, they actually suggested our consideration for a future cruise!

At a minimum, we expected the ship's Captain to contact us or at least come to our cabin to extend an apology and an explanation as to what type of action would be taken against this employee/assailant, but we failed to receive so much as a call or acknowledgement of this crime. We were merely handed a sheet of paper by Security, bearing the telephone phone numbers of the FBI and the local police department in New Orleans. That was it! That was Carnival's routine procedure of handling an attempted rape of two children.

When we disembarked that morning, we headed to the airport, where we contacted the New Orleans Police Department. Since it was Sunday, they suggested that it would be best for us to return home to California and continue dealing with the situation from there.

We spent day after day on the telephone, but to no avail. When we contacted Carnival's Guest Relations, the comment we received was, "Your girls are fine" and again, suggested that we book another cruise through Carnival. I replied, "You MUST be kidding!" Could they possibly be serious to think that we would take another cruise? We were all still in shock and in tears over this terrifying experience.

We have since interpreted this callous response as "robotic" and totally "unbelievable", but obviously, this is their normal course of business, when dealing with a crime.

As a result of Carnival's reaction (lack of action), as well as the reaction of the police in New Orleans, we saw no alternative but to consult with a local attorney, who filed a class action lawsuit against Carnival Cruise Line. After providing our attorney with the details and a photo of the assailant, she subpoenaed documents, believing this was not the first time that the employee had assaulted minors or other passengers. Obviously, he had planned this very well.

All we really wanted was written proof that this employee had been terminated, but due to employee privacy rights, Carnival claimed they were unable to release this information; therefore, as far as we know, this cabin steward may still be employed by Carnival Cruise Line. It's extremely important that potential passengers be aware of this, before considering a cruise vacation, especially with children.

For a parent, as well as the temporary guardian of my daughter's 12-year-old friend, this has been a total nightmare, and an emotional roller coaster for all of us. Although both families have continued to remain friends, as you well know, the entire experience will always remain imbedded in our minds.

The photo album of our 2004 Carnival Cruise vacation still remains empty. This cruise will always be a nightmare for all of us.

Clearly, there MUST be stricter employee screenings/background checks, improved hallway security with cameras, improved guest relations and crime reporting procedures. Until then, this is not a safe-haven for anyone planning a family vacation.

***

Statement for Shari Cecil

https://internationalcruisevictims.org/stories/shari-cecil/

On December 18, 2004, I was raped in my bunk by a fellow crew member, while docked at a U.S. port.

These are the statements made to me by my supervisor within the first 72 hours of being raped on board the 'Pride of Aloha', operated by Norwegian Cruise Line America, a U.S. flagged vessel with a U.S. crew sailing only in U.S. waters:

- "Bad things happen to good people."
- "You need to put it behind you and get back to work."
- "Just forget about it and get on with your life."
- "You don't have to be afraid of him."
- "We don't carry rape kits on board."
- "You're lucky this isn't an international ship. You would both just be fired and kicked off at the next port."
- "We don't know who the investigating authority is."

The following quotes came from the Maui Police Department and the Maui Memorial Hospital's Emergency Room Department:

- "It's not our jurisdiction – it happened on board. It's the Coast Guard that should investigate."
- "Since the investigating authority isn't here to order it, you can't have a rape kit."

When I offered to pay for the rape kit, I was told:

- "No, it must be ordered by the investigating authority and since they are not here to order it, you can't have one."

I went back to the ship, back to the same cabin, to the same bunk, where I had been raped. I put my soiled sheets and clothing in a plastic garbage bag. No one asked me to collect any evidence; I just couldn't stand to look at them anymore and buried them at the bottom of my locker. It was difficult for me to take a shower, because there had been no rape kit, and a shower would destroy any remaining evidence. There was nothing I could do, so I took a shower.

No one on board was willing to collect any of the evidence. Security told me to hang on to any evidence... they didn't want it, but assured me they would attempt to figure out who should investigate.

I continued to see my rapist in the gangways and in the crew mess. I continued to endure his comments of "Hello Shari, how are you?" At this point he was denying that he ever stepped foot in my cabin.

Meanwhile I had no alternative but to go back to work. It was extremely difficult for me to do this, but if I wanted to stay on board I had no choice. I had to stay on the ship to make sure they prosecuted my rapist. Other female crew members commented, "If they can do this to you they can do it to any of us. Please see this through for all of us."

Security still couldn't tell me who should investigate my rape. I called the U.S. Coast Guard and the FBI, both of which were unaware of any rape on board.

Over a week later, the Maui Police Department finally determined they were the investigating authority, but my rapist was never prosecuted. The Hotel Director informed me that as far as the company (NCLA) was concerned, they had decided to allow my rapist to finish out his contract; however, they simply would not re-hire him. They wanted me to know that the company had done all they could.

I knew nothing was going to happen to my rapist, but I told the Hotel Director that I would like to see rape kits placed in the medical center on board. He told me, "Our attorneys are looking into it and couldn't discuss it further." I knew talking about the rape would hurt me, in more ways than one; therefore, I did what my supervisors had instructed me to do and forgot about the rape.

I had worked so hard and had given up so much to make it on board. I went back to college at the age of 44, and achieved a 4.0 GPA. I also completed Coast Guard training, which included full-gear firefighting and water survival training, and received my MMD (Merchant Mariner's Document) as an Ordinary Seaman. I had put all my personal belongings in storage and said goodbye to my parents, children and grandchildren. It wasn't easy to begin my new career at 46 years old. My ultimate goal was to become an officer and save money for a future back on land with my daughter. Being that I had made it through all of this, I felt that I could certainly make it through a rape. I refused to give up so easily. I stayed with it and worked hard at trying to forget the rape.

In November 2005, I received my promotion to officer with a challenging job on board. My position included the responsibilities of crew welfare, the crew common areas, crew cabin assignments, crew purchases, entertainment, and orientation of new crew members. It was an extremely demanding role, but I was still living my dream.

We sailed into San Francisco in May 2006 for dry dock. I was exhausted. Around midnight a crew member with an illegal passkey entered my cabin and startled me out of a deep sleep. I asked him what he was doing. He apologized and left my cabin, but unfortunately, the damage had already been done. I could no longer sleep and continued to be extremely anxious.

After three days of no sleep, I broke down and went to the medical center. I found the nurse on board, the same nurse who was on board when I was raped, and explained my situation. I thought that maybe I just needed 24-hours off to get some sleep and pull myself together. I couldn't understand why I was crying or why I seemed to be having a panic attack. This had never happened to me before.

When I awoke, the ship's doctor asked to speak with me. He asked me to confirm a few things for him, specifically the sexual assault that occurred while on the ship. When I confirmed this, he asked if I had received any counselling before I was re-assigned to the exact same ship. I confirmed that no counselling had been provided, and that I had been re-assigned to the same ship. He immediately informed me that I was no longer "Fit for Duty" and I was "Medically Disembarked". I was released from the ship before it sailed that evening, and have been in therapy and unable to work ever since. I was diagnosed with Post Traumatic Stress Disorder (PTSD).

The symptoms of this disorder are horrible, especially to someone who has always been as outgoing as me.

My whole life and personality have changed (not for the better). I am no longer the same outgoing person. I can no longer tolerate being around people. Crowds are especially difficult for me, as well as issues with safety. This affects my entire life… from employment to the ability of attending large and small gatherings.

All of my previous jobs have been working with the public. Before I went to sea, I operated a mobile music service and sang in front of thousands of people. I no longer sing and rarely leave my house. I physically become anxious around other people, and have been haunted with the inability to sleep. When I am finally able to sleep, I have nightmares of being back on board that ship. There are other symptoms too, but the hardest thing for me to accept is the change in my personality; however, with the help of counselling, I am continuing to work on it… but it will take a very, very long time.

Through public awareness of what happened to me, my goal is to assist others. Attempting to forget about a rape is not the correct approach for any victim to take, as it will resurface years later and affect your life in so many negative ways. Under no circumstances should a victim ever accept an order or suggestion to "forget about it and get on with your life". Always remember that it was not your fault! And no matter how difficult it may be, victims must speak up and seek professional help.

***

Statement from a Grieving Mother

Cruise from Hell By Elle

https://internationalcruisevictims.org/stories/my-innocent-teenage-daughter/

About three years ago my family went on the proverbial "cruise from Hell." After it ended, we went back home and tried to suppress our memories; we haven't been able to talk about it until now. We are doing so only because, judging from our experience, cruise ships are anything but the safe venue for fun and sun that the cruise line ad campaigns promote, and we want people to know this.

We were booked on the Grand Princess of Princess Cruises, which left Galveston, Texas, for a week's cruise to Mexico and Central America. With me were my grandmother, parents, husband, two daughters, ages 16 and 8. We'll call my older daughter Lizzie; my younger one, Sophie.

As the ship left port, a dance party was already underway on deck. My two daughters wanted to go there just as soon as we checked into our stateroom. I escorted them there; people of all ages were dancing, only the adults seemed to have liquor, and crew and security staff were present. So I thought things were all right, but stayed and watched what was going on anyway.

As my girls danced with each other, I noticed that six or eight young men, apparently in their mid- to late-teens, were standing around in a group, "checking out the action" but not bothering anyone or causing trouble. Even so, acting on what might have been mother's instinct, I took note of them. One of the boys in particular put me on edge, though there was no reason for it: he looked to be about 19, dark-ish (like a Middle Easterner) but with blue eyes, well-dressed, and good-looking; I thought of him as the "handsome one."

The boys were staring at Lizzie. I have to say that she is extremely attractive, with blond hair, green eyes, and a good figure; she is also a dancer, and so stood out among the crowd on deck, even though it was crowded.

Lizzie has proven herself to be level-headed, responsible, and trustworthy. So, although I felt a bit uncomfortable with this situation, I decided I was being over-protective and shrugged it off.

Missing from the Teen Center

Around 9 that evening — on the first night of the cruise — Lizzie decided to go to the teen center on ship. I kick myself now for encouraging her to go and meet some other kids, as she was just a bit reluctant. I escorted her to the center.

The teen center was on one of the lower decks. There was a kind of coffee shop nearby. When we got there, some 40 kids were milling around and four or five crew members, probably in their 20s, were supervising. They said that kids had to be signed in and out of the center by a responsible adult, and that no kid could leave without being signed out. I agreed with my daughter that I would come back for her at 11 p.m.

When I did, there were only about 8 kids still there. My daughter Lizzie was not one of them; she was nowhere to be seen. I asked one crew member who was still there where she was, and was told that she and some other kids left to get a soft drink or something like that, probably at the cafe next door. So much for signing in and out! Later on, I tried to find the names of the young people who had been in the teen center at that time, only to be told that the list was not available.

(I want to point out here that the group of boys who I had seen staring at Lizzie on deck earlier, at the dance party, were in that restaurant before she and the other kids from the teen center went in. It may also be significant that she left with two other girls, one of whom had no apparent connection to any of the boys but who later was found to be the girlfriend of the "handsome one.")

I picked up the house phone and called my cabin, telling my family that Lizzie was missing. Already I felt sick with fear, and when my parents and husband came down we split up. My father and I began roaming around the ship, searching. I asked other passengers if they had seen my daughter; as I did, crew and security kept telling me: "Settle down." There were a good number of security personnel around (the staff member at the teen center with whom I talked had made some calls), but they seemed more concerned about publicity than about my daughter. I shouted back that I would settle down once Lizzie was safely with me.

"I put too much of that drug in her drink..."

Meanwhile, in what I still think of as something like divine intervention, my husband, who was walking down another corridor, passed the closed door to a stateroom and heard a group of young men inside the room talking in frantic tones. They were saying things like: "What do we do now? I put too much of that drug in her drink... what do we do? What are we going to do with her?" One of them said, "I put her in a hole."

My husband became frantic. He went to the security center... where two security workers tried to keep him quiet and told him not to disturb the other passengers. He couldn't believe what they were saying, and that they showed no interest at all in the conversation he had overheard.

My mother then met up with my husband and the two security officers, and all four went back to that stateroom where the conversation had been overheard. When they knocked on the door, a boy with curly black hair answered, seeming very nervous. My mother started shouting, "What have you done with my baby? Where is my daughter?"

The boys in the room were the "handsome one" and the

others who had been at the dance party on deck. They insisted they had no idea what she was talking about… but when my husband said, "Funny thing… I was walking by your room when I heard you saying, 'What are we going to do with her?'" Their faces turned ashen white. Even so, they kept saying they didn't know anything.

At this time it was early in the morning, maybe around 1 a.m. No public announcement had been made about Lizzie's disappearance — no such announcement was ever made — and the security people said they could not begin knocking on cabin doors, as it would be an "invasion of privacy." They did tell the boys to go to the security office and give statements — the next day! I have never seen any statements, if any were ever given.

At this point, we had been searching for two hours with no results. I was getting angrier and angrier that nothing was being done. Some crew were sent to stay with us and keep us quiet. I finally broke away from them and went up to any other passengers I could see, telling them that my daughter had disappeared and describing her appearance. Few of them seemed very interested.

Another hour had gone by. At this time, the picture of my daughter that was on her boarding pass had been copied, and crew members were handing it out to the few passengers who were still awake and moving about the ship. I was as determined as ever to keep searching, and made sure that security understood I was not giving up!

Finally a crew member said the whole ship was going to be searched. We were near Belize, our first stop, at this time, and preparations were being made to anchor the ship to allow a full search.

"Mommy, Mommy, where am I?"

Some ten minutes or so went by, and I was walking down a staircase, still searching. I saw a group of 10 or 12 crew standing together. As I approached, they moved aside… and there was

Lizzie, my missing daughter! At that point, I thought she was the most beautiful sight I ever had seen!

But not all was well with her. As I rushed to her, I noticed that her eyes were black and dilated. She was mumbling, slurring her words, "Mommy, Mommy, where am I? What happened? Mommy, I don't feel good."

We took her to the infirmary, where the doctor carried out blood tests. We heard him say, "Oh, my God! It's evident she's been drugged."

(This is bizarre: About three weeks after the cruise was over we got a letter from the cruise line confirming that my daughter had consumed a date-rape drug. But five days after that, we got a second letter, also from the cruise line, saying that nothing had happened.)

At this stage, our trust in Princess Cruises had been shattered. We asked to take custody of the blood sample so that we could have it checked by people who were independent of the cruise line. But this was refused; one security guard said, "When there's a crime on board, the evidence is ours, not yours." Please note that he used the word "crime."

When we got home, we had our own doctors test for evidence of sexual assault. Thank God, there was none.

In the meantime, we left the infirmary and returned to our cabin. Lizzie slept until 4 the next afternoon, and woke up with a severe headache. The ship's medical staff never did any follow-up tests or checked on her for the rest of the voyage.

Some strange things happened that next day. One boy who was on some kind of baseball team outing said that he had seen my daughter, looking "really out of it," in an elevator with that group of boys, who looked "very nervous."

Also that day, the phone rang in our cabin. When I picked it up, I heard the voice of a boy who seemed almost ready to cry. "I am so glad you got your daughter back," he said.

"Who is this? Who is this?" I asked.

He replied, "I can't say, but I'm just glad you got her back," and then hung up.

For the rest of the trip, our family stayed together. On several occasions, the group of young men who had watched our daughter at the dance party crossed our path; when that happened, they looked and acted as though they had seen a ghost.

I said before that my husband had an encounter with two security guards. One afternoon, when our family was alone on deck, the younger of them came up to us and said to Lizzie, "I am so glad your Mom got you back." He then said to me, "I know what happened on the ship and you know what happened on the ship, and that's all I've got to say," and quickly walked away.

As for the older one, the one who seemed to be in charge… the day after Lizzie was found, he said to her: "Where have you been, you little slut?" Both my husband and I heard this: to this day, I don't know how we managed not to tear this man apart for that remark.

This same security guard also told us that at no time could we approach the group of boys seen on an elevator with my daughter. We could not even talk with them, he said. And later, throughout the voyage, on several occasions we saw him laughing and talking with those boys.

Human Trafficking?

So what DID happen on the ship? And why?

When I saw Lizzie and ran down the stairs to her, one of the crew said, "I found her on the bottom of the ship in a cubbyhole." My family were never allowed to go to see that cubbyhole; we have no idea how far it was from the teen center. But I know that Lizzie's clothes and hair were damp when we got her back. (She said that she does not remember anything clearly after sitting down with the boys in the cafe and drinking a cup of tea.)

We were told that there was no videotape coverage of the cargo area, the crew area, or the passageways and elevators inside the ship. So if these boys drugged my daughter in the cafe, as we believe, and brought her by elevator to that out-of-the-way storage area, there was nothing on tape to prove it.

But one question stays in my mind: How would these boys have known about the existence of this cubbyhole? Why would they bring her there, rather than to a cabin?

Some people believe that human trafficking is a myth. Others concede that it can happen, but certainly not on a cruise ship. Passengers can't just disappear, can they?

Well, they do. Moving someone from a ship against their will does not seem preposterous to me... especially since we know that laundry, trash, supplies and such things are taken off and brought on ship when it is in port. Would someone find it worthwhile to take a girl from a ship and sell her into sexual slavery?

I cannot say, but I wonder how it can be that a passenger reported seeing my daughter in an elevator with the group of boys, and yet nothing was done about it. My family was told that because this incident happened in international waters, we had no legal recourse. Our daughter was drugged, kidnapped, and isolated, and we could do nothing.

As I said before, we were so thankful to have Lizzie back that we just tried to protect ourselves for the rest of the cruise. We did not think about anything else.

What we can do now is share our story, and hope that the public listens. My heart goes out to every family that has lost a loved one during a cruise, and has never gotten answers. For three hours I inhabited your world; for three hours my family and I were in Hell. I know that some of you have never left it, and am so sorry for your plight.

Tips for a Safer Cruise

https://internationalcruisevictims.org/

https://internationalcruisevictims.org/dont-snooze-before-you-cruise/

- Purchase additional Travel Insurance.
- Carefully read the fine print on your cruise ticket, as this is your contract and once you purchase it you are obliged to the cruise line's terms and conditions.
- Go online before you depart on your cruise and check where all the embassy offices are located and make a record of their contact information in case you need to contact them.
- Know the Emergency Signal: The emergency signal on a ship is seven short blasts followed by one long blast. Knowing the emergency signal when you hear it can make a difference by giving you valuable extra minutes that other people may not have if they're standing around wondering what that noise is.
- Cruise ships offer unlimited alcohol but be careful of how much you consume and don't fall victim by having to be at the mercy of a total stranger to help you back to your cabin.
- NEVER under any circumstance go into the "CREW ONLY" areas, even if a crew member invites you, DON'T go and politely decline the invitation as once down there you will be at the mercy of the crew member and his or her intentions may not be as honest as they might appear to be. ALWAYS stay in the areas designated for passengers.
- In a closed environment such as a cruise ship you will be

subjected to more contact with people who may have contagious diseases, so always wash your hands and be conscious about what you touch aboard, as it may be contaminated with all types of germs from other passengers of crew.

- Just because you're on vacation doesn't mean you can let your guard down around strangers. No matter how much you think you've gotten to know someone in a few days on a ship, remember, they're still strangers and you need to use caution in what you tell them and how much you trust them.

- Be vigilant: Use the buddy system on the ship and set rules for your children who can be particularly vulnerable. Be aware of your surroundings, especially in public places, such as swimming pools, casinos and nightclubs.

- Always check your cabin or stateroom thoroughly when you enter, making sure there is no place someone can be hiding, including the bathroom and closet, keeping the front door fully open in case you need to make a run for it, ensuring you can escape with ease if required.

- Never let your room/boarding pass key out of your sight and NEVER EVER divulge your room number to anyone on board.

- Remember there is a drug called the "Date Rape Drug" that is widely available and anyone can slip it into your drink if you are not aware, so ONLY drink beverages that you have witnessed being prepared and don't be embarrassed to ASK for an unopened bottle. The number one crime reported on board cruise ships is sexual assaults. Medical personnel onboard are actually considered "independent contractors." Because of this, the cruise lines are not even vicariously liable for the care they provide.

Acknowledgments and Special Thank You

The author would like to give a special thank you to the following people for their assistance in the making of this novel.

The International Cruise Victims Organisation

Kendall Carver - *for opening my eyes into the world of the International Cruise Victims Association and giving me access to all of your information, data and recourses to help me write this book. You are greatly missed my friend.*

Jamie Barnett - *for following on Kendall's legacy and continuing to be the voice of the International Cruise Victims Association.*

Jim Walker - *for all your help with the maritime laws and the legal information needed to fill in the blanks for this book.*

Betsy Benitez - *for helping with the compilation of Mr Walker's information for this book.*

Jane Lindemuth Fitzpatrick - *for all your help with the proofreading and editing of this book.*

Nadezhda Todorova Nuza - *for your patience during my three years of research and writing this book.*

*Available worldwide
online and in all good bookstores*

www.mtp.agency

www.facebook.com/mtp.agency

@mtp_agency

www.ingramcontent.com/pod-product-compliance
Lightning Source LLC
LaVergne TN
LVHW091534060526
838200LV00036B/608